If she could avoid the Parkers, reach Twilight by any other route, she would.

But the tiny town had only one road in and the same road out. And to get there Karen had to skirt a border of the massive Parker Ranch. She itched to floor the accelerator. To fly along this part of her journey and put it quickly behind her.

"This is a travesty!" Karen could still hear Mae Parker, the family's matriarch, telling that to any wedding guest who'd listen.

But it hadn't been her fault! She'd done nothing except fall in love and agree to marry one of them. It was *them,* the Parkers, who'd—

Trying to shake off the painful memory, Karen took a deep breath and glanced out the car's window. Somewhere between this narrow strip of road and those distant mountains lay the heart of the Parker Ranch. She'd never seen ranch headquarters, only heard about it from her former fiancé. Since he was descended from a Parker who'd left years ago to make his way in the city, he and his family were referred to as "off-ranch Parkers."

But a Parker was a Parker. They were all extensions of the same arrogant clan. People she had good reason to never, *ever* want to see again.

ABOUT THE AUTHOR

The history of the West has always fascinated Ginger Chambers. The struggles faced by people trying to make their lives in an often hostile environment meant that small towns sometimes sprang up, prospered and then failed, leaving their remains for new generations to wonder at. She decided to write about such a town—the fictional Twilight, Texas—and the tenacious few who still call it home.

A proud native Texan, Ginger now lives in Northern California. This is her fourth story involving the Parkers of West Texas. Watch for upcoming books!

Books by Ginger Chambers

HARLEQUIN SUPERROMANCE
601—TILL SEPTEMBER
647—FATHER TAKES A WIFE
680—A MATCH MADE IN TEXAS
730—WEST TEXAS WEDDINGS
778—TEXAS LAWMAN

Don't miss any of our special offers. Write to us at the following address for information on our newest releases.

Harlequin Reader Service
U.S.: 3010 Walden Ave., P.O. Box 1325, Buffalo, NY 14269
Canadian: P.O. Box 609, Fort Erie, Ont. L2A 5X3

TWILIGHT, TEXAS
Ginger Chambers

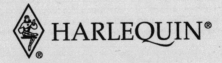

HARLEQUIN®

TORONTO • NEW YORK • LONDON
AMSTERDAM • PARIS • SYDNEY • HAMBURG
STOCKHOLM • ATHENS • TOKYO • MILAN • MADRID
PRAGUE • WARSAW • BUDAPEST • AUCKLAND

ISBN 0-373-70820-3

TWILIGHT, TEXAS

Copyright © 1999 by Ginger Chambers.

For Chris, who also loves "old things"

CHAPTER ONE

"I'M REALLY GOING TO MISS you, Karen," Rachel Anderson said from her perch on the kitchen stool.

"I'll only be gone a week."

"I know. That's what you keep telling everyone. But I've had one of my dreams, remember? And if there's anything I've learned to trust in life it's my dreams. You should, too. I was right about Jim Singleton winning a car and George Davis's long-lost brother showing up."

Karen Latham straightened from rummaging through the refrigerator for perishables to look directly into the soulful face of her friend. "What about Mrs. Meyer? She's still single."

"I never set a date for when she'd get married again. Just said that she would."

"She's seventy-four!"

"Romance can happen at any age!"

Karen extended a questionable wedge of cheese. "Do you think this has had it?"

Rachel sniffed, grimaced, and the reject went into the trash.

"All right," Karen said, still smiling as she shut the door. "That's it. Everything else should be fine."

"And if you do turn out to be away longer, I'll check it again when I water your plants."

"I *won't* be away longer," Karen insisted.

"Maybe that's what my subconscious is trying to tell you—you should!"

"Shouldn't the pizza be here by now?" Karen asked, hoping to change the subject.

"Martin's pressing you for an answer, isn't he?"

"And I can't forget to empty the trash. Not with that smelly—"

"Karen!"

Karen sighed. "Yes…yes, he is."

"If you want my opinion, I say put the man out of his misery. Marry him!"

"It's more complicated than that."

"Isn't it always?" Rachel retorted.

The doorbell rang and Karen hurried to answer it. But instead of the expected delivery boy, she found a tall blond man with a pleasant face and a nice smile standing on her doorstep. "I know we've already said our goodbyes," Martin explained, "but I wanted to see you again to—"

"Aha! At last!" Rachel rushed up to peek over Karen's shoulder. Her jubilation flagged, though, when she recognized the caller. "Ah-no! Martin! Did they lose our order, do you think?"

Martin Frederick stiffened the instant Rachel appeared. For some reason the pair had to strain to be civil.

"Would you like to come in?" Karen asked in an attempt to bridge the gap.

"Yes, why not?" Rachel agreed. "We'll be glad to share our meal…*if* it ever gets here!"

"I've already eaten. I only came by to—"

"I can disappear awhile if you two want," Rachel interrupted him yet again.

"No," Karen said quickly. Too quickly? "That would be silly."

Martin stubbornly completed his thought. "To tell you to have a safe trip and not to forget to call."

"Oh, isn't that sweet!" Rachel mocked. "A man who cares."

An angry light flashed in Martin's eyes, but before he could respond, Karen stepped outside and closed the door, shutting Rachel inside.

"I promise to call as soon as I get there," she said.

Martin's good humor was instantly revived as he touched one of the loose chestnut curls resting on her shoulder. "Are you sure this place even *has* a telephone?"

"I'm positive."

"Considering it's a veritable ghost town…" His words grew husky as he bent to kiss her.

Karen let him do it. She felt a pleasant tingle, but nothing more, and quickly pulled away. "I have to finish packing," she said.

"And I have to get back to the restaurant." Still, he tarried. "I'm going to miss you, Karen. This week will feel like forever."

"I—I have to go." Karen stepped back, but he grabbed her to deliver a harder kiss.

"Forever!" he swore, before setting her free.

Karen's heart was pounding and her breathing was shallow as she escaped back inside…but for the wrong reason! She looked up to find Rachel studying her.

"The man's besotted," Rachel said.

"I wish you two would be nicer to each other."

"I'm nice!" Rachel defended herself.

The doorbell rang again. Martin, needing more re-assurance?

This time the caller was the delivery boy, and after the necessary exchange of money, the two women brought the aromatic box to the kitchen table.

"Just how big is this place you're going to, any-way?" Rachel asked, helping herself to a thick cheesy slice. "This 'ghost town'?"

Karen passed her a paper napkin and took one for herself. "Well, technically, Twilight's not a ghost town. It sort of is and sort of isn't. People live there. So it's not really abandoned."

"How many people?" Rachel asked.

"Around twelve."

"Whoo-hoo! Big time!" Rachel chuckled as she took another bite.

"Did you ever see the old movie *Justice at Sun-down?*"

"With a young Gary Cooper? I think so."

"Actually, it starred Henry Ives."

Rachel frowned. "I always get them confused. Both long and lean with those carved features and enough sex appeal to melt the screen. Didn't some-thing unusual happen to Henry Ives? I can't remem-ber."

"He drowned while making his next movie. Some-time in the late thirties. Anyway, *Justice at Sundown* is about an event from Twilight's past. An outlaw stopped running from a pursuing posse long enough to rescue a child from an abandoned well, only to be hanged for his trouble. I've played by that well. It's just across the street from my aunt's antique shop."

"The shop she left to you."

Karen nodded. She'd spent every summer from

ages six through thirteen with her father's older sister in the tiny West Texas "ghost town" while her parents went on their yearly anthropological study trips to Central America. She'd played without restraint in that wild and isolated place and made friends with the town's scant citizenry—experiencing a freedom she'd never known in the more cloistered confines of her parents' academic world. It was hard to imagine Twilight without Augusta, just as it would be hard to imagine what her own life would've become without her aunt's liberating influence.

"Did your aunt qualify as a town eccentric?" Rachel asked, grinning. "Places like that usually have one or two."

"Aunt Augusta lived her own life, that's for sure. She did things her way whether other people thought it strange or not. She was also one of the sweetest people you'd ever want to meet. She'd have given away her last penny—although she had so many it never would have come to that. My uncle left her nicely provided for. She never had to worry."

"Which was how she could afford to run an antique shop in the middle of nowhere. She didn't have to make a living!"

"Exactly. She could've lived anywhere, but she chose Twilight."

"Is it even on the Texas map?"

"I'm not sure. An occasional tourist sometimes finds their way there, but they're usually fans of the old movie. That's how they know about it."

"Or they're lost."

Karen smiled. "Well, that, too."

They ate in silence for a time before Rachel asked,

"Did Mr. Griffin say anything when you told him you were leaving this weekend? Or did he just grunt?"

"He grunted."

"Typical. Would it hurt the man to wish you luck or to tell the truth—that he's going to miss you?"

"He's not a very demonstrative person."

Rachel dabbed at her mouth with the napkin. "You realize, of course, he'll want to have first look at your aunt's collection and will probably expect an outrageous discount if he finds anything he considers worthwhile."

Karen shrugged. "I'm not exactly sure what I'm going to do with it. If there's enough I could keep it myself and open my own place. Karen's Collectibles—doesn't that have a nice ring?"

Rachel's eyes opened wider. "Your own place? Here in Kerrville? Mr. Griffin would— You know he has a fit every time a new shop opens."

"Probably not here. Comfort's just down the road, so's Mountain Home." Karen named two neighboring Central Texas communities.

"What about Martin?"

"What does one thing have to do with the other? I could marry Martin and still—"

"Can I come work for you?" Rachel cut in with a grin.

Karen smiled. "It's all pie in the sky, Rach. I haven't been to Twilight in ten years, not since I was eighteen, and that was just for a short visit. After I stopped spending my summers there, Aunt Augusta would come by our place in Austin when she was out on buying trips. I don't have any idea what she might've left me. It could be a few things. It could be more. I won't know until I get there." She motioned at the remaining pizza. "Why don't you take this home, too, okay? No use leaving it to spoil."

"Home delivery isn't something you'll be getting a lot of out there, I suppose. What else will you be doing without? Electricity?"

"Twilight has electricity."

"But no fast-food places."

Karen smiled dryly. "I'll manage to survive for a week."

"Or more," Rachel added with a teasing twinkle. She stood up. "I'd better get going. Let you finish getting ready."

The telephone rang, but for the moment they ignored it.

"You take care," Rachel said, reaching out for a hug. "Don't do anything I wouldn't do. Then again…"

"Don't *you* forget the eggs and milk."

Karen continued to smile as Rachel left by the back door, a pizza box in one hand and a grocery bag in the other. Her good mood lasted until she picked up the phone and heard her mother's sharp tones traveling over the long-distance lines from Austin.

"Karen!" Gemma Latham said shortly. "Your father's told me what you told him last night. For the life of me I can't understand why you want to do this. Your aunt left you a few things…fine. Surely some kind of arrangement could be made to have whatever it is sent on. *You* don't have to go to West Texas to get it. What about the Parkers? What if you— What if one of them—" Her mother paused, reorganizing her thoughts. "Twilight is how far from the Parker Ranch? Fifty miles? Fifty miles is nothing in a place like that!"

"It's more like seventy miles, Mother. And the Parkers have absolutely no interest in Twilight. During all the summers I spent there I never once heard the name."

Her mother made an impatient sound. "I'm asking you to *think* about what you're doing, Karen. You've made a good life for yourself in Kerrville. Not the one that your father and I wanted for you, but it seems to be what you want. Why hand those people an opportunity to hurt you again? You more than anyone know what they're like. What the Parkers are capable of!"

The Parkers—the one subject guaranteed to rattle her mother's coolly competent persona. The mere mention of the name could set her spinning so far out of control that her academic peers and her students would have a hard time recognizing her.

Karen cradled the phone closer to her ear. "It's what I want to do, Mother. It's something I—I need to do."

Her mother was quick to sense an underlying tension. "Why?" she demanded. "Has something happened you haven't told—"

"I want to be on my own for a while, that's all," Karen broke in.

After a short silence Gemma returned to her cause. "Still…to go to Twilight! When you know they're so close by!"

"They don't want to see me any more than I want to see them. I'm sure of that."

"They should still be apologizing!" her mother snapped.

"Yes, they should," Karen agreed.

"I don't like it," Gemma said. "I *do not* approve. But if you must, keep in touch."

Karen let the handset slide back into place. Only instead of releasing it, she stood still, her hand outstretched. Where the Parkers were concerned, her mother could be wholly unreasonable. But in this instance, was she right?

Why was she so stubbornly determined to make this trip? Because she felt it only right to go herself to claim what her aunt Augusta had left her and also because it provided a convenient break from Martin's growing insistence? Or, on some deeper level, was it because she felt she still had something to prove to the Parkers? To herself?

She shook her head, denying the last thought. No. What had happened between her and the Parkers was well and truly in the past. It no longer had importance. *They* no longer were important.

"Not any of them!" she said aloud to the empty room. And was pleased by her certainty.

KAREN'S INDIFFERENCE to the Parkers lasted through the night and for most of the next day. While she had other things to think about—gathering her gear, loading it in the car, negotiating the interstate—she was fine. It was only as she abandoned the well-constructed highway for a narrower two-lane blacktop and then, later, turned onto an even narrower stretch of blacktop that the hairs on the back of her neck began to prickle. If she could reach Twilight by any other route she would, but her choice was severely limited. The tiny town had only one road in and the same road out. And to reach that road she had to skirt a border of the massive Parker Ranch.

When she was a child, the mile after mile of sun-baked land belonging to the Parkers had looked little different from the landscape she and her parents had been traveling through for what seemed forever. Dusty-beige rocks, distant waves of pyramid-shaped hills and jagged mountains that were even farther away. The mesquite, sage, yucca and creosote bushes… But now that she knew it was theirs…

Her foot itched to floor the accelerator. To fly along this part of her journey and put it quickly behind her. But she made herself keep within the speed limit and was relieved she had when a Briggs County sheriff's patrol car materialized out of nowhere to pass her in the opposite lane. Not that she expected the Parkers to be disturbed if word somehow filtered out that one of their county deputies had issued her a speeding ticket. Her ill treatment at their hands had been a minor thing to them—a small snag in the rich tapestry of their lives. In her own life it had caused chaos.

"This is a travesty! A complete and total travesty!" She could still hear Mae Parker, the family's matriarch, announce it to any and all who'd listen.

But it hadn't been her fault! She'd done nothing except fall in love and agree to marry one of them! It was *them,* the Parkers, who'd—

Memories came rushing back in an avalanche of pain—overwhelming her with recollections that she'd spent years avoiding because of their power to hurt. She saw herself as she had been then: barely twenty-one, dressed in her beautiful fairy-tale white wedding gown in a church packed with friends and relatives, following her attendants down the aisle, her hand resting lightly on her father's arm—only to arrive at the altar to find the groom missing!

She'd been startled at first, then calmed herself. Alex had been highly nervous the evening before, which she'd put down to prewedding jitters—something she also was experiencing. He hadn't eaten all that day, he'd confided to her. She doubted he was in much better condition now. So when the minister leaned close to murmur that on hearing the first notes of the Wedding March, Alex had excused himself, Karen encouraged her father to go through with the traditional parting kiss before seating himself next to her mother. Then she'd waited, along with everyone else, for Alex's return.

As the delay lengthened, nervous movements could be detected throughout the church, along with self-conscious whispers. Karen smiled reassurance to her attendants and the groomsmen, but finally gave up when she herself became concerned. She remembered shooting a panic-stricken look at Alex's older brother, Lee Parker, the best man. He had a similar slim, yet muscular, build, the same dark hair and strongly carved features, but with pale blue eyes instead of Alex's near black.

"I'll see what the holdup is," he'd responded, sotto voce.

Karen's gaze had clung to his tuxedo-clad back as he walked away. She didn't much care for him, because shortly after their first meeting two days before, he'd made it plain he disapproved of the marriage. At this moment, though, he carried all her hopes. She didn't understand what was happening, why Alex had hurried away and not come back. Was he ill? Did he need help? Should she go to him? What should she do? She glanced at the minister and, with a jolt, read compassion in his eyes. He felt sorry for her!

Did that mean he thought Alex wasn't going to return? But that couldn't happen! Alex would be there!

Strained moment followed strained moment. Whispers grew louder. Even the attendants and groomsmen had started to fidget. Then Lee Parker opened the side door and reentered the church…alone.

As he walked toward Karen, his expression gave nothing away. In front of the suddenly hushed crowd he stopped and said quietly, "Alex is gone. I looked everywhere, but he's—" His words ended on a shrug.

Karen couldn't take it in. Alex was gone? Gone where? Where would he go when—

"He's…gone?" she echoed, because she had to say something.

Lee Parker's lips were a thin line. He nodded.

Karen would never forget his eyes, those pale blue chips of Arctic ice that sent a chill straight to her soul. They held hers steadily, condemning her for daring to think that she could be one of them. As if becoming a Parker had been her ultimate goal!

"The Parkers" this! "The Parkers" that! Karen had had more than enough of the name during the past few months. Every decision her parents made about the wedding had been with an eye to impressing "the Parkers!" Wealthy, powerful, influential, an old-line Texas family… Karen had been blissfully unaware of the name's significance until after meeting Alex. And even then, it hadn't meant anything to her one way or the other.

At first, both sets of parents had resisted the engagement, protesting that Alex and Karen were too young. But faced with the young couple's determination, they had given in. It was afterward that the difficulties began, a direct result of her parents' closer involvement with Alex's parents during the early stages of planning the wedding. They seemed to sense a certain "disdain"—Gemma's bitter description. As if, in the Parkers' opinion, Karen would never measure up.

From that point things had gotten a little strange. The wedding became a sort of proving ground, where no expense was spared. "Only the best," became her parents' watchword.

Karen remembered the pain etched on their faces when she'd turned to look at them in the crowded church. The worst had happened. She'd been stood up! Every bride's nightmare. Every bride's parents' nightmare.

What happened after was a blur. She remembered a strong arm wrapping around her shoulders and then being whisked out the church's side exit. She remembered being held, her face pressed into a solid chest. She remembered the muted roar inside the church as people reacted. Then her parents dragging her away. Their anger, their outrage, the blame...

Karen took a deep breath, trying to recover from the terrible memory.

It was odd, but even after all these years she couldn't find it in herself to blame Alex. Just as her parents had at first pointed out, they'd been far too immature to make such a serious commitment.

Alex was fun, irreverent. He'd brought the first sparks of real joy into her life since she'd been forced to trade her childhood summers for what she considered the steamroll into academia. Her parents had wanted her to follow in their footsteps. They'd insisted that she fill all her spare time during her teenage years with accelerated study programs, with any and all forms of preparation for her approaching college education. Then during college—at, of course, what they considered the state's best university in Austin, where both had tenured professorships—she was expected to excel. They wanted to see a PhD attached to her name, just as one was attached to each of theirs. When she'd met Alex and he'd eventually proposed, she later realized she'd seen it as a way out. She didn't want her parents' life. She wanted her own!

She had no idea, either then or now, what Alex had wanted. She wasn't sure if he'd known himself. His mother had dreamed of him becoming a top-notch lawyer, with a partnership in a top-notch firm, and she'd been concerned that an early marriage would interfere. She'd also expected him to find a bride who'd bring something of substance to the union. Equally strong social status. Equal, if not greater, wealth. Karen brought neither. Her parents were respected experts in their field, which lent them a certain cachet, but their standing would be of only temporary interest to the social set of which Jessica Parker, Alex's mother, was a devotee. Especially since they were as far from great wealth as most teachers.

The weeks following the aborted wedding had been gruesome. The telephone calls, her parents' mortified attempts at explanation, the need to return all the gifts. Karen had been drowning in the feeling that she'd somehow let down her parents. That in the end she *hadn't* been good enough. And worrying about the money, most of it drawn from their savings, that her parents had funneled into something that had evaporated into thin air. All because of the haughty callousness of the high-and-mighty Parkers.

Karen had never again heard from Alex. He might've dropped off the face of the earth. She learned months later that Mae Parker had tried to contact her the next day, as had Lee. But they had been turned away by her parents, who, incensed that their daughter had been treated so badly, were fierce guardians of her privacy.

Karen glanced out the car's window at the passing scenery. Somewhere between this narrow strip of road and those distant mountains lay the heart of the Parker Ranch. She'd never seen ranch headquarters, only heard about it from Alex. Since Alex descended from a Parker who'd years ago left West Texas to make his way in an opposite corner of the state, he, his brother, his parents and those like them were referred to as "off-ranch Parkers." This was in contrast to those who continued to live on the ranch.

But a Parker was a Parker, off-ranch or on. They were all extensions of the same arrogant clan. People she had good reason to never *ever* want to come into contact with again.

CHAPTER TWO

KAREN ARRIVED TO FIND Twilight unchanged. Weathered wood buildings, some set side against side in a single row, some standing alone—most fronted by covered plank sidewalks, low-railed balconies and the occasional hitching post at the edge of the street. The tiny town looked like exactly what it was—a relic from the days of the Old West.

If she hadn't been leaning against the open door of her late-model car, she might have thought herself transported back in time to another age, when Twilight was a popular stopping place for late-nineteenth-century travelers. Any second now, a wagon piled high with a settler's wordly goods might lurch up the hard-packed road. Or a stagecoach, coated with dust, could roll to a stop and disgorge its passengers—also coated with dust—whose first destination would be the much needed refreshment of the well. Soldiers, trappers, Indian fighters, railroad men. Twilight had been a godsend in the arid and hostile land...until the spring failed.

A hot August breeze kicked up swirls of dust, peppering Karen's bare legs. She could do with a little water herself, she thought. Where was everyone? Doors were closed, not a soul was about. From the summers she'd spent here, she knew visitors were always promptly greeted.

She stepped away from the car and called, "Hello? *Hello!*"

A dog trotted out of an alleyway, stopped short and barked, the dark hair at the back of his neck bristling.

Karen clapped her hands. "C'mere, boy. It's okay. I'm a friend."

The dog barked even louder, before turning to run back the way he'd come.

A hand-lettered sign, faded by time, hung from the balcony of the nearest building. The Twilight Mercantile, it proclaimed proudly. Karen glanced from it to the neighboring establishment on the right. The Lady Slipper Saloon flowed in Spencerian script down a pair of plaques on either side of a matching set of doors.

Karen knew both places well. The saloon was owned and operated by John and Bette Danson. The mercantile, closed since the owner got fed up and abandoned it in the spring of 1910, had been one of her favorite haunts as a child. According to local lore, the mercantile's owner had walked away with only his hat. Much of the original stock remained—bolts of cloth, shelves of cooking supplies, buttons and brooms and a very old cash register. Karen had played there for hours, pretending to be the clerk, waiting on customers only she could see.

When hunger or thirst intruded, she'd run next door to the saloon, hopping up on one of the red leather bar stools to eat a snack of ice cream, pop and chips— or whatever surprise Bette might produce—or hurry for a meal at her aunt's apartment above the antique shop, which abutted the mercantile on its other side.

In comparison, the sign announcing Augusta's shop was simple—Antiques was all it said. Karen hadn't seen the place in years. Too many years, she now realized with a pang of nostalgia as she walked toward it.

On a whim she tried the shop's door, only to find it locked. Frowning, she tried the mercantile's, then the saloon's. They, too, were locked. Odd, she thought, her frown deepening. People didn't secure their doors here. The only person who might steal from them would be a neighbor, and that just didn't happen.

She'd written a letter to John and Bette, telling them of her plans to come claim her inheritance, and she'd received a reply. From them. From Twilight. She hadn't told them the exact date of her arrival, not knowing it at the time. But she hadn't thought it necessary. Twilight didn't run on a time schedule. Things happened here when they happened, and that was that. No one worried, no one cared. *So…where was everyone?*

Karen returned to the antique shop and, shielding her eyes, tried to see inside. She was disappointed when her view was blocked by what looked to be the back of a very large chest.

"Hello?" she tried again, turning to project her voice into the distance.

A series of barks answered. It sounded like the same dog.

Her frustration mounting, Karen returned to her car and plopped down in the driver's seat. What was she to do? What else *could* she do? Wait, of course. But for how long?

It was as if Twilight suddenly had become what her aunt had always affectionately termed it—a ghost town. With only her and the dog to—

"You that TV-show person?" a gruff voice demanded from nearby.

Karen almost jumped out of her skin. She jerked her head around to see a scruffy desert rat staring at her through the open passenger window. He was old and bent with an unkempt white beard, leathery skin, a ragged hat jammed low over flyaway white hair and the brightest of blue eyes peering at her through a squint.

Old Pete Tunny! Twilight's eldest citizen. No one knew exactly how old Pete was. He could easily be anywhere from sixty to a hundred. Just as no one knew where he'd come from or how long he'd been there. It was as if he'd always lived in Twilight, a leftover from the old days. He had a ramshackle shack on the far edge of town but preferred to spend his time wandering the distant foothills. Karen had gotten to know him well the summer he'd broken a bone in his foot and had to stay put so it could heal. He was a natural storyteller and had taught her to whittle while she listened to his tales.

His bright eyes narrowed even more. "You look kinda familiar. Like maybe I should know you. But I don't watch TV. Don't hold with it. Rots a person's brain. Turns it to vegetable mush!" He waited for a reply, obviously hoping for a spirited defense.

Karen grinned, the dimples in each cheek deepening. "I *should* look familiar to you, Pete. I'm Karen...Karen Latham! Augusta's niece."

Pete Tunny blinked, then the white hairs around his mouth quivered into a smile. "You're Karen? Nah! Little Karen's no bigger than a bar of used soap!" He paused. "You sure got her dimples, though! And her big brown eyes." His smile grew wider. "Karen, you say?"

He hurried around the car to meet her as she stepped out. She was examined up and down—from her shoulder-length chestnut curls and slim body in shorts and a white cotton shirt to the sandals encasing her feet. "Still not much bigger than a bar of used soap!" he decreed. "But you're her, all right! All growed up!"

"It's been a lot of years, Pete," Karen answered, giving him the quick hug she knew was all he'd allow. Pete wasn't much on shows of affection. "Too many years," she continued. "How are you? Still up to the same old things?" She was happier to see him than she would have thought possible even this morning. He was someone from Twilight. He made the town real again. Brought it to life.

Pete had to clear his throat. "Yeah...yeah...same ol' same ol'. You know how it is. I get restless if I don't make it out often enough. Had to stay put more'n I wanted this summer. But somebody had to be here to try'n bang some sense into these fools' heads! If your aunt hadda been here I coulda lit out, but she wasn't, so I had to stay."

"I don't—" Karen began, when he interrupted her.

"She'da told 'em right for right, that's for sure! Then they wouldna gone off with those movie folk, lettin' 'em wine 'em and dine 'em so's they can sweet-talk 'em into doin' whatever it is they want!"

Karen was more confused than ever. Frowning, she said, "You're going to have to start from the beginning, Pete. I don't understand."

Pete waved a hand. "Aw, that stuff turns my stomach if I even think about it! When they get back

they'll all be ready to talk, don't you worry!'' He
motioned for her to follow him. ''C'mon. Come to
my place and I'll fix you up with a nice strong cup
of coffee and you can tell me what all you been doin'
with yourself since you growed up.'' His expression
sobered. ''We were all cut up terrible about Augusta's
passing. It was like the best part of this town went
with her. Not been the same around here since. And
from the looks of it, it won't be for some time to
come, neither. Maybe *never*. Not if certain people get
their way.'' He threw Karen an estimating look,
grinned and patted her shoulder. ''But you're here
again, ain't ya, gal? Maybe you can change things
back to the way they were. Yep, maybe you just
can!''

Movie people, TV people...what was going on?
Karen wondered as she tried to keep up with Pete's
shuffling gait.

KAREN WAS SITTING in Pete's one-room shack, a cup
of freshly brewed coffee in her hand, chuckling at one
of his outrageous stories, when the rumble of a large
engine broke into their conversation. It drew closer,
switched to idle, then shut off.

''That's them back,'' Pete said in answer to her
questioning look.

''Back from where?'' she asked.

''The big city. Come on. You can bring that with
you, if you want.'' He indicated her chipped cup. ''I
wanna see their faces when they find out you're
here.'' He took hold of her arm and pulled her across
the room.

''They're my friends, too, Pete,'' Karen sputtered,
managing to leave the cup on a rough wood table by

the door. Something was wrong in Twilight...out of kilter. Something she knew nothing about. Something she wasn't sure she *wanted* to know about.

The dog who'd barked at her earlier jumped out of the way as Pete pulled her outside. They'd disturbed his nap.

"Don't make no difference," Pete replied, dismissing her protest as he brought her back to the spot where he'd found her.

A large charter bus was now parked in front of the saloon, not far from Karen's much smaller car, and passengers had started to climb out. They were led by a woman and two men—all in business suits, their hair cut in the latest styles—whose flashy confidence branded them as outsiders. Those who followed had more recognizable faces. John and Bette Danson, Joe and Rhonda Peterson, Isaac Jacobs, the Douglases, Mary O'Conner and her son, Benny, Carmelita Lopez and a strikingly pretty young woman with dark eyes and dark hair who was laughing up at an equally dark and handsome young man carrying an infant.

Seemingly content, they remained in a loose cluster around the outsiders. The woman, a sleek blonde with a smoothly cut bob and large gold earrings, was speaking to them.

"So you see," she said, obviously continuing a line of thought clearly started inside the bus, "we truly mean it when we say we don't want *anything* to change in the town's appearance. With the exception of the music hall, of course, and we're only doing that in order to reassure Mr. Armstrong nothing will go wrong during the media premiere. A number of very important people will be here that day and Mr. Armstrong is the nervous type. He likes to have all the angles worked out ahead of time. He doesn't appreciate surprises.'' She flashed a smile. "This town is perfect as it is! Why would you want to change it?''

A murmur cascaded through the group, which stopped only when Pete, his grip tightening on Karen's arm, shouted, "Exactly! Why change it? These folks don't care a fig about Twilight. All they wanna do is use it for their pree-miere! They're comin' here, tellin' you this 'n that, makin' all kinds of promises, lettin' you think we'll get rich, and they don't mean a word they say. So why listen to 'em? Why not tell 'em to get lost…like Augusta would?'' Pete thrust Karen forward. "If you don't believe me, ask this little lady. She'll tell you true enough what Augusta'd say!''

All eyes fixed on Karen. Most in puzzlement, a few in slow recognition. The outsiders looked at her with suspicion.

"Karen?'' Bette Danson ventured. She, like everyone else, was dressed in her best, not her typical jeans and T-shirt.

It had been ten years since Bette and Karen had met during Karen's last visit to Twilight. She'd come along with her parents on the promise that they'd stop by the little town while in transit to the funeral of a colleague in El Paso. They'd had car trouble, though, and because of the press of time were forced to cut their stay to barely a half hour. As they were about to leave Bette had rushed over to greet Karen effusively, then waved goodbye, arm in arm with Augusta, from in front of the antique shop.

In her late fifties, Bette still had the same bright red hair and wiry frame of her youth. She moved with purpose toward Karen, not stopping until she was directly in front of her. Then she, too, paused to look her up and down.

Karen waited. Her return to Twilight seemed to have come at a bad time. She wondered why Bette and John hadn't warned her.

Her old friend's aloofness quickly melted and she was enveloped in a warm embrace.

Pete growled with disapproval.

"Oh, hush, you ol' fool!" Bette chided.

"I'm not an ol' fool!" Pete retorted. "I'm the only one who knows enough to understand what's goin' on around here! And you'll all be sorry if you don't listen!" His last warning drew groans from the crowd, as if they'd heard it all before and were tired of the repetition.

The blonde hurried over. "And who is this?" she asked. "A member of the town we've somehow missed?" She extended a beautifully cared-for hand. "My name is Melanie Taylor. I'm special assistant to Mr. Raymond Armstrong of Cryer Studios in Hollywood. I'm sure you've heard of us. And you're—"

"It's none of your damned business who she is!" Pete snarled.

"She's Karen Latham, Augusta Latham-Lamb's niece," Bette said.

Melanie Taylor had a quick mind. "Augusta Latham-Lamb, the antiques dealer I spoke with several months ago and who's since passed away. On behalf of Cryer Studios, let me extend our heartfelt sympathy, Ms. Latham. Your aunt was a very special person. She didn't miss a trick, did she? Which must have come in handy in her chosen field."

"She knew exactly what you are!" Pete exploded, lunging forward.

John Danson and Joe Peterson caught Pete before he could get near the studio representative. Gently but firmly, they spirited him down the street.

"All right! All right!" he cried, shaking them off after a point. "That's enough! I'm not about to hang around where I'm not wanted! But you mark my word," he shouted to the others. "You better listen to what that little gal over there has to say. She's got more of Augusta in her than she knows. Always has had. She'll tell you straight. She'll—" His words became indecipherable as he turned to stomp away.

"My goodness," Melanie Taylor said with a laugh, sharing a slightly derisive look with her Hollywood companions. "He's quite a character, isn't he? So very...colorful. Just what we need, if only he'd stop making such a fuss."

John Danson came to stand beside his wife. Tall, with thinning gray hair, he managed to look dignified in a dark suit, which it was apparent he wasn't at all at ease wearing. "We apologize for the outburst, Miss Taylor...Melanie," he corrected quickly at her waggled finger. "Pete's just...bein' Pete." His gaze settled on Karen and he widened his apology. "Not a very happy welcome for you, either, huh, Karen? Gettin' plunked down in the middle of all this. Just the luck of the draw, I s'pose."

"There's no need to apologize," Karen murmured, offering a flickering smile. She still didn't know what was going on here but was even less anxious to find out. Pete seemed to think she could work some kind of miracle, while the others were under the spell of this "movie person," to paraphrase Pete.

She was starting to wonder how she could sidestep the moment, when Melanie Taylor again took charge. "Now, to continue," the representative said, her earrings swinging as she rejoined the others, "I'm sure we can come to some kind of agreement. If only we…"

John trotted ahead to open the saloon doors, and the woman expertly herded everyone inside. Everyone except Bette, who remained at Karen's side.

Bette smiled slightly. "Sometimes I wish this new movie had never been made. All it's done is get people riled."

"What new movie?" Karen asked.

"You mean you don't know? John and I thought maybe that was the real reason you were coming back. Cryer Studios has remade *Justice at Sundown*. Not around here, thank goodness. Someplace out in Arizona, where, I'm told, the townfolk had their lives turned upside down for a good six months. We're just up for the movie's pre-premiere. That Raymond Armstrong person Melanie keeps referring to thinks it would be a grand idea to have the movie's first showing in the actual location where the story took place. Not the real premiere, mind you. They'll have *that* out in California a week or two later. No, this is a special one—a junket, I think they call it—for the press. To help publicize the picture, whip up interest."

Karen frowned. "So why does Pete—"

Bette's gesture was exasperated. "Who knows?"

"If it's not a good idea, the town could refuse."

"Try telling that to John and Joe and Isaac and Hank, not to mention Rhonda and Mary and Carmelita and Pepper! John wants it so much he stays awake nights planning all the things he can do to turn it into something even bigger!''

"Pete's the only person against it?''

"Besides me. And I'm not *that* against it. I just want the hubbub to be over.''

"Pete said something about TV?''

Bette rolled her eyes. "That's something else John's gone and done. He's invited a TV crew here, too, to film everything that goes on. I never knew I was married to such a mover and shaker.''

"John?'' Karen repeated, smiling. John Danson had always been a quiet, easygoing type of person. A hard worker, but very much at his own pace.

"The man has scraps of paper with ideas scribbled on them all over the place. That's what Melanie Taylor's working so hard to head off. The townfolk, with John leading them, really want to do this thing up. John lived near Virginia City out in Nevada when he was a youngster, and he'd like Twilight to bring in tourists the same way. He wants to spruce the place up, open some old buildings and turn them into museums and restaurants and such like...and the movie people don't want him to touch anything. I keep telling him 'They want it just the way it is, John,' but will he listen? He even thinks he can get them to contribute to the cause!''

"But would Twilight be Twilight with hordes of tourists coming through?''

"They're not thinking about that. All they can see is ways of making this movie thing profitable. You should hear 'em talk.''

They turned to follow the others inside. "And Aunt Augusta knew about this before she died?'' Karen asked.

"Sure she did," Bette said.

"Which side was she on?"

"She never said."

Ragtime music flowed from the player piano as drinks were handed out all around. A product of the past century, the Lady Slipper Saloon was dominated by a beautifully crafted bar that stretched the length of the room. With the rich patina of wood lovingly cared for through the years and ornate scroll carvings spiraling up the sides, it had a look seldom duplicated in the modern world. The remaining walls of the saloon were cluttered with framed photographs mottled by age, signs advertising old-time consumer products, numerous sets of deer antlers, a stuffed coyote and a collection of branding irons. An array of tables and chairs invited patrons to linger.

John had removed his jacket, rolled up his sleeves and was pulling beer from old-fashioned taps. Foam ran over the top and down the sides as he filled one large mug after another.

"Karen?" A shy touch on Karen's arm drew her attention. Carmelita Lopez stood across from her—a little older, a little wider, but just as sweet and unassuming.

"Carmelita!" Karen cried. "How are you? I'm so happy to see you again!"

Carmelita's dark eyes glowed as she pulled away from a hug and said in her soft Tex-Mex accent, "We knew you were coming but not when. I'm not sure I would have known you, if Bette hadn't said your name. You've grown so…and are so beautiful!" She brought forward the pretty young woman Karen had seen getting out of the bus. "*This* is my Juanita! You remember little Juanita? She used to follow you around, making a terrible pest.''

Karen blinked. The last time she'd seen Juanita, the girl had been four or five to Karen's thirteen. It shouldn't be a surprise that Juanita was now a grown woman of nineteen or twenty. But like Carmelita's memories of her, Karen's memories of Juanita had received a jolt.

''And *this*,'' Carmelita went on, reaching around Juanita to bring forward someone else, ''is her husband, Diego, and their baby, Jesse.''

The three made a striking picture, Diego with the sleeping babe in arms and Juanita standing by him, fiercely proud.

''Hello,'' Karen said, still reeling from the shock of time's passage.

A smile glimmered shyly in Diego's dark eyes. But as it spread to his mouth, his strong, handsome Aztec features were diminished by the disclosure of several missing teeth. His smile lasted only a second.

Juanita edged closer, protective of her young husband. ''Diego is *muy macho*,'' she declared.

''I'm sure he is,'' Karen murmured. Then, bending over the infant, she said, ''Jesse? Is that his name?''

Juanita nodded, her gaze steady.

Did she remember the times Karen had evaded playing with her, feeling the wide chasm of their years? Juanita had been next thing to an infant as far as she, a newly minted teenager, had been concerned. Someone to entertain and be entertained by on occasion, but not all the time, as the little girl seemed to want. Karen's last summer in Twilight had been blighted by Juanita's persistent pursuit.

"He's very handsome," Karen said. "Like his father," she added, and smiled warmly at them all.

"Yes," Juanita agreed softly, "he is." She clasped Karen's hand and squeezed it lightly, as if signaling her willingness for a new beginning.

Mary O'Conner barged over, interrupting them. As usual, she swept aside anyone in her way without a thought as to how they might feel about it.

"Karen!" she boomed above the saloon noise. "Good to have you here! Almost but not quite the same as having Augusta back! Lordy, we *do* miss that woman. You gonna be around long? It'll be great to see the rooms above the antique shop lit up at night again!" All the while she was talking, Mary O'Conner pumped Karen's hand. She was a large woman, bold of body and spirit. But for someone who gave such an outward display of force, Karen had long ago learned that Mary had an extremely soft center, particularly where it concerned her son, Benny.

Karen's gaze wandered over to where Benny sat at the player piano, working the foot pedals. Benny was physically in his forties—a fully adult man—but mentally he wasn't much more than eight. He was quiet and kept mostly to himself while helping his mother with her pottery making.

"I plan to stay a week," Karen said, her attention returning to Mary.

Mary grinned. "Might turn out to be a tad longer than that! I don't envy you what you have ahead. But then you love old things, just like your aunt did. So you probably won't mind."

Before Karen could question her meaning, Mary sailed on to another port, accosting Isaac Jacobs as he sat alone at a table.

Rhonda Peterson and Pepper Douglas hurried over to Karen to say hello, welcoming her back into the fold, while their husbands huddled with John at the bar.

"We've been havin' such an excitin' time!" Pepper Douglas exclaimed, her silver blond hair caught in an elaborate single plat from the crown of her head to her waist. She was the only woman to have maintained her usual look for the dinner, but since that was a flamboyant cowgirl chic, she fit right in. Pepper had been a rodeo barrel racer in her younger days, and her husband, Hank, had been a bronc rider. That was, until Hank got hurt worse than usual and they'd been forced to retire. They turned up in Twilight a few years after Karen began her summer vacations there. Pepper was fun to be around, the complete opposite to Hank's more dour demeanor. "Only you should've come in time to go to dinner with us," Pepper said. "Melanie and her friends took us to one of the swankiest places. There was fountains and waterfalls and plants like in a jungle, only behind glass—"

"It's called an atrium," Rhonda Peterson supplied.

"Whatever! It was beautiful! And the food... mmm! A little bit of heaven, that's what Hank said. And I agree." Then, with her green eyes dancing, she confided, "And you shoulda seen the waiters! Cutest little things! It's a good thing ol' Hank has had his brand on me for so long. Otherwise, I might've been tempted to stray!"

"You could get a ticket straight to hell for sayin' something like that, Pepper Douglas," Rhonda scolded.

"What makes you think I haven't already picked one up?" Pepper retorted.

"A waiter? Or a ticket? I'm gettin' confused!"

The two women laughed together in easy friendship, their merriment stopping only when Melanie Taylor, having been assisted onto a chair so everyone in the room could see her, called for quiet.

Melanie preened for a moment before saying, "Now, do we finally have an agreement? You promise not to make any change in the town's appearance before the preview, and we promise to place an agreed-upon sum in a special account, which will be used for whatever purpose the town deems worthy. No strings attached."

"We'd like that in writin', please," Hank Douglas drawled.

"That could take a while," Melanie said.

"Time's not our problem, ma'am," Hank returned.

Melanie didn't bother to hide her irritation. "Look! This is a good deal! I don't understand why, when you want what we want, we can't work something out!"

"Are you *afraid* to put it in writing?" Mary O'Conner challenged, taking up the cause.

"It's not that." Melanie looked for help from her two slick companions. She stooped while one whispered something in her ear, then smiled brightly as she straightened. "There's no reason why we can't draw up a preliminary agreement. Would that be satisfactory?"

The room erupted, many voices giving opinions at the same time. Karen looked at Bette, who jerked her head toward the door.

Karen quickly followed her outside.

"I can't take much more of this," Bette said tightly as she leaned back against the mercantile's front door.

"Sounds like the studio is trying to get away without paying," Karen said.

"Now, don't you start!" Bette snapped, before quickly apologizing, "I'm sorry. My nerves are starting to go. This back-and-forth business has been dragging on for too long. Whether the town should let the studio hold the preview here, whether or not we should try to make them pay for the privilege, what— if they agree to pay—we should do with the money, how we can turn it into more." She sighed deeply.

"And people think living in a tiny place like this is simple," Karen said sympathetically.

"That's the thing," Bette said. "It used to be! That's what I liked about it."

Karen thought about Rachel, whose quick response would've been that nothing in life is *ever* simple. Which reminded her of her promise to Martin. "Oh, Bette! Could I use your phone? I told someone I'd call to let him know I got here safely."

"Sounds serious," Bette said.

Karen shrugged.

"Come on." Bette straightened. "We'll go around back so we won't have to wade through that mob again. And while you're making your call, I'll root around to find where John put Augusta's key. We locked everything up knowing we'd be away for the day. If we could've counted on Pete, we'd've left it open, but you know him. The man gets a wild hair idea to leave and he's gone in a second."

Karen followed Bette along the sidewalk, then down a familiar alleyway, until soon they were at the rear of the buildings. The noise from the saloon was more muted here, allowing the peace that came from living in such splendid isolation to settle back in place.

It was easy, from this vantage point, to understand Bette's and Pete's reluctance to see Twilight change, but Karen couldn't help wondering about her aunt. If she was still alive, would Augusta have approved the majority's plan? Or would she, like Pete, have fought openly against it?

Karen didn't know. She was just glad she wouldn't be here long enough to have to choose a side.

CHAPTER THREE

"OH...MY...HEAVEN!" Karen breathed as she gazed at the objects, large and small, that had been crowded, many one on top the other, into the antique shop. Tables, chairs, bookcases, armoires, bed frames, benches, buffets, lamps, dolls, glassware, pottery, ceramic figurines...and that was just what she saw at first glance! Very little space was left for a person to stand.

"Augusta kind of lost it this past year," Bette said. "John tried to get her to slow down, but she wouldn't listen. It was like she knew she didn't have long and was determined to do as much as possible while she still could. Diego and Benny did all the heavy lifting."

Karen slumped against the door frame. "I never expected—"

"Wait till you see the storage shed out back," Bette warned. "It's packed, too. And if it had a drawer, she put things in it." Bette opened a drawer at random and inside were numerous small items wrapped in tissue.

"My...heaven," Karen repeated.

Bette smiled. "We thought you'd be surprised."

"I was planning to stay for a week, maybe a little more. But this—"

"You could always go back and forth for a while, until you have it all sorted out."

Karen shook her head, not in disagreement but in awe. "A good friend of mine said I'd be here a lot longer than I thought. She has...dreams."

"Well, she's right about this one. Could take you a month, maybe more, even working full-time."

A month! Karen recoiled from the thought. She couldn't take that long off work! But then, if she ever was serious about going into business for herself, wasn't this the time? She could sell some of the more valuable pieces, use the proceeds as a start-up fund, maintain the rest as stock and—

She reined in her racing thoughts. Her aunt's shop had always been an eclectic mix of collectibles as well as true antiques, leaning more toward general interest than Mr. Griffin's rustic hill-country specialties. In order even to begin to know what she had here, she was going to have to examine each piece, consult her aunt's extensive reference library and probably talk to numerous experts. Over the past four or five years she'd increased her knowledge of antiques, but mostly in the area she dealt with as a shop assistant on a day-to-day basis. She'd have to take her time with this lot. Not rush anything, either in going through the legacy or in making up her mind about the advisability of opening her own store. And there was always Martin. What would he—

Mentally, she caught her breath. What was she to say to him? He wasn't going to like the idea of her being away so long.

"This is pretty," Bette said, studying the porcelain figurine of a ballet dancer. "But I'd never buy it. Nice things have a way of holding you back. Clipping your wings, when what you'd really rather do is fly away.''

''Fly away?'' Karen repeated, coming out of her daze.

Bette replaced the dancer on a crowded shelf. ''Sometimes I'd like nothing better. But then, I'm still trying to work through this mess we've gotten ourselves into…and I don't mean Augusta's clutter!''

''How long before Twilight's big night?'' Karen asked, understanding her reference instantly.

''Fifteen days. That's why they're in such a hurry to get this agreement lined up. The whole thing was a brainstorm of this Raymond Armstrong person, and for it to work, they have to get moving *fast*. You probably heard they want to fix up the music hall for the showing. On the inside only, of course. Redo the wiring, recondition the floor. They'll supply their own chairs, too—our old ones don't seem to be good enough—and replace the old velvet stage curtain with a new one. Not to mention rigging up their own fancy generators, because they're afraid the whole thing will put too much of a strain on our puny little power lines.''

''How many people will attend, do you know?''

''I've no idea. The movie's stars, of course, and their fancy friends. The director, the producers, *Melanie* and her staff—''

''You don't like her very much, do you?''

''She flirts with John.''

''Surely it doesn't mean anything.''

Bette lifted her eyebrows. ''John thinks it's cute. *I* don't.'' She resumed her head count. ''Not to mention all the media types—critics and celebrity journalists and such that they're going to bring along, hoping for

good reviews and lots of publicity. That's why John
and the others see this as the perfect opportunity to
show off the town. To let people know we're here
and get them to want to come visit us. John's making
big plans to put out signs advertising Twilight on the
interstate—right after our showing and before the big
one in Hollywood. He's planning to put them up as
far west as Balmorhea and east as Sonora. Then
they'll stake out some other smaller signs along the
highway here, leading them in. John's already ordered
T-shirts and caps and coffee mugs and bumper stickers—all those touristy kinds of things that'll have
Twilight's name on them. Isaac Jacobs designed the
town logo. It looks pretty good, actually.''

Isaac Jacobs was Twilight's resident artist. Independent, almost to the point of being a hermit, he
painted and occasionally sold primitive-style land-
scapes.

Bette continued, frowning, ''We've been told the
studio will provide travel trailers for everyone staying
the night. The whole thing's supposed to last a couple
of days. The studio wants to entertain 'em real good.
Then when the stars get here, they'll do a lot of interviews. John's concern is for after. If tourists show
up like he hopes, they'll need a place to spend the
night, too. That's why he's looking to renovate inside
the old hotel. Just a few rooms at first, and more
later…if things work out. At one time he considered
using our extra rooms, but I put a stop to that right
quick. It's bad enough he's offered to put up that TV
crew that's coming. I will *not* have a bunch of tourists
parading through my home at all hours of the day and
night!''

John and Bette lived in the apartment above the

saloon, which was rumored to have had a shady history. There were at least six bedrooms in the flat—far more than the Dansons needed. The ones not in use, Bette kept locked. Still, Karen could respect her feelings.

"I'm surprised he even asked," she murmured.

"John's done a lot of silly things lately," Bette returned. Then, looking at the clutter awaiting Karen's attention, she said, "Well, I'll leave you to it. Lucky for you Augusta left the upstairs a lot straighter than this. I checked. I didn't want you to get here and not be able to set foot inside. You know where she kept everything, so you shouldn't have any trouble. But if you do, give a holler. I'm not far away."

Karen accompanied Bette outside, hugged her warmly and watched as she went in through the saloon's back door.

Karen's gaze then traveled slowly over the open area comprising the buildings' backyards, from one end of town to the other. Storage sheds, an old garage or two, a broken-down corral, several upended metal drums for burning trash, a rusting car, bits of this and that. Beyond this, the otherwise barren landscape went on and on. It had all seemed so romantic to her as a child, so very different from life in her parents well-ordered home in a well-cared-for neighborhood near the university. Now the romanticism was gone. She was seeing it through adult eyes—seeing things as they truly were.

People she'd always assumed had all the answers were suddenly just ordinary human beings in search of answers themselves. Bette had seemed so strong and steady in the past. Now she seemed...uncertain. John had changed, Juanita had grown up.

Karen climbed the long flight of exterior stairs that led to her aunt's apartment and found, true to Bette's word, the neatly appointed rooms in perfect order. She drew a long breath, then smiled at the light fragrance of lilacs that still lingered in the air. Augusta's favorite scent.

Tears threatened, even though she knew her aunt would disapprove. She'd died at a comfortable age, doing what she liked best, on one of her antique scouting trips. *What could be better?* Augusta would challenge. Still, as Karen moved about the rooms, paying homage by touching this and that, it was through a misty haze. As that Melanie person had said, Augusta had been a special person. Someone Karen would miss always.

She found a photograph of her aunt and herself on a small table. It had been taken the last summer she'd spent in Twilight, shortly after they'd successfully created a flower bed in the hardscrabble earth by the shop's back door. Both were smeared with dirt and grime, yet they were grinning happily into the camera, their arms flung across each other's shoulders. She'd been thirteen, Augusta in her early sixties.

Karen ran a finger over her aunt's beloved face, then did as Augusta would have wanted—she put her sadness behind her and got on with the necessities of settling in.

Her first chore was to move the car around back so she could carry her things upstairs to the bedroom that had always been hers when she visited.

It, too, was exactly as she'd left it. Her aunt hadn't changed a thing. Unicorns were still the main theme, playing on shelves in ceramic form, on walls in print and paint, on a lamp base, on a music box, in glass and crystal. She'd mentioned in a letter once that she liked unicorns and had arrived the next summer to find Augusta had filled the room with them, having scoured the state for the collection. Once again a pang of loss tugged at Karen's heart.

After she finished unpacking, she considered starting on the jumble downstairs, but abbreviated sleep the night before and the long and, in part, harrowing journey here, not to mention the discord she'd discovered upon her arrival, had exhausted her. First thing tomorrow she'd attack it and have a look at that storage shed, too.

Her body urged her into bed, no matter the hour. But the special quality to the light filtering into the room through the airy curtains reminded her of yet another childhood treasure. An unobstructed view from her bedroom window of one of nature's extravaganzas—a West Texas sunset.

She was just in time. The sky was resplendent with reds, pinks, purples, gold and silver, all shifting and changing in intensity and brilliance against a collection of feathery clouds as the sun slowly sank beneath the horizon.

Karen didn't move until the last flicker of color faded. In fact, she barely breathed.

"SEE? WHAT'D I TELL YOU? Sunsets out here are pretty amazing." A smile tugged at Lee Parker's lips as he stood beside his fellow crew members on a rise providing a panoramic view of the area.

"Whoa!" his camera-soundman Manny Cruz exclaimed in his best California hip. "That's some kinda special, dude!"

Lee transferred his gaze to Diane, Manny's wife,

who worked as his research assistant. Diane was a cute blonde with short hair, an upturned nose and a natural plumpness that looked good on her.

"I agree," she said, smiling.

Manny dropped his role-playing as he motioned to the impressive complex at the center of the valley. "So's that!" he said.

The headquarters of the Parker Ranch. A ranch so large it was measured in hundreds of sections, which had to be divided into nine work divisions in order to keep them all straight. It only seemed fitting that the headquarters itself would be massive. A family compound with houses set around a U-shaped drive and tree-filled courtyard, a work area with bunkhouse and outbuildings and barn and, continuing left, an expansive collection of corrals, chutes and pens, where cowboys prepared daily for many of the down-and-dirty jobs of ranch life. The complex covered a good half mile. Possibly more.

"I agree with that, too," Diane echoed. She tore her gaze away to look at Lee. "Why didn't you tell us your folks own such a large chunk of West Texas?"

"Because my folks don't own it. It belongs to the family. There's a bunch of us, so there's lots of shares."

"Who are those people down there, then?"

"They're on-ranch Parkers. They live and work there year round. I'm an off-ranch Parker. All I do is visit occasionally and vote my one share."

"*And* collect a dividend?" she guessed.

"Yep," he agreed.

Diane tsked. "Now, don't get started with those cowboy 'yeps' and 'nopes.' Tell us about it!"

"It's pretty simple," Lee replied. "Two Parker brothers came here shortly before the Civil War to make themselves a ranch. Took a lot of doing by them and their descendants, but what you see is the result."

Diane grumbled, "I'd probably have to strangle you to get the full story."

"Next time I have a chance I'll search out the family history book. It tells all about it."

Diane brightened. "A history book?"

"Now you've done it," Manny complained, grinning. "She won't rest until she's read it. Then she'll want to do a show—"

"I love history!" Diane defended herself.

"So do we!" Manny returned. "Only we know when to take a break!"

"I *was* taking a break—with you, remember?—until Simon Legree here called and—"

"We better get going," Lee broke in. "I promised Mae we'd be in before dark. And she's not a person you make promises to lightly."

"What would she do?" Manny teased. "Have your head?"

"She might," Lee said, with just enough seriousness to make his friends wonder. They might as well be prepared, he thought, even though he himself hadn't been. Because he'd missed the annual family get-together-and-stock-holders meeting for the past number of years while building "Western Rambles" into the respected series it was today, he'd been caught off guard to hear Mae still sounding so full of spit and vinegar. She'd passed her eighty-eighth birthday, after all. But there she was, still on a high after recently overseeing her great-niece Jodie's marriage to the local sheriff.

"You should've been here a week ago," Mae informed him during his call to tell the family of his upcoming visit. "We put together a nice little wedding, even if it was on fairly quick notice. Groom stayed put, at least," she'd added in an obvious dig at his younger brother. She hadn't forgotten the terrible insult Alex had inflicted on the Parker name. Neither had he. Alex, on the other hand, seemed to have developed a convenient case of amnesia about the entire event.

"Mae..." Diane mused as she climbed into the rear of the sturdy off-road vehicle they used to transport themselves and their equipment from one shooting location to the next. "You've mentioned her before. She's...what to you?"

Lee settled behind the wheel. "A distant cousin. My great-grandfather and her father were brothers. But she's more than that. She runs the family. You'll see what I mean when you meet her."

"You're just chock-full of surprises, aren't you?" Diane muttered as she shoved a duffel bag back into place among the other gear after it fell against her shoulder. "What else are you not telling us?"

She was kidding, but had hit a little closer to the truth than Lee felt comfortable with.

"Who, me?" he asked innocently. "Surprises?"

Once Manny had climbed into the front passenger seat and secured himself, Lee swung the Range Rover back onto the narrow road.

This was the way they'd spent a good portion of their lives over the past five years. After lining up the subjects they wanted to cover for the series' upcoming season and making all the various arrangements— which at times held some of the same logistical challenges as moving a small army—they set off on two three-month-long sorties during the year to visit those places and people of interest, gather as much information as they could on-site, record it, then take the raw footage back to their headquarters in San Francisco, where they would later edit it into half-hour shows.

They hadn't taken any time off in two years until now, when they'd tried to allot themselves three weeks. Barely a week into their vacations, though, Lee had stopped by the office in San Francisco to collect the mail and found the letter from Twilight, Texas, informing him of the remake of *Justice at Sundown*. The letter had gone on to detail the studio's interest in holding a junket in the same town where the rescue and hanging had actually occurred, then finally rambled on at great lengths to describe the town, its history and its interesting characters.

Lee had almost tossed the letter aside. On another occasion they might have given it some consideration, but with the junket's date so close, and Manny and Diane in Maui, and him…well, him blissfully staying put in the Bay Area, it wasn't going to work. Then a name had caught his eye: *Augusta Latham-Lamb*. She was listed as one of Twilight's interesting characters. A deceased character, it turned out as Lee read more closely, whose niece, Karen, would soon be coming to take possession of her aunt's antique shop. The letter writer had then moved on to another town character, but Lee's attention didn't follow. Augusta Latham-Lamb and Karen…*Latham?* The same Karen Latham his brother had left standing at the altar?

Lee had straightened instantly, trying to stretch his memory back seven years. He'd been seated next to an Aunt Augusta at the wedding rehearsal dinner. She'd wanted to talk about antiques and where she was from—some tiny little place in Texas. A veritable ghost town was the way she'd described it. It all fit!

Lee had then started to play with the possibilities. Traveling to Twilight to cover the preparation for the movie remake's junket could be a legitimate action. They could show the effect of both the old and new versions of the movie on the tiny town and its people and throw in a more rounded view of the town's history, not to mention the area's. Where the heck *was* Twilight, Texas, anyway? It had a slightly familiar buzz, but he couldn't place it. Didn't matter, though. He could look it up. He started to plan, developing the idea, then made the intrusive telephone call to the Cruzes.

"It's now or never," he'd explained to Diane. "You remember the original *Justice at Sundown*, don't you? It was pretty big. I've put feelers out and it's rumored this new version will be big, too. It stars Johnny Mehan as the outlaw hero, Andrea Wright and Paul Colins. All heavy hitters. It should give us some good numbers if we get the timing right. I was thinking we could rush it through, or at the very least slot it at the beginning of this season's schedule. Possibly even market it as a 'Western Rambles' special, while interest in the movie is high. What do you think?"

There was a short pause, then she said, "I'll tell Manny to change out of his swim trunks and back into jeans. When do you want us there? And where's there?"

He could always count on Diane to have a quick nose for a story. She frequently ferreted out information that no one else thought existed.

He'd experienced a twinge of conscience at not telling her and Manny the truth about his personal reasons for wanting to do the show, but he wasn't sure what good it would do. Karen Latham might still be as unwilling to listen as she had been seven years ago. He could seek her out, apologize for what his brother had done—she'd stare at him like he was one of the poisonous snakes she probably still thought all Parkers to be. Then he'd slither off, do the show, and they'd leave town. But he had to at least *try* to talk to her. Her face, her eyes had haunted him for months after the aborted wedding. They still did on occasion. He couldn't forget her, the way Alex had.

Dusk had settled into night by the time they rolled to a stop in front of the two-story stone house at the head of the Parker compound. Intricately tooled black wrought-iron railings framed porches on both the upper and lower levels.

The front door swung open as they piled out of the truck, spilling enough light to reveal that Mae herself had come to greet them.

Lee moved quickly, taking the two steps onto the porch in an easy hop. But as he reached for Mae, she lifted her cane and held it between them.

"I was beginnin' to think you'd got lost," she complained. "It's so long since you've been here."

"I'd never forget the way. You know that."

"Humph!" she snorted, then, lowering the cane, she allowed his affection.

She'd changed little in the years since Lee had seen her—the same snowy white hair pulled into a smooth knot on top her head, the same hawklike black eyes, the no-nonsense set to her mouth, the intimidating force of her personality. For more than the thirty-six years since his birth, Mae's influence had radiated outward from the ranch to the Parkers living in other sections of the state. She kept apprised of their movements and acted when she thought necessary. Up until the time of her eightieth birthday, she'd actively ridden the divisions of the ranch, refusing to stop until a fall and doctor's orders had forced her off her horse. Some years earlier she'd even managed the ranch when no one else was a ready candidate. The cane was new, though. As was the hidden fragility he sensed in her body when he held her close.

She patted his shoulder as he pulled away. "Glad to see you, Lee," she said gruffly. "You're looking good."

"So are you," Lee said.

"No, I'm not." She allowed a wisp of a smile to touch her lips. "But I appreciate you sayin' so." She looked at the Cruzes, giving them a glance of quick estimation as they stood on the path, hesitant to intrude. "These folks your friends?" she demanded of Lee. "Tell 'em to come inside. I can't see 'em good enough out there."

They filed inside the house Lee had become familiar with through the years. The foyer's Spanish influence of pristine white walls, black wrought-iron sconces and chandelier and colorful rugs on the dark gray stone floor spilled into a living room, where a huge fireplace dominated the longest wall, sheer curtains graced the windows, and two overstuffed sofas offered an alternative to several straight-back chairs.

Mae chose one of the chairs, her posture, as always, exceptional.

Lee sensed the Cruzes' uncertainty as they chose

seats on one of the sofas. He tried to lighten the moment by introducing them.

Mae nodded acknowledgment, then, leveling her gaze on him, said, "You are plannin' to stay the night. You wouldn't come all this way and *not*. Am I right?"

They had planned no such thing. They were only going to stop by for a short visit, then move on, arriving in Twilight late but expected. Lee, on his own, would then make other trips back to the ranch if it fit into their schedule.

While he groped for words, Mae continued, "I have two perfectly fine bedrooms upstairs that Marie, Marie's my housekeeper," she explained to the Cruzes, "has spent hours freshening. I won't take no for an answer, Lee. You and your friends look tired. A good night's sleep is the best cure for that."

"They're expecting us in Twilight, Mae," Lee said, holding out.

Her expression was imperious. "I haven't seen you in five years. I want to catch up on things, get to know what you're doing."

"The show keeps me busy, Mae. Keeps *us* busy."

"Too busy to visit with your relations when you have a perfectly good opportunity?" Turning again to Diane and Manny, she smiled pleasantly and said, "You must be hungry after traveling all day."

The irrepressible Manny broke into a huge grin. "I could eat," he said.

Diane shot Lee a look, telling him the decision was his, before she dealt with her husband. "You can *always* eat! You're a bottomless pit, Manny Cruz. Honestly, if I ate the way you did, I'd be bigger than a house!"

"I like to see a person enjoy a good meal," Mae said with approval. "It means they've been working hard."

Diane giggled. "All Manny's worked hard today is his mouth. He's talked our ears off! When he wasn't talking, he was singing. And he *can't* sing!"

"I sound just like Garth Brooks," Manny bragged.

"In your dreams!" Diane shot back.

Lee saw that Mae's smile held real amusement as she watched the byplay between his two friends. She liked them instinctively and they, in turn, seemed to like her. All it took was surviving the first shock of exposure to her strong personality.

"All right," he said. "One night. But that's all we can spare. I'll let them know in Twilight that we've been delayed."

"Twilight," Mae repeated, frowning. "I still can't understand why that place is of interest to you. Pretty no-account from what I remember."

"It's not us, Mae," Lee explained patiently, as if they hadn't been through this before when he'd first told her what they were planning. He hadn't mentioned Karen Latham to her, either, feeling it was better to keep the young woman's presence to himself. "It's the movie studio. They're the ones with the big ideas."

"I haven't seen Twilight in years," Mae reflected.

"It's not far away, is it?" Diane asked, addressing Mae directly for the first time.

"Next county over. About…sixty or seventy miles."

"Long miles," Lee said.

Mae nodded. "Everything's long out here. Probably take a couple of hours to drive." She regarded

Lee curiously, "You ever get out there when you were visiting us?"

"You kept me too busy working, Mae," Lee said, smiling. Then he explained to his friends, "When I turned fourteen, my dad sent me to the ranch to learn a few things. Like how to ride and rope and work cattle."

"Things every Parker should know," Mae agreed.

"I liked it, so I came back for a few years. Even worked on a couple of roundups."

"Fall roundup's coming soon. You're welcome to work that one, too, if you want. Rafe'd be glad for the help."

"Who's Rafe?" Manny asked.

"Another cousin," Lee said. "He manages the ranch, now that—" He stopped, unsure if even after all these years the transference of management was still a sore point with Mae.

"And does a damn fine job of it, too!" Mae said robustly. "Better'n me."

"They'll meet him later...right, Mae?" Lee asked.

"They'll meet everyone," she replied. "They're all coming to dinner."

Lee caught the quick glance Diane exchanged with Manny and had to smother a grin. By the end of the night they'd've had their fill of being in the same house with so many strong-willed Parkers.

"You can use the phone in my office," Mae said, standing up. "You know the way. I'll tell Marie to get us all something cold to drink. Then you can take your friends to their room. They might like to freshen up. You, too, of course. In the meantime," she said to the newcomers, "make yourselves comfortable. I'll be back shortly."

Typically, Mae had handed everyone their assignments and expected them to be carried out.

Lee used the phone on the credenza behind Mae's rosewood desk and was just hanging up from making his excuses to John Danson in Twilight, when Mae entered the room.

She needed no preamble to get to the point. "I've seen this show you're involved in. A neighbor made a tape and sent it over. We don't get public television channels out here unless we have one of those fancy satellite dishes, which we don't. So I hadn't seen it until last night." Her dark eyes, holding his, narrowed. "I didn't know what to expect. I knew you'd won some awards with it, but—" she took a breath "—I wasn't prepared to be so proud of you. You did a really fine job with those people trying to get back on their feet after being flooded out of their houses last year. Showed the good and the bad, and that even in terrible times, people can still find things to laugh about. I liked it."

Lee had never received a compliment from Mae. She'd approved of his seemingly inborn ability to handle a horse and a rope and the fact that he'd held his ground in tight situations with an ornery cow. But she'd never gone so far as to actually tell him he'd done well. He was surprised by how good it made him feel. He smiled broadly. "Thank you, Mae. But it wasn't just me. Diane and Manny—"

"I like them, too."

"Not all of our shows are so serious," he cautioned.

"I know. I saw the one about the ostrich farmer. It was silly, but the youngsters enjoyed it. They learned something, too.'' She paused, then said, ''That brother of yours. What's he up to now?''

''He's a lawyer with a big firm in Dallas.''

''No, I mean what's he really up to? I know what he does for a living.''

''He's working on marriage number four.''

Mae shook her head in disgust. ''Your momma spoiled him. She tried to spoil you, too, but your daddy sent you out here. We took it out of you in about five minutes.''

Lee grinned. ''So that's what you were doing. I thought I was going through boot camp for cowboys!''

''Cowboys don't go to boot camp!''

''I know that…now.''

Mae smiled in spite of herself, and as they returned to the living room, she allowed Lee to place his arm around her shoulders.

''The Parker charm,'' Mae said as she resumed her seat. ''You have it in spades. Like you have the look, except for those pale eyes.''

All Lee's life his eyes had set him apart from his dark-haired, dark-eyed father, brother and cousins. His mother had mentioned something about having a great-grandfather from Denmark, but he'd never met the man.

''Never you mind,'' Mae murmured, as if offering comfort for an ongoing disappointment. ''They look good on TV.''

Which tickled Lee so much he couldn't help laughing. And without fully knowing why, the others joined in.

CHAPTER FOUR

KAREN SAT CROSS-LEGGED on the floor amid an array of small articles she'd spent most of the morning unwrapping and dividing into groups. At arm's reach was a large plastic bag for the temporary disposal of tissue paper and, beside that, several drawers, all empty but one.

At first the job of going through her aunt's things had seemed overwhelming. She knew her aunt had never been good at keeping formal records, so it would be of little use to look for any kind of list to refer to. She was fully on her own. Where did she start? How did she go about it? She'd never organized an estate before. In the end, she let simple expediency be her guide. She could only deal with what she could reach, so she'd started by removing some of the lighter pieces stacked atop others. Not cataloging anything herself yet, just creating a space to work. Then, since none of the chests or bureaus blocking the way could be moved until they were emptied, she'd begun going through drawers.

It was just like Christmas, since she had no idea what each lovingly wrapped bundle would reveal. Her aunt had given no special regard to value or uniqueness. A tin whistle distributed in the forties or fifties as a child's merchandising prize was tucked next to an exquisite lady's gold pocket watch dating from the turn of the century. Trash and treasure, a casual observer might presume. But Karen knew better. Her aunt either was aware the tin whistle had value or was speculating that someday in the future it would.

Where Mr. Griffin dealt only with sure things, her aunt combined whimsy with purpose. She knew a sure thing when she saw it, but she also took chances. Mostly because she enjoyed playing the game.

When the last drawer from the last imposing chest was emptied, Karen planned to rewrap all the articles as carefully as her aunt had and pack them in the cardboard boxes she'd found broken down and flattened into a stack in the antique shop's broom closet. Only this time, each article and each box would be numbered and listed correspondingly in a notebook, so she could find an item when she wanted to examine it in more detail.

She'd just reached for another tissued bundle and was opening it when a car drove up out front. Heavy doors opened and closed, and voices rang out—more visitors to Twilight. Karen's first instinct was to go look out the front window, but the room was still so solidly packed she couldn't even see the front window, much less look out of it. Quelling her curiosity, she stayed where she was and draped an intricately constructed rhinestone necklace across the back of her hand. It was nicely made, and upon closer examination through a loupe, she recognized the name of a well-known costume jewelry manufacturer on the clasp.

She added it to the jewelry group, then reached for another bundle—which turned out to contain a Kennedy-Johnson political button from the 1960 presidential race.

Her aunt had been extremely proud of her button collection, even to the point of attending numerous political rallies sponsored by both parties across the state in order to collect more. Karen unwrapped one after another. A Nixon-Agnew, a Carter-Mondale, an Eisenhower, a Franklin D. Roosevelt, a Hoover…numerous state and local office hopefuls. Some buttons were in better condition than others, but all could be considered above average. A few were even pristine. Karen was careful to rewrap them immediately, before assigning them their own grouping.

Several hours later she was still hard at work, having emptied two additional chests, manhandled them out of the way against a wall and taken several boxes upstairs to her aunt's apartment—the only place with enough extra space for storage. A light tap sounded on the back door, before Bette, calling her name, let herself inside.

When she saw Karen on the floor, Bette shook her head. "You've got to be kidding! With all these chairs? Why aren't you using one of them?"

Karen grinned. "It's easier to be in the middle of everything."

"Looks like you're making a good start," Bette said, glancing around.

"Don't you mean, 'It's messier now than it was before'?" Karen teased.

Bette rooted around for a chair. "That's always the way when you're organizing something. The mess gets worse before it gets better. I'm taking a break," she announced. "Those TV people have finally gotten here. They were supposed to come last night but didn't make it. Which was probably a good thing, since the argument with Melanie carried on until sometime around midnight. Did the noise keep you awake?'' When Karen shook her head, Bette continued, ''By that time Melanie had finally had enough and told John and the others to either take her offer or leave it—the studio wasn't going to dicker anymore. Of course, they took it. She used her little portable fax machine thingie and the agreement came back signed by Raymond Armstrong. Now it's a done deal. It's happening.''

''I don't know whether to be happy or sad,'' Karen murmured.

Bette shrugged. ''Me too. But that's neither here nor there. Pretty soon this place will be crawling with workers. There is one good thing that's happened, though. Melanie and her little friends are gone. They left with the bus. We shouldn't be seeing any more of them until just before the preview.''

''That's something,'' Karen agreed.

Bette was quiet for a moment, then she said, ''I have an idea. I'm making a big meal for the TV people tonight. Why don't you come have dinner with us? Be a friendly face at the table. I'm sure John would appreciate it. And so would I.''

''I thought I'd work as long as I could today. There's so much—'' She glanced around.

''None of it's going to go anywhere.''

That was a line of reasoning she couldn't argue with. She smiled. ''Sure, dinner sounds fine.'' Then her smile lessened. ''Bette? Aunt Augusta was happy during the last part of her life, wasn't she?''

''Augusta was one of the happiest people I knew. Never let much of anything get her down. The only time I ever saw her cry was that first summer you didn't visit. When your parents—''

"She cried?" Karen said.

"Having you out here livened up her whole year. She took it hard when you couldn't come anymore. I think she looked on you more as a daughter than a niece. But she got over it. I only saw her cry the once."

Augusta and her husband had never had children. In the way youngsters plunge innocently into murky adult waters, Karen had once asked why. Her aunt replied that she couldn't have children, something to do with the way she was made. She'd stated it matter-of-factly, as if it weren't really a concern, but now Karen couldn't help wondering if her aunt had been masking her true feelings. It made her sad to think that Augusta had missed her so badly. Though she, too, had cried in Austin, wanting to be in Twilight.

"You…scattered her ashes?" Karen asked, not wanting to talk about the task, but feeling the necessity.

Bette nodded. "John and I did. Out in the desert. Just like she asked in her will."

Karen's chin lowered. "My parents had a service for her in Austin. A number of her friends in the trade attended."

"She had a good life. She'd be the first to say it."

Another moment passed, then Bette slapped her jeans-clad knees and stood up. "I guess I'd better get going. That dinner's not going to cook itself."

"Can I help?" Karen offered.

Bette smiled. "Nope, I can handle it. Just come on over about seven. John's out with them now, showing them around. Playing host."

Again there was an odd little undercurrent in Bette's tone.

"What are they like?" she asked, following her outside. It felt good to move around.

"They're nice enough. Friendly. Interested. Two of 'em are married, and the other one...well, you'll see for yourself tonight. All I can say is, now I understand why the show's a success. You ever see it? 'Western Rambles.' They go to all kinds of places, talking to people, showing things of interest—anyplace west of the Mississippi River. Get it?"

Karen nodded. She got it, but she'd never seen the show.

"John just had to have a satellite dish," Bette continued. "That's how we see it. It's back there, on the other side of the garage. Looks like a space alien planted it." Her gaze settled on the storage shed in Augusta's backyard. "You take a look in that place yet?"

"Oh, yes."

Bette chuckled dryly. "I'm surprised you're still here. Maybe Pete has a point. You do have a lot of Augusta in you."

"She's my ideal," Karen answered softly.

"Mine, too," Bette agreed. "Well...see you at seven."

Karen gave an airy little wave and went back inside. But instead of returning to work, she sat in the same chair that Bette had and stared blankly at the tightly packed room.

Talking about her aunt had rekindled her previous melancholy. The cremation, the service in Austin...each brought a guilty reminder of the times she could have come back to Twilight to see her aunt and hadn't.

Augusta had been quick to offer sanctuary after the

aborted wedding, but the close proximity of the Parker Ranch had kept Karen away. She'd been too
freshly wounded, her spirit too fragile. Then later,
once she'd grown stronger and moved out of her parents' home, she'd been preoccupied with the need to
create a life for herself in Kerrville.

Create a life...

Since the summer she was six, Karen had often
viewed herself as two different people. The Karen
who lived in Austin, a rising-star student—at least in
her parents' estimation—and the Karen who lived the
life of a wild child during her vacations in Twilight.
Today, all grown-up, she was the Karen who lived a
relatively quiet life in Kerrville, worked in a rather
staid antique shop, had a boyfriend who was pressing
her to accept his marriage proposal. And the Karen
who...who what? Life didn't seem to be the same in
Twilight, and consequently, little remained of her previous personality here. Her carefree days had been
permanently altered by adulthood and her aunt's
death. This world had changed and was about to
change even more. And she had no idea where she
fit into it all. Or even if she did.

She was unsure about other things, as well.
Whether or not she wanted to continue working in the
staid antique shop for a man who derived little pleasure from life besides a nice profit. If she wanted to
continue living in Kerrville—a wonderful place in
and of itself, but where she was starting to feel smoth-
ered. By Martin? By his need to bind her to him?

She cared for him. He was a wonderful person.
Kind and gentle...she admired him greatly. Only he
wanted an answer. An answer she couldn't yet give.

Was caring enough? Was love? Her only experience of love was with Alex. And look where that had gotten her. She needed time to think, to figure things out—just as Rachel had advised. Rachel, who was far wiser in many ways than most people realized.

Now, as Rachel had foreseen, her stay in Twilight would have to be extended. In the end, she'd have the time she needed to—

Her thoughts suddenly stopped. A major consideration about opening her own place was the need to find a suitable location. It would have to be someplace large enough, someplace she could afford and in a setting that held promise. But she already had that! Right here!

Augusta had left her this building as well as the stock inside it. She owned it free and clear. And if, through John's efforts, the town became well known enough for tourists to start to pour in instead of trickle—

Karen again forced her thoughts to an abrupt halt. No one knew exactly how this tourist-enticement thing was going to work out. People might come, and then again, they might not. In either event, would she want to live permanently in a place so far away from modern conveniences? Even if it was her aunt's beloved Twilight?

Karen took a deep breath and was reminded again of Bette's cryptic words. Did she, too, want to fly away? To escape from the complications of her life?

If only she could.

THE "WESTERN RAMBLES" CREW was given a grand tour of Twilight. They saw the saloon downstairs from the apartment they would share with John Danson and his wife, the mercantile store, the music hall where the remake of *Justice at Sundown* would have its first showing in a short fourteen days. They saw the famous well where the outlaw Nate Barlow had rescued a small child from a slow and agonizing death, and whose own death quickly followed.

Diane was particularly intrigued with the well. Built of indigenous stones, it stood about four feet high and was nearly that wide in diameter, with a weathered wood crossbeam, iron hand crank and a worn rope from which the bucket had long ago broken free. For safety's sake the deep shaft had been covered with cut semicircles of wood, which were weighted down with several large rocks.

"Does it still have water?" Diane asked.

"Oh, maybe a little," John Danson answered pleasantly. "The spring was said to have dried up, but it kept the town goin' for another twenty or so years. Actually, we use another well now, a more modern one that's been drilled and redrilled a couple of times."

"So it was only a rumor that the spring dried up completely?" Manny asked curiously.

"Nah, it quit sure enough, but it started again a little while later. Only thing was, it wasn't near as generous, and the water was said to have tasted funny."

"That must have been quite a blow to the people living here," Diane said.

"Place never was the same. Stage started takin' another route, other people did, too. Things just kinda petered out after that. People started movin' away. Here, you wanna take a look?" Without waiting for a reply, John lifted the rocks and dropped them on the ground near their feet, then dragged away the wooden covers.

A musty, damp, earthy smell emanated from within the dark hole. All three newcomers peered over the edge, but there wasn't much to see.

Still fascinated, Diane asked, "How deep is it?"

As the conversation continued, Lee let his gaze wander over the picturesque little western town, taking it in from one end to the other. It certainly had an interesting look, one he thought the viewers of "Western Rambles" would appreciate. They'd also appreciate its engaging history and the aspirations of its present-day residents for a brighter future. Even discounting the movie and the press junket, there was more than enough material to do a show here.

His gaze caught on a nondescript sign printed on the window two doors down from the saloon. Antiques, it stated without fanfare. So that was Augusta Latham-Lamb's "little place," as he remembered her terming it. Where Karen Latham would be taking possession of her legacy. Was she there yet? It had a closed look that made him wonder. He also wondered how he'd be able to bring her name casually into the conversation to find out. His attention returned to the others.

"What about you?" Diane, ever the curious researcher, continued to pump their source. "How did you and your wife end up here, Mr. Danson?"

"Call me John. Everybody does." Deep creases formed along the sides of the man's cheeks when he smiled. "Bette and I just happened on the place one day and decided to stay. Bette doesn't like cities and I don't much care for 'em, either."

"Were you fans of the old movie?" Manny asked.

"Nope. Hadn't even ever heard of it. Guess it was fate that brought us here." With Manny and Lee's help, he worked the wood covers back into position and replaced the rocks. "I'm glad somebody did, though," he continued. "Otherwise, we wouldn't be havin' all this excitement. You wanna see the hotel? Nothin' much there yet, but when we're done it'll look real fine. We're plannin' to keep it to period as much as we can. Folks appreciate that."

As they moved away from the well and into the street, angling toward the far end of town, Lee asked, "Didn't you tell us Cryer Studios wants the place to stay exactly as it is, at least until after the preview?"

John grinned. "On the outside, sure. But we never said we wouldn't work on the *inside*. Lots of stuff we can do there."

"Two weeks isn't a very long time, John," Manny said.

"I've done carpentry work, so have some of the others. We can have the lower floor and a few rooms upstairs finished for the first tourists who might want to spend the night. Then later we'll do more and start workin' on some of the other places, too, so we can open 'em up for shops and such. After the preview, that is."

Lee found his opportunity as they neared the antique shop. "An antique store...way out here?" he said.

John stopped walking. "That's Augusta's place. I told you about her in my letter, didn't I? Augusta Latham-Lamb? She was the true heart of this place. Loved it more'n the rest of us put together. It's too bad she's not here anymore to—"

"That's right," Lee interrupted him, pretending

that his memory had just been jogged. "She's the woman who died recently. And her—was it her niece who was coming to take over for her?"

"Karen." John nodded. "Karen Latham. She's in there right now, matter of fact, makin' a start on goin' through her aunt's things. Augusta left her the works, but I'm not sure whether she'll be stayin' or not. Sure would like her to. Do you want to meet her? I doubt she'd mind if we—"

"No, no," Lee refused quickly, "we can wait." Then he reminded John, "You were taking us to the hotel?"

He felt Diane's quick look even as Manny and John started off again.

When Lee went to follow them, Diane held him back. "What's going on?" she demanded, frowning.

"We're being shown around town, aren't we?" he answered drolly.

"No, I mean...who's this Augusta person and this Karen?"

"Didn't you read the letter?"

"You never showed me the letter."

"They were in it."

Her frown intensified. "Why are you so interested in them?"

Before he could answer, raised voices from down the street caught their attention. Several other Twilight residents had joined John and Manny, and one, a strongly built woman, was gesturing emphatically.

"Maybe we'd better get down there," Lee suggested.

They arrived in time to hear a long, lanky man in his late forties drawl sternly, "Mary, you know that's just not right. Joe here has had claim to that well from the time he took over his daddy's place.''

The woman's face was flushed. ''I checked my papers first thing this morning and I *know* what I saw, Hank. I'll be glad to show 'em to you! Benny and I own that well. It's ours!''

''No, it ain't!'' another man—Joe?—contradicted her. He, like Hank, was tall, but he had a potbelly and a thatch of unruly cotton yellow hair. ''The well comes with my house. I live closest to it. It's mine! Mine and Rhonda's.'' He indicated a woman who stood a foot or two behind him, her arms crossed over her chest, her expression miserable.

''*I* have papers!'' Mary insisted.

''So do I!''

''Show 'em to me!''

Joe scowled. ''You know I can't. They got burned up when the shed caught fire.''

''Then Benny and I—''

John, who seemed caught totally by surprise at the ferocity of the argument, stepped in to mediate. ''Hey…hey. We have company here. We don't need to be airin' our dirty linen in public. Let's just everybody settle down.''

''I wouldn't've thought a thing of it,'' Mary steamed on. ''But he had to start talking last night like he owned the well, when I know he doesn't!''

''I do!'' Joe repeated his claim.

''These are the TV people!'' John cut in desperately. ''''Western Rambles,' remember? They're here to report on what they see. Do you want 'em to report *this?*'' He paused when the combatants looked startled. ''Yeah, I thought not! Tourists won't want to come to Twilight to hear us arguing. So stop your snarlin' and snappin' and introduce yourselves before they get disgusted and go away. You know we're all in this together. Share and share alike.''

The change was miraculous. Where seconds before they'd been engaged in heated battle, now all animosity faded. Even Rhonda brightened, stepping forward to stand arm in arm with her husband.

John introduced the crew. ''This is Lee Parker and the Cruzes—Manny and Diane. And this—''

''I'm Mary...Mary O'Conner,'' the large woman said with full confidence. ''Nice to meet you.'' She gave them each a firm handshake and took it on herself to introduce the others. ''This here's Joe and Rhonda Peterson, and that's Hank Douglas.'' More handshakes followed, along with a self-conscious little smile from Rhonda.

''Parker, you say?'' Joe repeated slowly, his head tipping to one side. ''Are you any kin to the Parkers over Briggs County way?''

''We're not the ones supposed to be askin' questions, Joe,'' Rhonda scolded softly, then turned to the newcomers. ''We're honored you decided to visit Twilight. I really like your show. I watch it every week. We—we all do!''

''Thank you.'' Lee spoke for his crew.

''I was on my way to show 'em the hotel,'' John explained quickly, seemingly anxious to prevent anything else from going wrong. ''Then I thought I'd take 'em to the cemetery.''

''The cemetery?'' Lee echoed.

''Where Nate Barlow's buried,'' John said, rushing on. ''You know.'' He frowned at Hank, pressing for corroboration.

Hank's puzzled expression cleared. "Oh...oh, yeah. Nate Barlow!"

"Ol' Nate Barlow, our town hero," John said. "Man in a hurry who didn't hurry enough! Rescued a couple of kids, though. Maybe that was enough to save his eternal soul. I can just see him at the Pearly Gates, tellin' St. Peter all about it."

"A *couple* of kids?" Diane questioned. "I thought it was one."

John started to pull away. "One, two...who can be sure? I've heard it more'n one way." He motioned for the TV crew to follow. "Personally, I like to think there was two kids. Better heaven insurance for ol' Nate."

They left the townspeople standing in the street. Ten minutes later when they came outside the hotel, everyone else was gone.

John glanced at his watch. "I'm not used to wearing this thing. Only put it on after this movie business came up. Bette said to be home for six-thirty so we'll have time to wash up. We still can make it to the cemetery if you wanna see it."

"Is it, like, Twilight's Boot Hill?" Manny asked, winking at Diane.

"Well, sort of. More the town's cemetery. Nate Barlow's the only outlaw I know of who's buried there."

"Then sure we do," Manny said.

Once again they fell into step beside their guide as he took them the rest of the distance down the town's main street, turning at the other side of the hotel onto a less traveled path that led to the burial place. As they passed a small shack set a short distance off the

path, a scruffy old man came to stand in his doorway
and glare at them.

"Who's that?" Manny asked.

"Old Pete," John said tersely. "Don't pay any attention to him. He's a little…addled."

The others turned away, but Lee couldn't resist a
longer look. To his surprise the old man lifted a hand
and, very deliberately, gave him the finger.

Lee had to fight to contain a bark of laughter and
as a result nearly lost his footing.

Diane, who reached to help steady him, demanded,
"What's *wrong* with you?"

"Nothing. Absolutely nothing," Lee replied.

Of course Diane didn't believe him, and with a hiss
of displeasure at what she must have seen as his stubborn intractability, she pressed on in the wake of her
husband.

As he brought up the rear, Lee realized he was
beginning to feel a growing excitement about this
shoot. With or without Karen Latham, it was starting
to look interesting!

CHAPTER FIVE

As SEVEN O'CLOCK DREW nearer, Karen wished she hadn't agreed to dinner at Bette and John's. She was aching with exhaustion. She hadn't worked with such uninterrupted concentration since she'd been at university trying to finish one of her numerous projects. Yet she couldn't just not show up. She'd given Bette her word.

With a light groan she abandoned the comfort of a long soak in her aunt's clawfoot tub and donned a summery dress. It wasn't as if it would be more work. All she had to do was sit there, smile and occasionally ask what could be taken for an intelligent question. As soon as she could, she'd make an excuse for an early withdrawal, stumble back to her aunt's apartment and fall into bed and sleep. Ah, bliss!

As Bette had done earlier at the shop, she tapped perfunctorily on the saloon's rear door before letting herself inside. Since the Lady Slipper was closed for business, no one was there to greet her. John had considerately left a light on behind the bar, though, to help guide the way through the maze of tables and chairs to the stairway. At the top landing she knocked again, only this time she waited.

A woman in her early thirties with short blond hair and a round, pretty face opened the door. "Hello!" she said brightly. "You must be the neighbor. I'm

Diane... Diane Cruz. Bette's in the kitchen," she explained as Karen stepped inside. "Lee's helping her. At least he's supposed to be helping her. He thinks he can cook. But at least he knows he can't sing, which is something, believe me."

The casual use of a name from her past caused Karen to start slightly. It also intensified the Alice-in-Wonderland feeling of entering a conversation late. "I'm sorry," she murmured, "I don't—"

Diane instantly apologized. "No, it's me. Different conversation, different house, different people. Things get a little confused when you're on the road so much."

John was in the living room in his easy chair, talking to a young man who also looked to be in his early thirties. Of mixed heritages—most obviously Hispanic and Asian—he had dusky skin, slightly almond-shaped brown eyes and dark brown hair that stood out straight from his head in a short clip. His smile was broad and open, and when he stood to greet her, his hand stretched to meet hers in unconditional friendship. Karen automatically liked him. He wasn't much taller than she was herself—five foot six or seven. Solidly built. Muscled without being overly muscled.

"Manny, this is—" Diane paused.

"Karen," Karen supplied. "Karen Latham."

"Manny Cruz, my husband," Diane said, completing the introduction.

Bette hurried in from the kitchen, flushed and laughing. "Oh, Karen, good! You're here! Everything's ready, I think. Lee's putting the finishing touches to the deviled eggs. I've never made them with curry powder before. They taste absolutely wonderful!''

"Curry powder?'' John echoed doubtfully.

"We didn't have any in our supplies,'' Bette bubbled on. "They did in theirs.'' She smiled at the Cruzes. "Lee said you have to be prepared to cook for yourselves when you're out on location.'' Again the name—Lee! "Everyone can come to the table now. We'll start serving in just a second.'' Then she disappeared back into the kitchen.

Bette's behavior was markedly different from the way it had been this afternoon. Almost as if she'd been starstruck.

"Nice to meet you.'' Manny grinned, shifting their handshake into an escort service to the dining room.

"Last I heard, we were havin' plain ol' roast beef and mashed potatoes,'' John commented dryly as he and Diane followed. "I didn't know things had turned so special. That boss of yours sure has a way about him to get Bette in such a state. I don't think I ever remember seein' her so twittery.''

"Lee's been known to charm the birds from trees,'' Diane said, equally as dryly.

"Lee?'' Karen managed to ask as she took her place at the table. If she didn't want to mimic her mother's continuing unreasonableness she was going to have to *do* something to desensitize herself to that name. Numerous people had it. She couldn't keep reacting every time—

The door from the kitchen opened and a tall, muscularly lean man with thick dark hair, light eyes and far-too-familiar features strode into the room carrying a serving tray, Bette close behind him.

"Lee Parker,'' Diane confirmed. She might have

been making an announcement instead of answering Karen's question.

Karen felt herself freeze. Then shock slid into a kind of surreal disbelief. It was him? *It was him!*

He didn't seem the least surprised. In fact he said, "Hello, Karen," as if nothing untoward ever had occurred between them.

Karen couldn't move, couldn't look away. Her mind screamed, *Don't just sit there! Do something!* But nothing happened.

Bette removed the tray from Lee Parker's grasp and set it awkwardly on the table. "Do you two know each other?" she asked.

"Wh—what are you doing here?" Karen said in a strangled whisper.

But before he could answer—before he could speak to her again—she jerked away from the table and hurled herself from the room.

A loud sound pounded against her ears as she ran back onto the landing, down the stairs and out of the saloon. The sound followed her into her aunt's apartment as moisture wet her cheeks.

Like a terrified animal she pressed herself against the door, trying to keep horror at bay.

He was here...*Lee Parker!* A member of the family she had never wanted to see again! One of the worst members! He and Mae—the way they'd—

An anger like none Karen had experienced before exploded from the depths of her body, exaggerated because it sprang from a rage she hadn't known was there. She began to shake, and the pounding in her ears increased.

"Karen?"

His voice. He was right outside the door.

"Karen, listen to me. I didn't mean for it to happen this way. I didn't set this up."

She didn't want to listen! She didn't want him there!

Go away! she screeched. Yet the words remained a prisoner of her mind.

"Karen! I know you're in there."

"Go away!" she finally managed to say, but strong emotion made it almost inaudible.

"I need to talk to you, Karen. It's not what you think. All those years ago— The Parkers. We aren't— We never—"

"The Parkers can go straight to *hell* for all I care! I don't want to have anything to do with you!"

"I never did anything to hurt you, Karen."

Karen's hands curled into fists as she continued to shake. He sounded so sincere, so reasonable. But she remembered the way he'd looked at her, as if she weren't good enough. It was something she hadn't been able to get out of her mind. She'd thought of it over and over for months following the aborted wedding. It had assumed almost more importance than what Alex had done. As had the suspicion that he'd played a large part in persuading Alex to disappear.

"Are you afraid to talk to me?" His challenge interrupted her thoughts. "I'd never have expected that. You didn't seem to be afraid of anything. Even my mother."

Karen bit her bottom lip.

"Or Mae. Mae didn't seem to bother you, either. You made quite an impression on her, did you know that?"

There were a thousand words she wanted to hurl

at him, none of them complimentary, but she wasn't going to play his game. Bette could, but *she* wouldn't.

She waited and he waited, one on either side of the old pine door.

Finally he said, "I guess I can't make you talk to me, huh? But you can listen. I tried to tell you this a long time ago...I'm sorry for what my brother did to you, Karen. My entire family is sorry. Alex was wrong to hurt you. He should never have let it go so far, not when he—"

"Go...away!" Karen repeated her order through tightly clenched teeth.

Time passed, and when he said nothing more, she was able to gain a little control. The trembling stopped, as did the pounding in her ears, which she now recognized as the rapid thudding of her heart. She made several quick swipes at the leftover moisture on her cheeks.

She was going to have to leave Twilight. If he was here, she couldn't be. First thing tomorrow she would load her things back in the car and go home to Kerrville.

"Karen?" Bette's call from the other side of the door made her start. "What happened, honey? I've never seen you so upset before. Do you *know* Lee Parker? What did he do to you?" A pause. "Honey, open the door. Please? Okay?"

"I'd rather not." Karen sniffed. "I'm sorry about your nice dinner."

"Oh, who cares about dinner! It's you we're worried about. Look, if Lee Parker did anything bad to you, we'll run him out of town so fast he won't know what hit him. You know everyone in town will be up in arms."

Karen thought about her already-decided-upon plan
to leave and the town's hoped-for future. They needed
Lee Parker and his show to see those plans fulfilled.
"Are you alone?" she asked.

"As the day I was born…well, minus my mother,
of course."

Karen opened the door slowly until she could see
Bette's concerned face. She sighed. "It wasn't him.
It was his brother. So you don't have to run him out
of town. He—he just apologized, too."

"It doesn't look like it helped much."

Karen tried to smile, but the tight little jerk of her
lips was a failure. "Like he said, it was a long time
ago. Tonight was…a surprise, that's all. I didn't expect—"

"Would you like me to keep you company for a
while?" Bette offered.

"No. I'm fine. And don't—don't tell anyone in
town. It won't help."

Bette's look was dubious but she relented. "Well,
you know where I am if you change your mind."

Karen closed the door and locked it. She didn't
trust Lee Parker not to be hiding somewhere so he
could force his way inside and make her feel even
worse.

She still couldn't believe him walking through that
kitchen door, carrying a tray and then nonchalantly
looking at her and saying, "Hello, Karen."

Even as she remembered it, his voice reverberated
through her nervous system and again made her
shake. Only this time her shaking was joined by a
near hysterical laughter as the old western cliché,
"This town ain't big enough for the two of us,
stranger," passed through her mind.

There was no question as to who would be getting out of town.

She would pack her things this very minute.

LEE TAPPED on the Cruzes' bedroom door when he saw a rim of light spilling out onto the edge of the hall runner. He hadn't come back right away after his attempted talk with Karen. He'd walked and thought and thought some more, trying to see if somehow he could have prevented what had happened all those years ago. Short of hog-tying his brother to make him stay put, he didn't see how he could have done anything.

The door opened and Manny looked out.

"Can I come in?" Lee asked. "You two still decent?"

Manny motioned him inside. The cameraman was in jeans and an undershirt and Diane was decorously wrapped in a robe—not that Lee hadn't seen them in less, and they him. Close conditions created their own kind of intimacy. The three knew one another far better than most.

"Do you finally want to tell us what's going on?" Diane asked from her place on the bed, sitting with two pillows supporting her back. "This shoot has been different from the first, hasn't it?"

Lee took the only chair while Manny continued to do his exercises, curling handheld dumbbells up and down in alternate short sweeps. He could feel their eyes on him. "You could say that," he admitted.

"Who is she to you?" Diane demanded.

"She almost married my brother."

"Almost?" Diane echoed.

"The ceremony was called off…when my brother bolted."

"Oh, God. How soon before the ceremony did it happen?"

"During it."

Diane was robbed of words. All she could do was stare at him, almost as if he were the guilty party.

"It wasn't me. I didn't do it," Lee defended.

"You were there, though," Manny said.

"I was best man."

Manny stopped exercising to whistle softly. "Transference…she blames you, dude."

Diane swung her feet from the bed, and dragging one of the pillows onto her lap, thumped it as if it were a man's face. "What happened? When the minister got to the part about, 'Do you take…' he took off? No wonder she was upset when she saw you!"

"I know she blames me. She blames all the Parkers. Mae and I both tried to talk to her, but her parents wouldn't let us."

"I can understand why," Diane said quickly.

"You knew she was in Twilight, didn't you?" Manny asked.

"Yes."

"Why didn't you tell us?"

Lee rubbed his hands together briefly. "It wasn't supposed to happen this way. I thought I'd find her…if she was here. All I knew was that she was *supposed* to be here. I'd apologize, and she'd either accept it or not accept it. Either way, the Parker honor would be upheld."

"You knew she was coming to dinner," Diane reminded him.

"I still thought I could talk with her."

"So...did you? You followed her out."

"I tried. Through her door."

Diane gave a funny little smile. "Through her door? That was a new experience for you."

Lee's eyes sparked. "I wasn't trying to hit on her!"

"Just talk to her," Manny murmured. He, too, was smiling oddly.

Lee rose abruptly. "I'll leave you two to it, then. I just didn't want you to think this was going to get in the way of what we planned to do here. If she doesn't want to have anything to do with the Parkers, she won't have to. I'll leave her strictly alone."

"After coming all this way to see her," Diane said.

"I didn't come all this way to—" He stopped, feeling foolish for having put himself in this position. "We came to do a show, remember, and that's what we're going to do."

"Yes, sir," Diane returned, giving him a smart little salute that she ruined with a giggle.

"Oh, yeah," Manny agreed. "Sure, man. Anything you say." Only he, too, was still grinning as he resumed exercising, sweeping the dumbbells up and down, up and down.

Dumbbell, Lee thought as he moved down the hall to his own room. The word had two meanings, only one of which applied to him and his mishandling of the meeting with Karen Latham. It couldn't have turned out worse.

"KAREN...KAREN," a hushed voice called from beneath her bedroom window.

At first Karen tried to ignore it. She had a good idea who her late-night caller was, and if she stayed still and didn't respond, maybe he'd go away.

"Karen…"

She threw the light cover off her legs and hurried to the window. He wasn't about to go away.

Pete peered up at her in the moonlight.

"It's late, Pete," she said, her words as hushed as his. Voices carried easily in the night.

"I knew you weren't sleepin'. I saw your light go out."

Karen swept a fall of curls away from her face. "Pete…please. I'm tired. I want to sleep. And tomorrow…I'll probably have to leave early."

Pete blinked. "You goin' somewhere?"

"I may. For a couple of weeks, then I'll come back."

His features assumed a stubborn look as he shook his woolly white head. "Uh-uh. Nah. It'll be too late then. The damage'll all be done."

"Pete," Karen pleaded desperately, "try to understand. There's nothing I can do to stop this movie thing from happening. The others want it. I can't—"

"I know that," he said shortly. "They're like horses with the bit between their teeth. Nothin's gonna get 'em to see sense now. But there's somethin' else…that bunch of TV people. I saw 'em late this afternoon. John was takin' 'em around…out to the cemetery and about. There's three of 'em. They'll probably start takin' pictures tomorrow. We gotta stop 'em!"

Karen closed her eyes. "Pete—"

"Your aunt Augusta woulda done it!"

"Are you sure about that? Are you really sure?"

"Sure I'm sure!" he claimed.

Karen sighed. "Pete, there's nothing I can do. I *have* to leave."

Pete stared at her for another moment, then, jaw jutting, he said, "Now I'm not so sure about you bein' like Augusta. Augusta never woulda run from a fight!" Whereupon he wheeled around and stomped away.

The moonlight allowed Karen to follow his shuffling gait before he disappeared into the shadows. His shoulders were hunched, his head lowered. She'd let him down.

Karen stretched out again in bed, an arm covering her eyes. What else could she do? She couldn't change anything. If she had that kind of power she'd change a few things for herself. She'd get rid of her confusion about what she should do in the present and in the future. She'd look into the years ahead and see if what she decided would be what she truly wanted in life. She'd change the past, too, so that Lee Parker and his relatives couldn't hurt her anymore. Had never hurt her. There wouldn't be a ruined wedding, because a wedding would never have been planned.

Pete had as good as called her a coward. Was she a coward? Her things were packed and waiting in the living room. All she had to do in the morning was pick them up, carry them to the car, tack up the note she was leaving for Bette, then go. As far away as she wanted. She never had to think about the Parkers again.

Only...was that the way it would actually work? Or would she, too, think of herself as having acted in a less-than-sterling way?

She moved uncomfortably, then moved again. Finally, after about a half hour, she sat up.

Sleep wasn't a commodity she was going to get very much of that night.

BY FIRST LIGHT OF MORNING Karen's bags were *un*-packed and everything put away again. She'd made a decision. She didn't care whether *he* was going to leave town or not, but *she* wasn't.

She was Augusta's niece. And like her aunt, she wouldn't run away. She'd conduct her business, he could conduct his...and if they happened to cross paths, she'd stare him down like the rat he was and dare him to so much as speak to her. She also was determined not to be like her mother. She could control herself. She could control her reactions.

She attacked her work in the antique shop with renewed vigor, and by the time she heard signs that the rest of the town was up and about, she'd already sorted through a trunk and several small trinket boxes and was ready to carry another labeled box upstairs.

On the trip down she saw Bette outside the saloon's back door and waved.

At first Bette seemed uncertain how to react, then, copying Karen's greeting, she walked over. "My goodness, you're up early," she said, her gaze moving carefully over the younger woman's face.

Karen withstood the scrutiny. "Lots to do," she said.

Bette frowned. "Everything's...all right? After last night, you're not—"

"I'm fine," Karen said, and even smiled, making her dimples deepen.

"Lee—" Bette stopped when she realized what she'd said, then, seeming to decide that the damage had already been done, started again. "Lee told us what his brother did. Augusta never breathed a word."

"She wouldn't."

"I never even knew you were engaged—and to a Parker! Oh, darn." She grimaced. "I did it again, didn't I?"

"It's all right. Like I said...I was surprised last night. I never expected—"

"Neither did I! That's what I was planning to tell you. I had no idea 'Western Rambles' had anything to do with one of the Parkers. But once that came out, I understood why the show's such a success. Everything those people put a hand to succeeds." Realizing that she'd committed yet another faux pas, Bette rushed on, as if that would somehow lessen the offense. "They want to talk to us. Not you, of course. You don't have to worry. Only the people who actually live here. We're all going to be in the show."

"Pete won't," Karen said.

"Well, no. Not unless he changes his ways. They want us to tell our stories—how we came to be here, what we do with our time, how we manage so far away from everything."

"I thought you didn't want them here."

"Well...they seem nice enough." She seemed to know the weakness of her argument and was embarrassed by it. "I've got to go. Lee was up early, but the Cruzes slept in. They'll be wanting their breakfast. Lee and I...we had a nice little talk this morning. He's not like his brother, Karen."

Karen couldn't fault Bette's earnestness but knew her old friend had no clue about what she was saying. Rather than contradicting her, though, Karen murmured, "No, I'm sure he's not." Adding only to herself, *He's worse!*

Just then Diane Cruz opened the saloon's back door and looked mildly startled to find the two of them together. "Oh, good…you're here, Karen! Saves a trip. You have a telephone call. It's your mother."

Karen groaned to herself. Leave it to her mother to call at just the wrong moment. Instinctively, she looked to Bette for help. She couldn't go inside the saloon. Not with Lee Parker there.

Bette said quickly, "He's gone out. There shouldn't be a problem."

Painfully aware of the way Diane Cruz had undoubtedly taken Bette's assurance, Karen said evenly, "It's all right. I don't care where he is." Then she sailed inside, head up, jaw set…and knees like jelly.

John and Bette had two telephone extensions—one upstairs in their living quarters and the other downstairs at the bar. Karen felt she'd managed quite enough when she made it to the bar. After smoothing her sweaty palms along the sides of her shorts, she picked up the phone by the till and said with as much conviction as she could muster, "Hello, Mom?"

Bette and Diane glanced at each other and withdrew upstairs to give her privacy.

"You didn't call," Gemma Latham complained. "Are you all right?"

"I'm fine, Mother." A quiet click signaled the upstairs extension had been hung up.

"You promised to keep in touch and you didn't. What are we supposed to think? It's the Parkers, isn't it?" Her mother launched into her pet grievance. "They've somehow discovered you're in Twilight and they're giving you a hard time. Is that it, Karen? Tell me. Because if it is, you just put whatever it is your aunt left you in the car and come home immediately. They have no right to bother you! No right at all!"

"I couldn't begin to put what Aunt Augusta left me in my car."

"Then leave it there! It's not important."

Karen couldn't tell her mother the truth. It would only upset her more. Instead she said, "A lot's going on in town, that's all. Everyone's excited because a movie studio—"

"I don't *care* about a movie studio!"

"And a TV crew—"

"I don't care about that, either. My concern is you. I wish you'd never gone back to that place. You know I've had a bad feeling about it all along."

"You and Rachel," Karen murmured wryly.

"Rachel?" Gemma seized on the name. "Isn't that your friend who says she has dreams?"

Karen could tell her mother didn't appreciate being included in the same category. "Rachel said I'd be here longer than a week, and as it turns out, I will. Aunt Augusta didn't leave me a few things. She left the shop and a storage building packed to bursting point. It's going to take weeks to go through everything."

"Weeks!" her mother echoed in disbelief.

"At least."

"With the Parkers nearby."

"Yes."

Her mother said flatly, "I never knew I'd raised a masochist."

"That's a little extreme, Mother. I'm not a masochist. I've just been given an opportunity…a chance, maybe, to do something *I* want for a change. And I'm not going to let anything, not even the Parkers, stand in my way!"

"I thought that's what you'd been doing all along—what you wanted."

Karen was robbed of breath. The jab hurt. Her rejection of the life her mother and father had plotted out for her, her engagement to Alex, her independent life in Kerrville—all had been her choice, yes. But each had been made as a reaction to someone else's plan for her. Not from her own considered reflection about what she truly wanted.

She closed her eyes, knowing her inner conflict was written on her face. Then she heard a noise—a boot scuffing against the old plank floor—and she immediately spun around. There he was. Lee Parker. Looking at her as he had so long ago, with those chips of Arctic ice for eyes, his expression giving nothing away.

She spun around again, presenting him with her back, even as her gaze flew to the mirrored shelves. His view of her had been perfect. Once again he'd been privy to a private moment of her life. A moment of vulnerability when her soul had been exposed.

Her mother's voice broke through to her, demanding, "Karen! Do you hear me, Karen? Why don't you answer?"

CHAPTER SIX

KAREN KNEW SHE HAD TO SAY something, but no appropriate words came to mind. Instead, she said to her mother, "I—I have to go. Someone's calling me."

"Our conversation is *not* finished, Karen."

"I have nothing more to say."

"Well, I do! Karen—"

"I'll call you later, Mom. Don't worry. Everything's fine." Then she hung up, before Gemma could make another protest.

For several seconds she waited, fully expecting the phone to ring again. When it didn't—her mother probably being so put out with her that she'd stomped off to her lecture room to vent her anger on her students—Karen drew a shaky breath and prepared to face him.

Only he didn't give her enough time. Before she'd known that he'd even moved, he was hitching a seat at the bar directly behind her.

When she turned, Karen's startled senses absorbed everything about him. The strong, chiseled features that seemed so common among the Parkers—square jaw, straight nose, high cheekbones—the thick dark hair, long, lean body and stubbornly uncompromising attitude. Even dressed as he was in modern jeans and a white T-shirt, he fitted into these old-time surroundings as if he belonged.

"So," he began, his tone soft, cajoling, "*is* everything fine? I got the idea last night it wasn't."

Karen tossed her head. "Don't talk to me."

His eyes remained steady. "Is it?" he repeated.

"What do you think?"

"I'd say no, you're still p—"

"How did you know I was here?" she demanded tightly, suddenly remembering his lack of surprise.

He shrugged. "I just walked in and there you were...on the phone. Who was that? Your mother?"

"I meant yesterday...last night!"

"How is your mother?" he asked, instead of answering. "Still in fine fighting fettle, I take it? Why didn't you tell her I was here?"

She knew he was enjoying taunting her. She answered in kind. "I thought for your safety's sake it was best not to."

"I never did anything to you."

"You're a Parker!"

"But I'm not Alex."

"No, you're worse than Alex!"

His eyes lost a little of their teasing glint. "Now, how do you suppose that?"

"Think back!" she snapped.

He frowned. "I don't see— What was I supposed to do? Marry you myself?"

"Heaven forbid!" Karen shot back, even as a start of surprise tore through her. *That* had been the furthest thing from her mind!

He folded his arms and leaned back, smiling. "Now I think about it, maybe it wouldn't have been such a bad idea. We'd've been married...what? Seven years now? I wonder what that would be like."

Karen could feel her cheeks grow hot. She stomped out from behind the bar, ready to burst outside through the rear door, except John came in at just that moment and blocked her way. She plowed straight into him.

"Whoa, there!" John exclaimed, steadying her. "What's your hurry?" One look at her face had him glancing toward the bar. "Ah! You're hightailing it away from Lee again."

Lee sat there with a slight smile. Karen wanted to rip every shred of it from his face.

"She just turned me down flat, John," Lee said.

"Turned you down? What for?"

Karen didn't wait to hear what twisted lie Lee Parker would tell. She struggled out of John's hold and stalked past him. She couldn't stand to be in the same room with that horrible man for a second longer.

Loud banging noises were coming from the hotel at the end of the street. The beginning of John's refurbishment project. At the moment, though, Karen, like her mother, wasn't interested in what was going on in Twilight. She planned to bury herself in the work of cataloging her aunt's collection and would pay attention to nothing else. She wouldn't even leave the shop unless she had to. She'd hide from everything and every—

She pulled up short, both in stride and in thought. *Hide?* As if *she* had something to be ashamed of?

Squaring her shoulders, she turned back to the saloon. She needed to make a few calls of her own. To Mr. Griffin, to Rachel, to Martin. And she'd be darned if she'd let Lee Parker's presence stop her.

As she neared the door, for a split second her courage faltered, but she grabbed it, shoved it back in place and retraced her steps into the Lady Slipper.

JOHN DANSON SHOOK his head as he perched on a stool next to Lee. "Women sure can hold on to a grudge," he said.

"Particularly when they have a good reason," Lee agreed.

"That brother of yours…what's wrong with him? He blind or somethin'? Karen always was a pretty little thing and she's growed up even prettier. Sweet, too, on top of it."

Lee didn't know about the "sweet" part. Karen had never shown him that particular aspect of her personality. Not willingly, at any rate. He fingered one of the absorbent coasters scattered along the bar. Something about her sure got to him, though. A wistfulness, a need, a regret…all revealed inadvertently when her guard was down. "Alex's trouble is that he doesn't appreciate what he has while he has it."

"A lot of men are guilty of that." John looked at him curiously. "What'd Karen turn you down about? You never said."

Lee shrugged. "Just…an interview. For the show."

"That's too bad. I hate to see her left out. She's as much a part of Twilight as the rest of us. She used to come every summer, you know, to spend some time with her aunt while her parents—"

The sound of a cleared throat caused both men's heads to snap around. Karen stood in the doorway, her chin up, her brown eyes flashing. It was clear she'd overheard their discussion and didn't like it. "I need to make some calls,'' she said tightly. ''Is it all right if I use your telephone, John? I'll pay.''

''Of course,'' John said promptly, sliding off his stool.

She walked straight to the bar and moved behind it. She lifted the receiver, but before dialing, she requested coldly, ''A little privacy, please?''

Her irritated gaze included both men but focused longer on Lee.

Lee couldn't help smiling. Something sure had gotten into her since she'd beat a hasty retreat seconds before.

John touched his elbow. ''Wanna come see what we're doin' down at the hotel? Our supplies aren't set to arrive until tomorrow, but we thought we'd get a head start…lots of things we can do to get ready.''

''Sure,'' Lee said, pushing off to follow. But before leaving the saloon, he couldn't resist another look at Karen.

Her back was to him, her shoulders stiff. It was only when he checked the mirror, as he had previously, that he saw she wasn't nearly as disinterested as she seemed. She was watching him intently, so he gave her a little wink, and, surprised by the unexpectedness of it, she flushed and blinked.

A GROUP OF TOWNSMEN WERE hard at work at the hotel. Lee had met two of them before. The others he hadn't.

''Joe, Hank…you remember Lee,'' John called across the open space of the lobby. Friendly waves followed. John then included the others, singling them out one by one. ''This here's Isaac Jacobs…Diego Torres and Benny O'Conner.'' In an aside to Lee,

John said quietly, "Benny's a little slow in the mind department, like I wrote, but he's really good at helpin' out." Then more loudly, "That's right, huh, Benny? You do your part."

A plump man with gray hair sprinkled among his natural blond nodded seriously as he carried a bucket of debris outside. His features, holding no guile, were more like a boy's than a man's.

"You met his momma yesterday, Mary O'Conner," John said to Lee, managing to refer to, yet skirt, the argument about the well. "This here's Lee Parker," he continued with his introduction. "He's here with his TV crew and wants to talk to each and every one of you when the opportunity presents itself."

"You're the one who's gonna put Twilight on the map!" Isaac Jacobs said as he tore off a strip of peeling wallpaper.

"He'll make us famous," John agreed.

Lee laughed good-naturedly. "I don't know if I'd go that far."

"Sure you are," John said, slapping his back. "What's the use of us takin' all this trouble if Twilight's gonna stay a secret? We have to get the word out. And between you and our ol' friend Nate Barlow, it'll happen."

"What if it didn't?" Lee asked, stepping forward to help Diego Torres remove a stubborn length of scarred door molding.

The room suddenly went quiet, as if he'd said something outrageous in a holy place. Once again, John took the lead. "Nah. Not gonna happen. Twilight'll come into its own. People love the Old West. Love to see things the way they used to be. All we

have to do is be ready for 'em when they get here.''
And work resumed.

"Twilight's pretty far off the beaten track," Lee
said, still sticking with his line of inquiry. "Aren't
you worried it might be too far?"

"So's the Grand Canyon, but that don't stop people
from goin' there.''

Lee reached for another piece of cracked molding
once Diego loosened it from the wainscoting. "Still,
Twilight's not exactly the Grand Canyon.''

"It's more like Virginia City," John said, pitching
in to help Isaac gather discarded wallpaper. "I come
from near there, so I know how many people show
up each year. And the same thing can happen here.
I'm convinced of it.''

"Do you have an extra hammer?" Lee asked, grinning.

John stopped what he was doing to straighten.
"You don't need to do that. There's plenty of us
here.''

"Hard work never hurt anybody, someone I know
and respect always says." Lee didn't reveal that the
person was Mae. Nor did he add that he'd found
working alongside people allowed him to see them as
they were, not as they wanted him to think they were.
That way, when it came time for them to sit before
the camera, he knew exactly how to deal with them.

John said, "Well, sure. We won't turn you down.
We'll take all the help we can get!''

LEE ASSISTED IN THE HOTEL for the rest of the morning and promised the men he'd return from time to
time when he could. Then he rendezvoused with
Manny and Diane. Having worked as a team for five

years, they all knew the routine for the start of a shoot and the individual responsibilities that went with it. Lee pulled together a sense of the overall picture, Diane dug for details, and Manny saw to the cameras and sound equipment and tested background shots.

"Well, what do you think?" Lee asked as they sat around one of the tables in the empty saloon.

"I like it," Diane answered promptly.

"I do, too," Manny said, patting the shoulder-held technical marvel of a professional video camera he'd placed on the table next to them. "Got some good shots. Town photographs like a dream. Looks like a movie or a TV set." He narrowed his eyes. "What about you?"

"I like it, too. The people are friendly and interesting. They have good stories. So does the town."

An expectant pause followed and Lee knew they were thinking about his strained relationship with Karen Latham. Instead of addressing it, though, he said, "I've been wondering…what do you think about following through on this? Maybe stretching it into that full hour we talked about doing one day? We have plenty of material. We get to know the people, hear their dreams, give the town's history…then, instead of just talking about the preview, we cover it. Show all the preparation and its aftermath. How it affects the town. Our viewers will want to know what happens—if it looks like what these people are hoping to achieve will stand a good chance of working out for them."

Diane sat back and crossed her arms. "Which means spending two weeks here instead of one. What I want to know is, are you pushing to stay longer for the sake of the show, or because Karen Latham's here

and the two of you have all this unfinished business?''
She warded off his instant denial. ''No, I want you
to think about it before you answer. We've all worked
hard to make 'Western Rambles' a success. You most
of all. You've put your money into it as well as your
heart and soul. Not that I think it would be a bad
thing if Karen *is* the cause. I just want you to recognize it. Otherwise, things could get really confused
and that would be bad for the show.''

Lee took his time answering. ''Maybe it's a pride
thing, I don't know. Can you blame me for wanting
to show her that the Parkers aren't all bad? But she
hates my guts. I doubt another year would make a
difference.''

''There's more to it than that,'' Diane murmured.

''No.''

''I think you're full of it,'' she retorted.

Lee sat silent, while Manny snickered at his wife's
chutzpah.

Then Lee reached across to ruffle Diane's hair.
''Would you feel better if I tell you Jim Hinley called
earlier and gave us the go-ahead for an hour-long special—the one I pitched to him last week?''

Diane squeaked excitedly and jumped up to kiss
both Manny and Lee. ''I know you said something
about a special, but I never expected—''

''Still think it's a bad idea?'' Lee asked, teasing.
''He wants us to set up in halves, so it can fit into
our normal half-hour slot for reruns and syndication.''

''You're a genius!'' Diane exclaimed.

''How do you think our hosts are going to feel
about having us hang around for an extra week?''
Manny asked.

''It's more coverage for the town,'' Lee said.

"What about our living arrangements?"

"You talk to Bette, Lee," Diane urged. "She won't say no to you."

Lee sat back smiling. Everything about this shoot seemed to have a special luck going for it. They'd been playing around with the idea of a special for a year or more but had never found the proper vehicle. Now here it was, dropped in their laps. Both the opportunity and the approval. So why did he have this niggling feeling of unease? As if everything wasn't as hunky-dory as it seemed?

His gaze moved across to the bar, to the spot where Karen Latham had stood twice that morning using the telephone, and he suddenly realized *she* made him uneasy. But why...?

KAREN FINALLY MANAGED to clear a path to the antique shop's front door. She'd yet to go over everything she'd moved out of the way, but it was a psychological boost to step out onto the plank sidewalk and look around. The feat also helped with general working conditions by allowing an exchange of air, especially when she left the back door open, as well.

She'd worked steadily all morning and was just about to take a lunch break when Juanita stepped timidly inside.

"I saw the front door open," the pretty, dark-haired young woman said softly, "so I thought you wouldn't mind if I... I can leave if you're too busy," she offered quickly.

Karen straightened, stretching her spine. "I was just planning a break."

Juanita's dark eyes were large as she looked around. "Diego told me your aunt had many things, but I never thought... He moved them for her, you understand. He never came here alone. He wouldn't!''

"Bette told me he and Benny helped Aunt Augusta.''

"Yes, yes...that is right.'' She continued to look around, uncomfortable yet fascinated.

To help put her at ease, Karen asked, "Where's little Jesse?''

"At home with my mother. He's taking a nap.''

"Would you like to sit down?'' Karen offered. "Like Bette also said, I have plenty of chairs.''

Juanita shook her head.

Karen stretched her back again. It felt good not to be hunched over boxes and furniture. She glanced at the younger woman, wondering what had brought her here. To further ease the way she kidded lightly, "I still find it hard to think of you with a child of your own. I see you as a little girl. Little Juanita.''

A wisp of a smile touched Juanita's lips, then quickly disappeared.

Karen frowned. Maybe she needed a more direct approach. "Is something wrong? Is that why you're here?''

Juanita looked down at the floor, then out the door, before nodding.

"What is it?'' Karen asked.

Her gaze came back, anxious. "My mother—my mother and I are wondering, are you siding with Pete about the movie people? He says you are. That you're going to stop everything. That the town won't change, and no people will come!'' She grew more agitated as she continued to talk. "That's not good. Not good at all. We *need* these people to come. My mother is going to cook at the hotel. I am going to clean. And

Diego and I are going to run one of John's gift shops. We need them to come! We—''

"Juanita, wait! I can't stop the movie people. I've already told Pete that. As for everything else—''

"Pete says you'll stop the TV people, too!''

"How can I do that when it's what all of you want?''

"You'll find a way, he says!'' she cried.

Karen took a fresh tissue from her pocket and handed it to the younger woman, who dabbed at her cheeks. "Don't let what Pete says frighten you, Juanita,'' she urged. "Either you or your mother. He's happy for his life to stay the same, but he's not thinking of the rest of you.''

Juanita sniffed. "We don't need a lot of money. Just enough for Diego— We want the money so Diego can—''

She moved her fingers near her mouth and Karen understood. They wanted the extra income to repair Diego's mouth—to replace his missing teeth.

"My Diego,'' Juanita said simply, "is very proud.''

Karen felt both compassion for them and irritation with Pete. The people of this town had very little, and even though they seemed content here, most of them were merely subsisting. Did each of them have some secret need that they hoped the rebirth of Twilight would help fulfill? "Tell Diego—tell your mother— I have more than enough to keep me busy right here. I'm not going to try to stop anything.''

A small smile of relief touched Juanita's lips. She reached for Karen's hand, held it a second, then said she had to be on her way.

Karen walked with her to the front door, then

watched as she headed for the end of town to the trailers set on a plot of land opposite the hotel. One trailer—Carmelita's—had always been there. The second must now belong to Juanita and her family.

Construction noises continued from inside the hotel, which made Karen think of Lee Parker and John's invitation for him to come and watch them start working...which, in turn, made her shake her head and determinedly think of Pete.

Beneath her irritation with him she was worried. He seemed intent on fighting a battle he couldn't win. The old saw about not being able to stand in the way of progress well and truly fit what was happening here. If the people of Twilight wanted change, she didn't see how he could stop them. She had to have an honest and open talk with Pete, try to get him to see reason. She only hoped she could do a better job with him than she had with Mr. Griffin.

When she'd called Mr. Griffin earlier, he hadn't been pleased to hear that she wouldn't be back at work for several weeks. He'd grumbled and fussed, yet in the end, after she'd told him to go ahead and fill her position with someone else, he'd backed off, assuring her that her job would be held indefinitely. Even when she told him she didn't expect that, he'd insisted.

Rachel had laughed when she'd told her. "You probably put the fear of God into him that you weren't *ever* coming back." Then, after a pause, she'd said, "Or is that the truth...and you're not?"

"I almost came back this morning, actually," Karen had said wryly.

"You did?"

Still unsettled by Lee Parker's audacious wink,

Karen had gone on to say more than she'd meant to. "There's been a slight...crimp in my plans."

"Beyond the extra three weeks?"

"Someone I used to know showed up in town again."

She could feel her friend's quickening interest. "Who?"

Karen hadn't told Rachel about the aborted wedding. She'd kept that to herself. "Someone I'd rather not see," she said tightly.

"Ooh, sounds interesting. Does Martin know?"

"No. And there's no reason he should."

"You're not going to tell him?"

"No, and neither are you. This man's an—an outlaw! You wouldn't like him, either."

"I love outlaws, remember? My ex-husband—"

Karen had interrupted Rachel at that point, angry with herself for even mentioning him. She reminded her friend to water her plants and clear out the refrigerator for her own use if she wanted, then told her she'd call again when she knew more.

Her contact with Martin had been even briefer. In fact, she'd left a message on his answering machine, telling him of the unexpected extension of her stay and that she would get in touch again sometime next week.

After hanging up, she was amazed at how relieved she'd felt at having avoided talking to him personally. A feeling that had startled her with its intensity. And still did.

Karen turned back into the shop to resume her cataloging, but after several failed attempts, she dropped all pretense of work to examine her unsettled feelings.

What was wrong between her and Martin? He was

a good man, a nice man, a patient man. He cared deeply for her, swore he loved her. But was that good enough to base an entire lifetime together on, when she—

When she only *liked* him back?

A SHORT TIME LATER Karen had another visitor. In contrast to Juanita, this person was far from reticent. Mary O'Conner strode in through the front door and announced in her booming way that she wanted a word with Karen.

Almost before Karen could draw breath, Mary was charging, "What's this I hear about you interfering with Twilight's last chance to be something better? It's not right, you know, for you to show up after so much time away and try to tell the people who've been here day in and day out how to live their lives! I don't care if you are Augusta's niece. That doesn't give you any special privileges!"

Karen blinked at the woman's zeal. Mary had always been forceful, but in this instance she was fierce.

"Well?" Mary demanded impatiently. "Aren't you going to say anything?"

Karen got to her feet from her hands and knees, where she'd been examining the side panels of a writing table. Like so many of the other pieces of furniture, it would require further study. To gain a little time to think, she dusted her hands. Then she said evenly, "I think you need to check your facts, Mary. I'm not trying to do anything of the kind."

"Pete says you are!"

"And you automatically believe everything Pete says?"

Mary shifted her stance but maintained, "At times I do, yes."

Karen grinned slowly. "Then that means you believe his stories."

"No one believes Pete's stories!"

"I know. And that's exactly what this is. I'm not going to try to change what's happening in Twilight. Juanita was here just a little while ago asking that very same question. I told her what I'm telling you—I'm not."

"Well, Pete's positive you are."

"Pete's wrong. I'm sad things are going to be different. I'd like to see the town stay as it is. But that's like trying to make a cat stay a kitten or a dog a puppy. If you feed it, it'll grow. If someone—say, the movie people—shines a spotlight on Twilight, people are going to want to come see it. It's just human nature."

Mary's fierce expression dissolved, and to Karen's surprise, she enveloped her in a huge hug. "I can't tell you how happy this makes me!" Mary proclaimed. "And I can't say how much I hope you're right. It'd be a crying shame after all the work everyone's put into this for it not to come off. We're expecting a shipment of merchandise that John's ordered any day now. T-shirts and cups and all kinds of knickknacks with Twilight's name on 'em. Things tourists like, you know? We wanted to get 'em in early so we could sell some to the workers the studio's sending. They'll be a captive audience, so to speak," she added, grinning.

"Everyone's so committed to this," Karen murmured.

"Your aunt Augusta woulda been too. She'da understood the difference it's going to make in everyone's lives. You know what Hank wants? A pickup truck. One of those fancy ones with big wheels and a rack of lights on top. He's dreamed of owning one since his rodeo days. Says he's never had the wherewithal for a new truck before. All his have started out with at least a hundred thousand miles on 'em—new to him but not other people. And Pepper...what Pepper wants is this living room set she's been swooning over for years. One that'll look perfect in their trailer—remember, it's a double wide, so there's lots of room.''

Karen was beginning to understand even more. She studied Mary, who, when she let herself relax, was nowhere near as overwhelming a personality.

''What do you want, Mary?'' she asked. ''There must be something.''

Mary shot her a keen glance that again questioned her sincerity, before saying gruffly, ''I want what I always want—what's best for Benny. I'm not getting any younger, Karen. One day soon...'' She paused, then said, ''I just turned sixty-six. I know that's not considered hugely old in this day and age, but I also know I'm not going to be around forever. I want enough money outta this for Benny to be looked after proper when I'm gone. For him not to be put into some kind of state home. I want him to be happy and carefree all the time he has left, until the good Lord decides to call him to His bosom, too. I don't think that's too much to ask, do you?''

Karen murmured through a tight throat, ''No, I don't think that at all.''

Resuming her tough exterior, Mary demanded, ''So

I can tell the others you aren't going to try to stop us?''

''You can tell them that straight from me,'' Karen confirmed.

''Good,'' Mary said, and, satisfied, took herself off in her usual assertive manner.

CHAPTER SEVEN

"OLD PETE'S THE PERSON you really need to talk to,"
Bette said as she, Lee and Diane sat in her living
room the next morning after a leisurely breakfast.
John was already at the hotel awaiting delivery of his
building materials and Manny had gone off to scout
locations. "He knows more about Twilight's history
than the rest of us put together. He's been here forever."

"That's what someone else told me, too," Diane
said, flipping through her notebook. "Rhonda...
Rhonda Peterson. But she said he probably wouldn't
talk to us."

Bette agreed. "It's highly doubtful."

Lee twisted to set his empty coffee mug on the end
table. "Who's Old Pete?" he asked.

"Have you seen a white-haired old man around?
Could be anywhere from seventy to ninety, kinda
scruffy, usually has a black dog with him?"

Lee placed him instantly, especially remembering
the old man's in-your-face gesture. "Yes, we did.
You saw him, too, Diane, on the way to the cemetery.
John said he was—what was the word?—addled."

Bette grunted. "He's not addled. He's stubborn.
Pete doesn't want things in town to change."

"Why not?" Diane asked.

"Well, when you're a desert rat you like to be on your own."

"But he lives in town," Lee said.

"He has a place here. He spends most of his life out there." She indicated the vast arid land surrounding them. "At least, he used to. He's been slowing down over the past couple of years. This summer he's hardly gone out at all."

"Could he tell us anything about Nate Barlow?" Diane questioned. "I mean, if he's nearly ninety…"

"He probably could if he wanted. Like I said, he's stubborn."

"What about you?" Lee asked, smiling at his hostess. "We've heard you aren't particularly enamored of the changes, either."

Bette grew flustered. "Well, yes…that's true. But that—that was before I got to know you…all of you. I guess you could say I'm more of a middle-of-the-roader. Karen is, too."

"Karen?" Lee encouraged, despite the quick look he knew it would draw from Diane. He hadn't slept very well last night due to thoughts of her. Wondering why, other than being extremely nice to look at, she stayed in his mind so persistently. Maybe if he could make her understand that his brother wasn't a good representative of what the Parkers stood for, what they—

"She probably wouldn't like me telling you this," Bette said. "She wouldn't like me telling you anything, but she'd be the person to go through if you want to talk to Pete. She's the only one he'll come close to listening to."

Lee said dryly, "Too bad her idea of a good time is to see me staked naked on a fire-ant hill."

Bette frowned. "You know, I just can't understand about that. I know what your brother did and all, but—"

"Manny says it's transference," Diane contributed.

Lee looked at her from under his brow and drew a giggle. She, like Manny, knew he had little patience with psychobabble.

"Would you like me to bring it up with her?" Bette offered. "I could kind of ease into it."

Lee shook his head. "No, let us see what we can come up with on our own first. You're driving to the county seat a little later, aren't you, Diane? Into Davisville?"

When Diane nodded, Bette asked curiously, "What for?"

"I always try to gather as much archival information as I can about the area we're studying and I prefer to get it from local sources," Diane said. "Libraries, courthouses, newspapers…not to mention private collections. Some amazing information can turn up. Great old photographs, and sometimes something completely unexpected. Things we'd never learn without some deep digging."

"My goodness," Bette said, "I didn't realize putting on a television show was so much work!"

Diane laughed. "It's not so bad. I enjoy it. We all do."

"Still," Bette murmured. Then she brightened, "I suppose since you'll be staying longer in Twilight and doing an hour special, you'll have more time for old photographs. Did you know I have one? It's hanging on the wall in our bedroom. Been there from before John and I bought the place. Probably was taken not long after the turn of the century. It's a view down

the street from in front of the hotel. Shows the mercantile and the Lady Slipper...both a lot newer than
they look now. You can even see a bit of the well. I
hadn't thought about it before, but since you said—''

''May I see it?'' Diane asked, instantly interested.

The two women hurried out of the room, and Lee,
left alone, went to the window to investigate the engine noises he'd heard earlier. A small cluster of men
stood in the open area that passed as the hotel's backyard, talking with the driver of a flatbed truck. John's
building materials had arrived.

Activity of another sort soon caught Lee's eye.
Two doors down he saw Karen Latham struggling
with a large cardboard box as she tried to carry it up
the antique shop's exterior stairs.

He watched until he was sure she was in trouble.

SOMETHING WAS WRONG! Karen fumed as she moved
the box this way and that. No matter how hard she
pushed or pulled or tried to get it to swing to either
side, it wouldn't budge. She couldn't put it down,
either.

Perspiration broke from her pores as she grappled
with the box in the hot August sun. She'd put too
much in it—a double mistake, not only because the
box wasn't of top quality, being the last she'd had to
choose from, but because it was too heavy and awkward to deal with.

Mentally, she prepared to count. On three she
would give it a final sideways shove, which she hoped
would dislodge it. If it didn't, she sighed, she would
have to call for help from the men outside the hotel.
One...two...

Three had just formed in her mind when a presence

suddenly loomed behind her and long arms reached around her to relieve her of the load.

"Let go," a man's voice directed near her ear. "I have it."

Karen knew instantly who her rescuer was. And she instantly rejected his interference.

"Here...duck under," he said, lifting an elbow for her to escape.

Karen wanted to refuse. What right did he, of all people, have to tell her what to do? But short of standing there arguing, with him pressed rather intimately against her, she had no other option. She ducked under and out and scooted down several steps.

She watched as he wrested the box to each side, then up and down—to no avail, just like her.

"It's caught," he said, glancing back. "Can you see what on?"

"No," she said.

He smiled dryly. "That doesn't surprise me. You have to look."

"I'd rather not," she returned.

"Why? Because you'd have to get close?"

Karen retook two steps and carefully peered around the left railing. "Move it back a little," she instructed. "Yes. I see now. It's caught on a nail."

"Why won't it pull free?"

"Maybe the nail's caught on something inside. Maybe if we—" She brushed his arm and instantly recoiled.

"You want me to shake it?" he asked, openly amused.

Karen nodded.

Within seconds the box was free. "All right!" he cheered mildly.

Karen reached to take it back, but he'd already started up the remaining stairs.

"I can carry it from here," she said quickly, catching up.

"Why? When I've already got it?"

"I'd still rather—"

"We're almost to your place. What's the problem?"

Karen gritted her teeth, moved past him on the landing and motioned him into her aunt's apartment with an irritated flourish.

The small rooms were even smaller with his presence. He was taller than Alex, an inch or two over six foot, and a more substantial man. Still slim, yet— The difference between a man and a boy, came the unbidden thought, which Karen immediately repudiated.

"Over there will be fine," she said stiffly, pointing to the dining room, where she'd pushed the table aside to make space for numerous boxes. She knew she wouldn't be entertaining, so she'd have no need for the area.

He set the box in among the others and straightened, but he made no motion to leave. Instead, he surveyed her handiwork. "You've been busy," he said.

"Yes. Thank you for helping."

He ignored her dismissal. "So, this is Augusta's place."

Karen didn't reply.

He examined a Rookwood vase that had been one of her aunt's favorites. Arranged next to the vase on the sideboard was a small collection of paperweights, all manufactured by the same company. "Very nice," he approved.

"I have to get back to work," Karen said firmly.

"So do I." Still, he made no move. "I suppose people who deal in antiques have a hard time letting go. They love it. That's why they get into the business in the first place." He looked at her. "Was that the way it was with your aunt? I've heard she left you a lot of things."

"My aunt loved to collect," Karen agreed.

"Worth a lot?" he asked outrageously.

Karen snapped, "I don't see where that's any of your—"

"You're right. It's not. Just put it down to curiosity." He moved to a Navajo wool rug hanging on the wall. "This is nice, too. We did a segment on the women who make these out in Arizona—at least, the modern ones. Learned a lot about the people who're still living on reservations."

"I'm glad," Karen said.

He smiled at the shortness of her reply, which did funny things to her equilibrium—which she instantly insisted to herself was caused by stress and too much sun while she was out on the stairs.

He commented, "There seems to be an argument going on in town about the best course for Twilight's future. How do you think your aunt would feel about it?"

"I don't know."

"Bette said your position is the same as hers— middle-of-the-road."

"I don't live here."

"But if you did…"

He took a step in her direction and for some insane

reason her heart rate quickened. She couldn't prevent herself from backing up, which seemed to amuse him even more.

"I truly *don't* bite," he teased.

"Would you go now, please?" she requested tightly.

"After one more question." His humor faded. "Bette also said you're the person to help with Péte. That he'd listen if you asked him to talk to us. Do you think you could bury the hatchet long enough to act as intermediary?"

Karen was aghast at his nerve. "Is that what this is all about?" she demanded. "You want me to help you?" Her laugh was caustic. "No, Mr. Parker, I don't think so. I don't think so at all!"

"That's not—"

"I said no! Do you have a problem with that word? Haven't you ever heard it before? Or is it that being a Parker immunizes you from the disappointments the rest of us ordinary human beings have to face!"

"The Parkers aren't—" he defended.

"The Parkers are snobs of the worst sort. You don't think anyone else is good enough to breathe the same air. Does it ever get lonely up on Mount Olympus, Mr. Parker? I would imagine it's a huge bore to be a god."

The anger she'd exhibited previously had been only a warmup to what she felt now. She could hear herself spewing invective. Just like her mother, she'd lost control. She could no more stop herself than she could make yesterday be today. Because of the circumstances seven years ago, she'd never had the opportunity to release her anger. To rail against the Parkers *to* the Parkers about what they'd done to her—what

they'd done to her family. Almost two years had
passed before she'd been fully able to pick up the
pieces and resume an ordinary life. Before she'd been
able to see that she *was* good enough. That the problem wasn't hers, it was theirs!

Answering anger sparked in his eyes, which made
her happy, because that meant her hard thrusts had
hit home. He should suffer. They all should suffer
after everything they'd put her through.

He grabbed her arm and she was glad about that,
too. Let him assault her. She'd have him arrested in
a second. She'd—

"Did you love Alex that much?" he demanded
harshly, his face close enough that she could feel his
breath. "Well, you might as well know the truth—he
didn't love you. Not the way you wanted him to. I'd
just got through pulling him out of a mess with one
girl, when he told me he was engaged to you. Alex
thinks only of himself. He always has and always
will."

"That's not true!"

"It is! His behavior brings shame to the Parker
name. I don't enjoy saying that about my brother, but
it's a fact. And you should know it."

Karen continued to glare at him. She didn't want
to believe a word he said. She'd lived with her anger
for seven long years. She wasn't prepared to let go
of it so easily.

He said something indecipherable—she had no idea
what—and the next moment his mouth was fixed
firmly on hers.

Karen fought against him, trying everything she
knew to make the contact stop. Then her struggles
ceased. From the time she was a young girl, she'd

been taught to be the master of her sexuality. Taught that the mind could hold dominance over the body. And she'd believed it, living her life accordingly. Neither Alex nor Martin had ever seriously challenged this conviction. No man had. Until now.

A fireball of response burst through her, shocking her with its intensity. Suddenly, Lee was what she wanted. What she had to have. Now. This instant. She became consumed with an all-encompassing need. The kiss went on and on, becoming much more than a kiss—

Then some small niggle of responsibility broke through. *What was she doing? And with whom?* She dragged her mouth away from his, gasping for breath, and only in that second did she realize she stood braced against the wall, her clothing in disarray, his body pressed against hers, one hand fondling a breast while the other massaged the curve of her hip.

She shuddered, appalled by what had occurred. How had she ever come to let him—encouraged him, even—

He, too, seemed dazed by what had happened, but Karen chose not to acknowledge it. She needed someone to strike out against, someone to blame besides herself.

"Get your hands off me!" she said emphatically.

He jerked away and she almost lost her balance, not realizing how much she had been relying on him for support.

"Don't say a word," she ordered, when he seemed about to speak. "Just go!"

She could tell he wasn't accustomed to being dismissed in such a cold-blooded way, but she couldn't trust herself to address him in any other manner.

She made the mistake of meeting his eyes, and where before they'd haunted her with their iciness, she now worried that she'd never be able to forget the way they could smolder with thwarted passion.

Her body tingled, and for a brief second she wanted to melt against him again, to go back to the place they'd been before, where nothing mattered except each other, but her mind was back in charge now. The rebellion was quashed.

Without a word, he left as she requested, closing the door softly behind him.

When she was at last alone, Karen collapsed against the wall. She couldn't believe it. Her...him! It didn't seem possible. Instinctively, she ran a hand lightly over the breast he'd fondled, before moving it to the curve of her neck and her mouth, where his lips had created such pleasurable havoc.

It didn't seem possible that something like that could happen.

But it had.

LEE NEEDED SOMEWHERE to think. He felt just as shaken as Karen had looked.

It was insanity! The whole ten or fifteen minutes. How had the situation gotten away from him? He'd been talking to her about Augusta, about the town, about Pete. She'd taken deep offense when he'd asked her to help them, struck out angrily and made him angry in return. Then his anger had deserted him, and he'd found himself kissing her as if it were something he'd been longing to do for untold years.

She'd been close, he'd been close. He remembered the soft, sweet scent of flowers, and the next thing...

"So, there you are!" Diane cried, breaking into his thoughts. "What are you doing down here?"

He'd chosen a table in a far corner of the empty saloon to recover.

"We wondered where you'd disappeared to," Diane said. Then she leaned closer to examine him. "What's wrong? You look funny. Do you feel ill?"

"It's the light," Lee said gruffly.

Diane glanced around. "Why are you all the way back here? Someone could think you're hiding."

"Did the photograph hold up?" he asked. He needed a return to the business at hand, to get his boots planted firmly back on the ground, but this was a little too soon.

"We might be able to use it. There's more of the well showing than Bette remembered." She paused. "Are you sure you're all right?"

"Sure I'm sure. Why were you looking for me?"

Diane seemed disturbed by his curious demeanor, but she knew him well enough to sense when to leave things alone. "Bette asked if she could ride along with me to Davisville. I told her she could. You don't have any reason why she shouldn't, do you? You don't need her here for anything?"

"Not a thing."

"Good. I think she's looking forward to an outing." She sighed. "I truly don't know how these people do it. I know we see this all the time—the hardy folk who live in little out-of-the-way spots. Few, I might add, that are as 'out-of-the-way' as this. I also know we're on the road a lot ourselves. But we get to go back to San Francisco when we're done, where everything's just a short walk away. Food…what kind do you want? Theaters, museums…again, what kind do you want? I don't think I could live my life in such an isolated place. And I wonder how they can.''

''Who knows?'' Lee said shortly, shrugging. ''Who knows why anyone does anything?''

Then he stood up and walked away, leaving Diane to stare after him.

KAREN RESOLVED not to set foot outside her aunt's apartment for the rest of the day. She tried to busy herself by making a closer inspection of the contents of a few of the boxes already upstairs—a chore she would have to do eventually, anyway. But there was no way she could concentrate. All she could think about was that kiss.

Memory of how deeply her emotions had been stirred intensified her search for an answer. Lee claimed he wasn't like his brother, but he was. They had similar looks, similar builds. There also had to be something about being a Parker that fed into the mystique, as well—something more than confidence, arrogance and wealth. She'd once found Alex attractive, so naturally a flare-up of a similar nature should be expected when she was with a person who reminded her of him. Shouldn't it?

Except it had never been that way with Alex. He'd never made her want him with a desperation that caused her to feel she would *die* if they were to part too soon.

Nature was a funny thing, she thought as she fanned herself in the suddenly too warm room. It abhorred a vacuum yet didn't care what it used for filler. Martin had been a quiet presence in her life for these past two years. He was comfortable, safe. With him, she felt no physical pressures that unsettled her. Yes, that had to be it! A confluence of circumstance, with Lee Parker once again acting as catalyst. He'd been present years before at the worst moment of her life and was here now when she was stressed by the loss of her aunt, not to mention facing another set of far-reaching decisions about her future.

He seemed to have a knack for being where she didn't want him.

Short of breaking down the door, though, he wasn't going to get another chance at her anytime soon. When the moment was right, she'd emerge, in cool and complete control of herself, and *dare* him to bring up this morning.

Karen forced herself to go back to her aunt's extensive collection of reference books, and this time her concentration was better. She was able to work for hours, comparing marks and descriptions and sometimes published photographs with the articles that most interested her. It was much later before she heard a commotion out back that made her tear herself from her study.

The afternoon sun bore down on the trio of angry men standing just inside her aunt's backyard. John, Joe and Hank were talking loudly, with one or the other of them gesturing occasionally toward Pete's shack in the distance. Soon the crowd increased, as others heard the ruckus and came to join it.

"Somethin's got to be done about it," Hank said tightly.

"We just can't put up with it anymore!" Joe agreed.

"What's this? What's happened?" Mary demanded as she steamed up.

"Pete's took our nails!" Joe answered. "You can't fix anything without nails! And he knows it."

"It's not like it's the first bad thing he's done, neither," Hank added, scowling. "Man's gone off the deep end, I tell ya. We have to stop him before he messes everything up."

"We don't know Pete stole 'em," John said, trying to be reasonable.

"Who else woulda done it, then?" Joe demanded. "They were there. I saw 'em with my own two eyes."

"He's got to be stopped," Rhonda said, siding with her husband.

"Yes!" Carmelita agreed, her grandson, Jesse, balanced on a broad hip.

Karen didn't wait to hear more. She hurried downstairs.

"What's happened? What's wrong?" she asked urgently as she joined them, already knowing the answer but hoping to buy a little time.

"Pete's took our new nails!" Hank accused.

"I'm afraid he has," John said, looking pained. "They were there this mornin' and now they're gone. And Pete's the only suspect we've got. Nobody else would do it, only him."

"Maybe it's a mistake," Karen suggested, glancing hopefully from one to the other.

"Yeah," Joe said flatly, "it's a mistake. Just like when he hid the extension cord and made off with the hammers."

"And took all the screws out of the ladder," Hank added.

"He did that?" Mary gasped.

"I caught him doin' it!" Hank said.

Carmelita looked around. "Where is the TV crew? Do we want them to hear this?"

"They're all in different places. Not here, thank the good Lord," John said.

"Well, what are we going to do about it?" Mary demanded. "Call the sheriff?"

Karen's heart jumped again, just as it had when Carmelita asked about the TV crew. She couldn't believe the town would turn against Pete, but then, by his stubborn acts, it looked as if he'd given them just cause.

The idea of calling the sheriff seemed to bother everyone, even the most irritated. Pete was a citizen of Twilight. Its oldest citizen. He was one of them.

"Maybe—maybe we could try talkin' to him again," Hank muttered. "Tell him what'll happen if he does it again. That then we'll *have* to call the sheriff."

As soon as the words were out, every eye turned on Karen, who took a mental step back. She'd wanted to talk to Pete—to tell him to stop making the others think she felt as he did. But this? To officially warn him off?

"Would you do it, Karen? Would you talk to Pete?" Pepper asked, late to the group but already aware of what was going on.

"I...yes, I suppose," Karen said. "But he doesn't listen to me very well, either. He—"

"It's one last try," Hank said regretfully.

Karen nodded and the group dispersed—the men back to their work inside the hotel and the women to their various enterprises. All except for John, who asked if she wouldn't mind if he came upstairs with her for a minute.

"I want to get a good feel for Augusta again," John said, easing his lanky body into a chair. "We used to have these long talks, you know—her and me. About this and that...all sorts of things. She kept me pretty up-to-date with what you were doin'. I knew when you left the university—not why, she kept that to herself—when you moved to Kerrville, when you went to work in that antique place directly after." He rubbed a hand over his thinning gray hair. "That's why I feel I can talk to you straight about this. Not pull any punches. Just like I wouldn't with Augusta. The town's in a bad way, Karen. If this deal don't work out with the movie studio and with 'Western Rambles,' it'll probably die for real. We *need* to get tourists here. For sure, a lot more than we have now. Otherwise people are gonna start leavin', even people who've been in Twilight for years. It costs more to live here now than it used to—electricity costs more, water, the weekly trips for supplies. Taxes are up, too. It's all relative, of course, but our pocketbooks aren't growin' any. Pete doesn't see that. Everythin' he uses is pretty much the same as it's always been. His needs don't change. I hate like hell that we can't get him to see we're not bein' selfish. That all we're tryin' to do is survive!"

Karen perched on the footstool next to his chair. John had always been something of an uncle to her. At least, she'd looked on him that way, whether he knew it or not.

"I didn't know things were so bad. Aunt Augusta never said—"

"Augusta wanted to help out, but we wouldn't let her. To my way of thinkin', if you're a perfectly healthy adult, you should be able to stand on your own feet. That's the way the others feel, too. We're not askin' for a handout, just a break.''

"What can *I* do?" Karen asked.

"Talk to Pete like you said you would. Get him to see how our patience is startin' to wear thin…and what he'll end up doin' to the town if he doesn't stop it."

"I'll try," Karen promised.

John stood up and patted her lightly on the shoulder. "Augusta would be proud of you," he said. "But then, she always was. You couldn't do wrong in her eyes." The moment would have remained sweet if John hadn't continued. "Too bad she's not here to help you sort through this Parker problem you have. Almost every family's got at least one bad apple, and you seem to have had the misfortune of findin' one of theirs first thing."

Bumfuzzled by Karen's stunned reaction, John plodded on, making matters worse. "It's somethin' Bette says Lee feels strongly about. We were just talkin' about it in bed last night."

Karen walked stiltedly to the door and opened it. "I—I should probably get going if you want those nails back," she said.

John watched her as he moved past her onto the landing. "We'd sure appreciate it." Then, in an attempt to make amends for whatever it was he sensed he'd said or done wrong, he added, "I'm sorry if I butted in."

He looked so genuinely contrite that Karen couldn't resist giving him a quick hug…only to have her attention caught by a man who at that moment was walking through her aunt's backyard.

The man stopped, almost in midstride, and looked back at her.

Lee Parker! And she could see by the whimsical expression that suddenly flooded his features that if he'd been closer, he'd have made some kind of smart remark about her and John hugging.

John, noting her detachment, glanced around to see what she was looking at. Then in pleased surprise, he cried, "Lee! Just the person I wanted to see. I have an idea I wanna talk to you about—" And he broke away from Karen to hurry downstairs.

While John poured out his idea, Lee's gaze stayed fixed on Karen, whose own body went on instant alert. She found herself acutely aware of everything about him. The way his jeans were set low on his slim hips and fitted his long, strong legs. The way his T-shirt hugged what she could see of his chest. The way the plaid cotton shirt, worn loose and unbuttoned, hung from his wide shoulders. His thick dark hair and strongly chiseled features…and those pale, pale eyes that were in such stark contrast to his dark Parker looks.

She remembered how they'd smoldered with unfulfilled passion, and how, just moments before, that mouth had—

Her body burned as if a flame had stroked it. It trembled, ached.

And before she could embarrass herself completely, she shut the door.

CHAPTER EIGHT

KAREN MADE SURE Lee Parker was safely out of the way before she ventured outside. A part of her wanted to continue to hole up, the rest knew her mission couldn't wait.

She crossed the different backyards, then turned on an angle after the hotel and soon was on the path that led to Pete's place. As she drew near, the dog started to bark, but he made no real effort to intervene.

Pete stood unblinking in the doorway. "I thought you was leavin'," he said gruffly.

"I changed my mind."

The dog risked a speculative sniff of Karen's leg but scooted away when she reached to pet him. He was as leery of strangers as his owner.

"Why?" Pete demanded.

"For personal reasons," she answered.

He screwed up his face and squinted at her. "I know. I heard. It's about that TV man. You was plannin' on marryin' him once before and he left you standin' at the altar."

Strangely, the way Pete put it, it didn't hurt as much as it once had. She even managed a grim little grin and corrected, "It wasn't him, it was his brother."

Pete waved dismissal. "One's as good as the other."

Not exactly a sentiment Karen wanted to grapple with right then. "I'm not here because of *my* problems, Pete. May I come in? Or do we have to say everything we need like this?"

"I don't have nothin' to say."

"Do you realize the town is *this* close to calling the sheriff?" She measured a minute amount between her forefinger and thumb. "Is that what you want, Pete? To be arrested? To be put in jail?"

"Hell, no!"

"Then why are you sabotaging everything they try to do? Do you expect them to overlook it? They only have a short time left until the preview."

"You know what I think of the pree-view!" Pete exaggerated the word from orneriness.

"The whole area knows what you think. You've made yourself perfectly clear. But just because you don't want it doesn't mean it shouldn't be. You don't own Twilight, Pete, not any more than the rest of them do. You're outnumbered. The count is twelve to one."

"That only makes thirteen!" Pete snapped. "That's not enough."

"I wasn't counting baby Jesse or Aunt Augusta."

"You should have a vote."

"Pete," she said patiently, "I don't live here."

"You do now. So where's your vote? You have to take a side."

Just what she'd been hoping to avoid from the beginning! "Pete, it doesn't matter which side I'm on. Even if I'm with you, that still only makes two. And if I'm not—"

"You're not?" he returned, rocking back in surprise.

She sighed. "Can I come in, Pete? I feel funny talking like this, like we're not friends anymore."

"Maybe that's the way it is," he said stubbornly. "Maybe it's me that don't know you so good. I thought I did, but I sure can see now that I mighta been wrong."

"Pete, please," she pleaded. "Listen carefully. John says the town is going to become a *real* ghost town if something isn't done soon. People are going to move away because they can't afford to stay. They're your friends, Pete. Don't you care?"

"I don't have any friends," Pete grumbled.

Karen lost what little patience with him she had left. "No, you certainly don't! And from the way you've been acting, you don't deserve any, either! Did you take their nails so they couldn't work? Did you hide the extension cord, make off with the hammers? Did you remove all the screws from the ladder? That's something a child would do! Not a grown man! Not a man who's seen as much as you have, who's done as much. I always looked up to you, Pete. Cheered you for sticking to your way of life. Don't ruin it all with your stubbornness. You can't freeze Twilight in time. No matter how hard you try, it's not going to happen. Towns change, people change!"

"Augusta would be rollin' in her grave if she had one," Pete shot back.

"Aunt Augusta would've wanted what was best for the *people* of Twilight. If there was a chance to save the town, she'd be doing all she could to make sure it happened. You know that, Pete, and don't try to tell me you don't." She paused. "If Aunt Augusta was alive, she'd be standing right where I am now, trying to make you see sense."

Pete glared at her for a long moment before turning away from the door. From her position Karen could see him rummaging through a chest in the corner of the room. He withdrew a paper sack and brought it back with him.

"Give 'em their darned nails," he said tightly, transferring possession to her, "and tell 'em I hope every single one of 'em bends or breaks!"

The sack, with other smaller sacks inside, was heavier than Karen expected. She had to make a second effort at supporting it. "I'll tell them," she said. Then added with regret, "Try to understand, Pete. Try hard."

"I don't hafta understand nothin', 'cause I'm gettin' outta here. I don't wanna be around when the crazies take over."

She looked at him in alarm. "But you are coming back, aren't you? You wouldn't—"

"Maybe...maybe not." He shrugged. "I haven't decided."

"Pete—"

"Get on with ya. I've said all I'm gonna say."

And with that he closed the door, blocking her out of his life.

Karen looked around helplessly. Had she handled it anywhere near properly? Had she said everything she possibly could?

She started to move away, and once again the dog barked.

It gave him something to do.

BY LATE AFTERNOON Lee and Manny had settled on several locations for the practice run-throughs of the interviews they would start taping tomorrow. Lee had already arranged times with the chosen subjects—the idea being to use the most effusive and loquacious among the citizenry, so that those harboring misgivings could see how easy it was. Manny, as always, would film everything as a keeper, just in case they ran into a natural who might not be as natural in their "real" interview. It happened that way sometimes. People who were great during the run-through were as frightened as rabbits later on.

They were just about to take the rest of the afternoon off when the clamor of industrious hammering drew them to the hotel. Within minutes they were caught up, helping. Work had broadened from reclaiming the lobby to include refurbishment of the kitchen and the dining room. One or two of the men were in each area, doing what needed to be done. A ruined kitchen drainboard was being ripped apart and dilapidated cabinets were being taken down. The dining room was in the same state as the lobby yesterday, while in the gutted lobby, replacement trims were being put in place.

Manny gravitated to the demolition in the kitchen, while Lee took up a hammer and nails in the lobby.

"You can thank Karen for those," John said as he jockeyed a length of door trim into proper position.

Lee looked at the thin finishing nail. "For this?" he asked.

"She got 'em all back from Pete. He'd...uh...relieved us of our burden, so to speak. Almost had a riot. I wasn't gonna say nothin' but figured you'd have to be unconscious not to hear about it. We're all gettin' together after work today, havin' a little shindig to celebrate. You and your people are invited, too, of course."

"Is Karen coming?" Lee asked.

"You bet! Even if we have to drag her. She's the one we want to thank most for keepin' the lid on things. Pete's also taken himself off into the desert, so that means we can actually get some work done."

As he made his way toward the front door, Hank Douglas spotted Lee. "Pepper's gonna be up all night tryin' to decide what outfit to wear tomorrow. She's got two special ones and can't make up her mind."

"Tell her to relax," Lee called after him. "The camera will love her whatever she's wearing."

"Joe says Rhonda's havin' the same problem," John murmured. "She's drivin' him nuts, too."

Mary O'Conner also was included in the first round of interviews and had asked if Benny could sit in with her. Lee looked around for Benny and found him in the street in front of the hotel, steadying a two-by-four across a set of sawhorses for Hank to cut. Benny looked up and smiled, and smiling back, Lee couldn't help but think how Mary's love and devotion to her son was going to shine through.

"Western Rambles" was popular because it commemorated the positive facets of the human spirit—honesty, integrity, generosity, selflessness, cooperation—instead of the baser motives.

Lee had left network television to go off on his own because so much of what was done in the name of news was abhorrent to him. Putting a microphone into the face of a vulnerable person to demand an accounting or to question their up-to-that-second feelings—he'd done it, he'd hated it and he'd sworn never to do it again. "Western Rambles" had been his dream. It had taken years of slogging through one production job after another, but finally, it had happened.

"You off dreamin' somewheres?" John teased, breaking into Lee's thoughts.

Lee shook his head, trying to bring his mind back to the present. "I was just…thinking about Benny," he said.

John paused. "Yeah, it's a sad story. Mary's a handful, but maybe she's had to be, not to let anybody take advantage of that boy of hers. Not even his own dad. Did she tell ya? He left 'em shortly after Benny's accident, then showed up a few years later, thinkin' there might be an insurance settlement. Mary says she told him to get lost, but I'm bettin' there was a little more to it than that. I've seen her operate. And I sure don't want to be on her wrong side!"

Lee smiled. Mary and Mae would probably get along great.

AFTER HER TALK WITH PETE, Karen tried again to concentrate on sorting her aunt's collection. Numerous reference books lay open on the dining room table, the contents of a second box were scattered about on the floor, more pages in her notebook were filled with her neat handwriting. But a niggling recollection continued to vex her: what Lee had said about Alex having another girlfriend.

Because of the upset with Pete, her thoughts had been diverted. But it was something she couldn't forget. Lee had said he'd *just got through pulling him out of a mess with one girl, when he told me he was engaged to you.* By that, he'd intimated a short time frame between events. But she and Alex had dated each other exclusively for a whole year before they'd become engaged. And their engagement had lasted a further six months. It had taken that long to plan the wedding. If Lee was to be believed, it meant Alex had cheated on her up to and possibly even during their engagement.

Karen bit her lip. She didn't want to believe it, but it had the ring of truth. Then another thought struck her: had Alex abandoned her at their wedding to return to the other girl?

Not that it mattered all that much...

She stopped herself. *Shouldn't* it matter?

What was wrong with her that she felt only a mild displeasure with Alex? She should be directing as much intense anger toward him as she had with Lee. Even more. She should be throwing things! Breaking things! Why, for all these years, had her deepest resentments centered on Lee, and to a lesser degree on Mae?

Her mind skittered away from any uncomfortable answers and instead clung to the theory she'd maintained for seven years. The Parkers—the family—were to blame for everything. That was all there was to it.

A short time later someone knocked on the door, and she was surprised to find John, Bette, Carmelita and Joe clustered on the landing.

"Bette and I want you to come with us," John announced, grinning. "And just in case you turn stubborn, we've brought reinforcements."

"You want me to what?" Karen asked, confused.

"Come to the party we're havin' at the Lady Slipper," John explained. "You might say it's a Gettin'-Pete-Outta-Our-Hair party! We want to relax, have a

little fun. Things have been kinda tense for a while.
Now they're not.''

Joe, too, was grinning hugely. So were Bette and
Carmelita.

"Come on," Bette urged. "It'll do you good. You
need to get away from all these old things for a while
and have a good time."

"I *like* these old things," Karen said.

"You're the guest of honor," John explained, stepping around her to propel her toward the door. "You
have to be there."

Karen frowned. "Me? How? Why?"

"You got Pete to cooperate," Joe chimed in.

"I made him leave town! I'm not proud of that."

They spirited her down the stairs and across the
mercantile's backyard to the saloon.

"Who cares?" Joe said, his hand on her back, im-
pelling her onward.

"I care!" Karen protested, but her reply was lost
in the cheerful noises spilling outside.

Again the room was filled with music, the player
piano going full tilt, Benny joyfully pumping it.

A cheer went up as Karen entered, and John
quickly stationed himself behind the bar, where he
could pull beer and hand out soft drinks. Another
cheer was given.

"To Karen!" someone called.

"To Twilight!" someone else added.

"To all the tourists who'll soon be comin'!"
toasted yet another.

Karen's mood lightened in spite of herself. Everyone was so happy. So hopeful. It was hard not to be
swept along. To share in their enthusiasm.

She found herself at one end of the bar, a soft drink

in one hand, a noisemaker in the other. "Left over from last New Year's Eve!" John had explained as he'd tossed them around. The noise level had risen even higher.

"Would it be safe to offer my congratulations?" a familiar voice asked shortly after she felt someone slip onto the bar stool next to her.

Karen wanted to pretend that she hadn't heard him but knew it wouldn't work.

With her gaze anchored exactly where it had been, on Benny, she challenged, "Since when have you been worried about safety?"

He chuckled. "Not now, that's for sure. Maybe I should be wearing my flak jacket."

"When I'm not holding anything more dangerous than an eight-month-old noisemaker?"

"That might be all you *think* you're holding."

Her gaze switched suddenly to his. "Did Alex go back to that other girl? Is that why he left me in church?"

She hadn't meant to ask that. Not here, not now! Yet she somehow managed to hold eye contact, trying not to be aware of his magnetism, of his good looks...of her newfound awareness of him as a man. He *did* remind her of Alex. The same Parker looks, with an equal, if not more potent, measure of Parker charm. What was it his assistant had said about him? Lee could charm the birds from the trees if he wanted? He'd gotten around Bette's resistance. Was hers so easy to get around, too? She banned herself from making further comparisons. It was imperative that she remain cool, detached.

The smoldering smile left his eyes. He didn't like

to be reminded about what Alex had done to her. His reply was simple. "No."

"Could you expand on that?"

"No," he said, "he didn't go back to the other girl. That's not why he left you at the altar."

She took a breath. "More, please?"

"Are you a glutton for punishment, like your mother thinks?" When she didn't answer, he said flatly, "Alex left because the idea of marriage frightened him out of his mind. And that's quite a joke now, considering he's on his fourth marriage."

"His *fourth?*" she repeated, shocked.

"He takes a new set of vows every year or two. If he keeps to schedule, number four should be getting nervous."

"But he's only a year older than—"

"You are. I know."

"What's wrong with him? What's happened? That's not the way—the Alex I knew wouldn't—"

"The Alex you knew didn't bother to tell you to cancel the wedding. He canceled it himself, like a coward."

"If I don't hate him, why should you?"

"I don't hate him. I just know him for what he is."

"Because he shamed the *Parker* name."

He reacted to her disdain by frowning. "The Parker name stands for something, Karen. Something you never had an opportunity to see. All you got was the rough edge."

"As if you care!" she shot back. She felt herself tightening up, felt her detachment faltering.

"I care more than you might think."

She couldn't stand it any longer. She had to get out of there. Without a word she hopped off the stool and headed for the front door. She heard Lee call after her. Heard other people call her name, as well, but she didn't look back.

She knew she was calling attention to the two of them by her action. But if Pete had learned their story, so had everyone else. A secret was impossible to keep in a town this small. She was surprised the others hadn't already begun to question her about it.

Her sandals scuffed lightly on the plank sidewalk, then padded soundlessly across the hard-packed street to the well. As a child she'd played near it for hours. She'd had strict instructions never to touch the wooden covers and she hadn't. One look down into the seemingly bottomless pit had satisfied her curiosity and convinced her she didn't want to repeat the mistake of the unfortunate child who'd needed to be rescued.

The tree directly behind the well was even more gnarled than Karen remembered it, some of its branches now lifeless. But it still bore the initials she'd carved in its trunk near the lowest fork—a very small *KL*.

She ran her fingers over her childish effort and wondered at the others scattered around it. Who were these people who'd also left their marks for posterity? Stagecoach riders? Settlers heading west? The child who had fallen into the well?

"Karen?" A woman's soft voice called for her attention. "Is it all right if we talk?"

Karen looked up to see Lee's assistant. She tried but failed to remember her name.

"Diane," the newcomer supplied, almost as if she'd read her mind. "Diane Cruz. I don't blame you for not remembering, considering everything that happened.''

"Yes," Karen agreed tightly. "I did make a rather dramatic exit."

Diane tossed her short blond hair and laughed. "I'll say! It took us all a full minute to speak. We were so surprised. We didn't know. Lee hadn't told us."

Karen pushed some stray strands of hair away from her face. She didn't want to talk about Lee, or Alex, or her involvement with either of them.

"Is it naturally curly?" Diane asked, motioning to her hair.

Karen nodded.

"I've always wanted curly hair. I tried a permanent once, but it frizzed so badly I looked like a monster from a B horror movie. *Frizz Girl from the Black Lagoon!*" She giggled.

Karen smiled. "I'm sure it wasn't that bad."

"Oh, it was. Ask Manny."

Diane went to stand by the well, and after a moment Karen joined her. She missed having Rachel to talk to.

Diane mused, "I wonder what it was like when Nate Barlow jumped off his horse to get a drink and heard the child's cry for help? How it felt to have to make that kind of decision. Your life or the child's? If he'd ridden on, the child would more than likely have died. No one would have heard him."

"I've never really thought about it," Karen said, shrugging.

"It's just a story you've heard since you first came to Twilight."

"Yes."

"What about your aunt? Did she ever say anything about it?"

"Not really."

Diane worked a pebble through a small crack in the wooden covers. Moments later they heard a hollow-sounding splash.

"It's funny how things work out, isn't it?" Diane mused again, turning to look at her. "The town going downhill because the well fails them, the outlaw, the posse, the child, the 1939 movie, the current remake, the town possibly starting to prosper again—all because of what happened at the well. It's almost as if there's a plan. Do you believe in fate?"

Karen wondered what the woman was getting at. Diane seemed sweet, but she was also smart. And she'd had a reason for following her. Karen murmured, "As you say, when you look back, things often seem to have a purpose."

"May I ask you something personal?" Diane asked.

Karen nodded, tensing imperceptibly. Dusk was heavier, but her action was still visible.

"What do you have against Lee? I mean, other than being Alex's older brother. And other than being a Parker—neither of which he can help."

"Did he send you after me?" Karen demanded.

Diane smiled wryly. "Lee doesn't send anyone to plead his cause. He either pleads it himself or says to hell with it. I was just wondering, because you're the first person I've ever met who's reacted negatively to him. Most people take to him right away. It's a gift. Manny has it, too, but not as much as Lee. Do you know, Lee still gets calls from people we worked with the first season of 'Western Rambles'? They want to tell him what's going on in their lives. Not for the show, but because they continue to see him as a friend.''

''Why are you telling me this?'' Karen asked tightly.

Diane shrugged. ''He's my friend, too. I don't like to see him treated unfairly.''

''He's a Parker!'' Karen scoffed. ''I doubt he'll suffer.''

''I've met the Parker family. The ones who live on the ranch—Mae, Rafe and Shannon, Gib, Harriet and LeRoy, Christine and Morgan. Taken all together in one place, they're a bit—'' she smiled ''—over-whelming. But I like them. They're good people.''

''You've obviously never been on their wrong side.''

''And you were,'' Diane said.

''I'd rather not talk about it.''

Diane's blue eyes filled with sincerity. ''Manny and I have never met Alex, but I know brothers can be as different as night and day. Lee's a good man. A great boss. The best thing Manny and I both ever did was agree to work with him. He's always treated us fairly, with friendship, with respect…and not many bosses would do what he has—made his crew part-ners in the business. He has control, but we have a say. And we get a share of the profits. We're a real team.''

''Which underscores my skepticism.''

''I'm not saying this because Lee asked me to,'' Diane denied again.

''But you know which side your bread is buttered on, don't you? Can't you conceive he might not be as wonderful as you think? That none of the Parkers are?''

Diane shot back, ''And can't you conceive that he *is?*''

Karen turned to walk away. This day had been interminably long, with too much emotion swinging back and forth. She barely knew what she was saying anymore, what she was thinking. All she wanted was to go somewhere quiet.

Diane jogged a few steps to catch up with her. ''Karen, look,'' she said, falling into place at her side, ''I didn't mean for us to argue. Maybe we're both just a little prejudiced in our views. You've had one experience with the Parkers, I've had another. All I was trying to do was get you to give Lee a chance.''

A chance to do what? Karen wanted to counter. She was as close to tears now as she'd been after she and Lee— She thought again of her strong reaction to his kiss. Of the way she'd felt upon seeing him in the yard, of talking to him just now at the bar....

All right! Yes! She admitted to herself. There was some kind of attraction flaring between them that had nothing to do with her prior relationship with Alex. But that didn't mean she had to give in to it! She'd be crazy to give in to it!

She didn't notice when Diane broke away and returned to the saloon.

CHAPTER NINE

LEE SAT AT THE BAR, nursing a beer, when what he
wanted more than anything was to commit a little
mayhem on his baby brother. Like Mae said, their
mother had spoiled him. It didn't seem to matter to
Alex whom he alienated, whom he hurt…just so long
as he could skate out of it, worry-free. He'd been like
that as a boy and it had only gotten worse as he'd
grown older. Their mother had always made excuses
for him, taken his side. Maybe if once or twice he'd
been made to face up to what he'd done… Alex made
friends easily, particularly with women. They liked
the little-boy quality about him—until they had cause
to need more.

"Hey, man," Manny said, sliding onto the stool
Karen had abandoned moments before.

"Hey," Lee responded dispiritedly.

"Nice party."

"Yep."

Manny took a sip of his own brew, nodded in beat
to the old saloon song jangling from the piano, then
said, "She, uh, didn't look very pleased when she left
just now. Maybe what you should do is get her some
flowers."

"Some flowers," Lee repeated.

"Yeah, you know…women like flowers."

Lee broke into a slow smile. He always marveled

at the workings of Manny's mind. "And this is something you've gathered from your vast experience?"

"Well, sure."

"Tell me something," Lee said, shifting so he could see him better. "When Diane's mad at you—*really* mad—do flowers make her listen?"

"She's never been that mad at me before."

"Aw, come on!"

Manny shook his head. "Nope, she hasn't. I'd remember."

Since Lee had witnessed more than a few occasions when that just wasn't the case, he was set to argue. But noticing Manny's sideways glance and the slow grin that followed, he understood that his friend was merely trying to lift his mood.

Grinning, too, Lee drew back to deliver a feigned punch, just as John showed up to offer them another beer.

At their refusal John said, "Gotta keep a clear head for tomorrow, huh?"

"Yeah," Manny agreed. "We don't want to find out later that our shots are out of focus."

"Or the sound's missing." Lee laughed. "We did that once, remember? In Missoula, Montana. Right before you and Diane got married. You were in such a state you forgot to flip the right switch and we lost half a day's work!"

"Yeah, I remember." Manny smiled.

"How long have you two been married?" John asked.

"Four years," Manny replied.

"It's been twenty-eight for Bette and me."

"Whoa!" Manny fell back on his favorite expression.

Diane, unnoticed, had come up behind them. She slipped her arms around her husband's neck and teased, "I didn't know you and Lee had been married for four years!"

Manny howled, Lee chuckled and John went away laughing.

Diane enjoyed the moment, then, turning to Lee, said seriously, "There's something we need to talk about."

"Karen?" Lee guessed. He'd known Diane had followed her outside.

"No."

"What, then?"

"I'd rather not say…here. Just—later, okay?"

At that moment Rhonda and Pepper hurried over, wanting to consult about their interviews. "My outfit's mostly white and I'm startin' to wonder if I've made the right choice," Pepper said. "I do have a perfectly good blue one. What do you think? Y'all are the professionals."

"I told her the blue one," Rhonda said. "She'll fade away to nothing in white. Mine's mauve, more on the purple side? I thought it would go good with my eyes."

Diane drew the women away to advise them about their clothes and makeup, which was another part of her job. They wanted their interviewees to look natural, not fake. And too many people had the idea that more was better, in every way.

It was another hour before the party broke up and the crew could meet privately upstairs.

"What's up?" Lee asked as he took the chair opposite the Cruzes, who both sat on the foot of their bed.

"There's something funny about Nate Barlow," Diane said. "I've looked everywhere and I can't find a thing that definitely links him to Twilight. No newspaper articles about the rescue, nothing about him being hanged here."

Both Lee and Manny grew still.

"You're referring to contemporary records... records of the time," Lee said.

Diane nodded. "There's nothing. Some years later I found a reference to an account by a French journalist on a grand tour of the West, and in it he claims the story as real."

"What about documentation—death records, judicial records?"

"Record keeping was pretty spotty out here at the time. And then there was the usual courthouse fire. Honestly, it's hard to believe how many courthouses caught fire in the early days. Must have been all those papers in one place. But every time you really want something—"

Lee cut off her rant. "What did the French journalist have to say?"

"Pretty much the same story we hear today. How Nate Barlow was trying to outrun a posse, how he came upon the child in the well, how he got the kid out and the posse caught up with him and hung him on the spot." She paused. "Tonight, I was out by the well. There's a tree, but the limbs don't look strong enough to have been used to hang someone."

"Probably not the same tree," Manny murmured.

"Anything else?" Lee asked.

She took a deep breath. "The Frenchman mentioned another name."

"What name?" Lee pressed.

Diane paused. "He wrote about a Parker being in Twilight, too. The translation got a little funky at that point, as if parts of the writing in the original text were splotched or missing. There were blank spaces and numerous question marks to indicate confusion. But it definitely had a Parker, a Twilight and a posse, all mentioned right after the account of the hanging."

Lee drummed his fingers on the chair arm. "So what the hell does that mean?"

"I was hoping you'd know," Diane said.

"How would I know?"

"You're a Parker…and this wouldn't be the first thing you've held back from us on this shoot."

"I don't have the slightest idea," Lee replied. He was quiet a moment, then said, "Go back to the first part. Are you telling us you aren't sure if it even happened? If there really was a Nate Barlow? We saw his headstone in the cemetery, remember?"

"Oh, there was a Nate Barlow, all right," Diane reassured them. "He was a pretty rotten fellow from what I can see. Robbed stages, robbed banks, shot and killed a few people. I just don't see anything to confirm the rest of it. Him being a hero and all."

Lee rubbed a hand over his face. He was tired, and he hadn't expected anything like this. "Maybe you just need to look some more."

"I thought that, too. There's another town, closer to here actually, but not in the same county. It's the county seat of Briggs County—Del Norte."

"Del Norte," Lee repeated. He'd been there many times during his visits to the Parker ranch. Besides being the county seat, it was Briggs County's largest town—which still didn't mean it was all that large.

"I thought maybe I'd take a look there. See if I

can find anything. Just in case the old records were
sent to the wrong place when the parent county divided.''

"Did you say anything to Bette about this?"

"No."

"To anyone else?"

"Do I look like a fool? I did ask around a little,
just to see what people had been told, what they remembered.''

"And?"

"Everybody I talked to knows only the one account.''

"You didn't mention the Parker name."

Diane laughed. "I thought I'd let you handle that
one yourself."

He stood up. "I don't remember anything about it
in the family history. Shannon, Rafe's wife—she's the
one who put it together for Mae. I'll give her a call.
See what she has to say."

"Good idea," Diane said. "In the meantime we
keep this strictly between ourselves, right?"

"Right," Lee and Manny agreed in unison.

Lee started off to his room but was called back by
a troubled Diane.

"I don't really want to tell you this," she said just
outside the door, "but I may have made things worse
between you and Karen. She got angry with me because I defended you. But I couldn't just let her keep
thinking you're some kind of inhuman monster. I
tried to make it up with her, but I don't know. She
seemed kind of...distant at the end."

"Hey," he said quietly, "it's okay."

She shook her head. "No, I should have stayed out
of it. What business is it of mine, anyway?"

"You were just being a friend."

Her blue eyes held concern. "She means something to you, doesn't she? More than just your brother's—"

"I don't know what she means," Lee said honestly.

Diane read something in his face that made her bite her bottom lip. Then she whispered tightly, "I'm sorry," and went back inside.

Lee lay down on his own bed fully clothed. It had been an eventful day. Packed fuller than most. But then he didn't end most of his days wondering if, somehow, he might have managed to—

No. He wasn't in love with Karen Latham! It was…something else. He felt badly for her, ashamed of the way his brother had treated her.

A memory lingered of the way she'd looked all those years ago in her white wedding gown, innocent, vulnerable, in urgent need of protection. Like a delicate blossom about to be crushed. She'd turned to him for help, and all he could do was break the terrible news that Alex was gone. It was the hardest thing he'd done in his life up to that point. And it still stood alone in his mind as the most difficult.

Had he fallen in love with her a little bit then? Was that why he'd never forgotten her?

EXCITEMENT WHIPPED through Twilight like a fever the next morning. The "Western Rambles" crew was starting interviews. No one wanted to work during the tapings. Everyone planned to watch as first Pepper and Rhonda went before the camera, then Mary and Benny and, finally, John.

Karen considered herself immune to the illness. Her day's schedule called for her to resume her work downstairs in a continuing effort to clear and organize the crowded puzzle pieces that were her aunt's legacy.

She wasn't unaware of what was happening, though. Her bellwether was the cessation of construction, which resumed anywhere from a half hour to an hour later. By midafternoon she'd noted at least three such stoppages. It was only during the last that her curiosity became piqued enough to draw her to the front window.

A small crowd had gathered across the street at the well. She watched as Lee, still wearing jeans but with a far nicer shirt, spoke with John. He was motioning this way and that—at the well, at the tree behind it, toward the houses on either side and behind, then across the street to where she stood. Karen pulled away from the window. She didn't want him to see her standing there, watching! But she didn't have to worry. When she chanced to look again, he'd moved on to talk with Diane and Manny. Soon everything that needed to be resolved was resolved, and the interview started after one last check of the principals' mikes.

John, it seemed, was going to act as host—as if he were escorting Lee, and through him, the audience, around town for the first time. Karen saw them make several starts, then finally continue for a piece, while John told the story of the well. She saw him gesture, saw Manny lean over the cleared opening of the well, shining the shoulder-held camera's bright light toward the bottom.

The interview proceeded with numerous starts and stops, until finally they left the well—Manny walking backward, his camera lens fixed on the two men, while Diane, wearing a set of headphones, fiddled with the dials on a small black box.

The crowd followed, having become quickly educated about staying out of camera range. John and Lee stopped in front of the Lady Slipper to talk, but contrary to Karen's expectations, they didn't go inside. Instead, they started down the sidewalk...in her direction.

For a second she panicked. She was afraid they might try to come in. John, she knew, wouldn't think a thing of it. And Lee— She wouldn't put it past him to do something like that just to irritate her.

But after passing the mercantile, they also walked past the antique shop and ended up going all the way down the plank sidewalk to the hotel.

"Isn't this great?" Bette enthused, taking a moment to pop into the shop. "John's a wonder. I never knew—" She laughed. "I could be married to a big star and not know it!"

"He did look as if he were having a good time," Karen said, smiling.

"Oh, he is!" She gave Karen an estimating look. "Aren't you curious about how these things are done?"

"Not particularly," Karen fibbed.

"It's very interesting. Why don't you come along? We're heading out to the cemetery next to look at Nate Barlow's grave."

Karen frowned. "Nate Barlow?"

"Yeah. Nate Barlow...the outlaw. You know, the one at the well?"

"I know who Nate Barlow is. But I never knew he was buried in our cemetery."

"Where else would they have put him after they

hanged him?" Bette quipped. "Come see for yourself! His headstone took a tumble, John said, but he
found it and set it up again. It's there now, pretty as
you please."

"I might do that. Only...later."

"You know, Karen. It's really not right to hold
something against a person that he didn't do. That's
what Augusta would tell you."

"Aunt Augusta would understand."

Bette tilted her head. "Oh? She blamed Lee, too?"

Karen set her lips, unwilling to reply.

Bette glanced at the door, anxious to be away. Yet
she took time to say, "You seem to have a blind spot
where he's concerned, honey. It might not hurt to
figure out why." Then with a little wave she hurried
outside and broke into a trot to catch up with the
others.

Karen stared after her. A blind spot? What was
Bette trying to say? What did she suspect?

With the light of a new day, Karen had considered
herself better able to deal with yesterday's confusions.
She'd been caught off guard, she decided. She
couldn't be held responsible for anything she'd
thought or felt or done.

And most of all, she *wasn't* attracted to Lee Parker!

THE DAY'S WORK HAD GONE exceptionally well, the
crew agreed as they wrapped up shooting in late afternoon. Almost everything was a keeper. Rhonda and
Pepper had been both fun and uninhibited in telling
their stories—Pepper about her experiences in rodeo
barrel racing and Rhonda, surprisingly, as a real estate
agent. Then Mary had been more forthcoming than
Lee expected, showing them her specialty pottery

pieces and giving them a glimpse into the tragedy of Benny's accident, but mostly concentrating on how they'd moved beyond that to a satisfactory life in Twilight. Even Benny had been persuaded to say a few words. Then John had given them an introduction to the town and its history and the reasons why it remained so true in appearance to its past. Two of the people who'd been most reticent about being interviewed, Carmelita and her daughter, had come to him afterward and shyly told him that now they weren't nearly so afraid.

As always, they shot far more footage than they'd ever use, but it was better to have an embarrassment of riches than not to have enough to make up a good show. And with an hour to fill, Lee wanted plenty.

Tomorrow they would do the remaining preliminary interviews, some of which they expected to have to shoot over. Then they'd start to expand, chronicling the preparations for the movie's preview and recording the citizens' hopes and dreams for their tiny town. They needed to shoot interiors, too. Of the Lady Slipper Saloon, the mercantile, the hotel. And particularly of the dance hall—both before and after the studio workers performed their magic on what was now a big empty room in relatively seedy condition. John had also invited them to watch as they made the signs that would guide tourists along the roads to Twilight.

From this point they would record everything that happened in the tiny town, hoping to capture the increasing excitement, the pressures, the tensions, the hard work. They wanted their viewers to identify with these people, to pull for them in each and every way.

Only one thing could muddy the water—the question about Nate Barlow. In the midst of everything,

Diane planned to squeeze in a trip to Del Norte tomorrow, and Lee had to remember to call Shannon.

DIANE AND MANNY CALLED IT a day shortly after the evening meal and headed off for their bedroom.

"You must be exhausted, too," Bette said. She was curled up in an easy chair that matched the one John was stretched out in, fast asleep. He hadn't lasted ten minutes after sitting down.

Lee smiled. "Yeah, it wears you out."

Bette's gaze moved over her husband. "He had a great time today," she said.

"He's a natural," Lee agreed.

Bette started to say something else, hesitated, then hedged, "Now, you can tell me this is none of my business, but…you aren't married, are you?"

Lee had let his head fall back on the rear couch cushion to rest his neck. But at that question, he lifted it, curious. "No, why?"

Bette shrugged. "Well, I only wondered because, well…"

"Out with it, Bette," he teased.

"I was just wondering if that was the reason Karen's so dead set against you. Like maybe she once found you attractive, then discovered you were married…with six or eight kids or something."

Lee chuckled. "Not a wife, not a child."

"I'm sorry," she apologized quickly, embarrassed. "I really do need to learn to keep my mouth shut. I keep saying things I shouldn't!"

"What makes you think she might find me attractive? Or…did," Lee asked.

Bette shrugged again. "I don't know. It's just a

feeling. People sometimes pretend to hate what they love. You know, that kind of thing.''

''I'm afraid in her case hate is simply hate.''

''I've known her for a long time, remember,'' Bette said, frowning. ''I keep picking up on something when she talks about you.''

''She talks about me?'' Ridiculously, his heart had leaped. What was he? Sixteen? Still, he waited for the answer.

''Only when I bring you up myself, and then not very much. But it's just…something. Something's there.'' Her frown cleared. ''But I'm sure you don't need me to tell you that. You probably have women all over the country waiting for you to call.''

'''Western Rambles' keeps me pretty busy.''

''Not that busy, surely.''

''As you saw today, it takes up a lot of time.''

''You sound just like Karen. What's wrong with you young people today? Single-mindedness is good, but not to the point where you don't have an actual life! One day you're going to wake up, be my and John's age, and you'll wonder where in heck all that time went!''

''Tell me about Karen,'' Lee said, smiling.

Bette settled back comfortably in her chair. ''I've known her since she was little. Is that a good place to start? She was the cutest thing with those big brown eyes, those curls and those deep, deep dimples when she smiles.''

''She smiles?'' Lee asked facetiously.

''Of course she smiles!'' Bette grinned. ''Not at first, mind you. Her parents were older and highly educated. They expected a lot from her from an early age. When she was six—the first time I saw her—she was this quiet little thing. I was almost afraid to say boo to her, afraid she'd run away. Then after Augusta had had her for a few weeks, the real Karen started to bloom and she was this happy, carefree little child with a sunny disposition. Then she went away for the next school year and came back again all solemn. A few weeks later, the real Karen." Bette sighed. "It went on like that for the first few summers, until finally, it got to where just as soon as the dust settled from her parents' car leaving, she'd be our Karen again!"

"'Our' Karen?" he repeated.

"Augusta felt like her mother and I darned near felt like her aunt. Neither one of us hens had a little chick to call our own, so we kind of adopted Karen. Not that she ever knew it, of course. It was just something we did…quietlike, to ourselves."

"How long did she come here?" Lee asked, thinking of the coincidences in their lives—that both had spent a series of summers in nearly the same area of West Texas.

"Until she was thirteen. That's when Mother and Father decided she had to get serious about college and needed to study all the time. Can you imagine! At thirteen! She was still a baby! She should've been out and about, having fun. Coming to see us…"

"I met her parents."

"At the wedding, yes."

"They hate the Parkers, too, now."

Bette tipped her head. "Did you know? Except for Augusta, no one in Twilight knew a thing about that wedding. First time I knew was the other night when Karen ran out." She stopped to ponder. "I've been wondering about that...why Augusta failed to mention it."

Lee had a feeling he knew, but didn't see how he could say anything without causing hurt to his host and hostess. And he didn't want to do that. He liked them. They were true salt-of-the-earth types.

He pushed to his feet. "I feel like a walk. Want to come?"

Bette brightened, then glanced at John, still snoring softly in the chair. "I'd better not. I need to get my man off to bed before he wakes up with his back hurting him."

Lee nodded and turned for the door.

KAREN HAD A LOT of nervous energy she couldn't seem to shake. She should be tired enough to fall into bed and go straight to sleep again, as she had last night, even with all the tension and distress. This evening, though, her senses were on high alert. She was aware of everything. The faint scent of lilacs that lingered in her aunt's apartment, any little sound, a faraway voice wafting on the almost still air.

Part of her problem was that it was finally beginning to dawn on her just how valuable her aunt's collection was. Even at a conservative estimate, with a tremendous amount yet to be gone through, it had to be in the thousands of dollars. Possibly even the hundreds of thousands. One article after another—some of high individual value, many more with moderate to low value—it all added up. Her aunt had left her a small fortune!

Karen found that difficult to comprehend. Her parents had never been rich, but they'd never hurt for money, either. So, not having been without, she'd never particularly felt the need for great amounts of it. Of more importance to her was the ability to go her own way. To be independent. To make her own decisions. Even to fail. Her aunt's legacy would give her that independence. But at the same time, the prospect was slightly unsettling.

She had to get out of the apartment! She had to move, stretch her limbs. She didn't want to think about money, or independence, or the need for or lack of anything. Nothing. She wanted only to concentrate on putting one foot in front of the other, preferably in rapid succession.

Karen walked for about an hour, enjoying the peace, the quiet, the way the air cooled as dusk lengthened. True to her resolve, she hadn't thought about anything of importance...until she once again neared Twilight. Then Bette's comment about Nate Barlow's headstone made her curious, and she veered off onto the path that led to the cemetery.

As she passed Pete's shack she had an attack of conscience. How was he? Where was he? Was he all right? His great age had to make roughing it more difficult now. If he just wouldn't be so stubborn, so determined to stand in the way. But changing Pete was an impossibility. She could more easily flap her arms and fly.

The cemetery was set apart from the area around it by a low fence. Wild grasses grew in clumps, both within and without the boundary. Some graves were marked by old wooden crosses, some had standing headstones. None had current dates. No one had been buried there for the past thirty years.

Karen moved from headstone to headstone, reading the names of people from long ago. She was having no luck locating the one she was searching for until she reached the last row. It was a little away from the others, set off to the side...possibly segregated because even though he'd died a hero, he hadn't been one during the rest of his life.

Nate Barlow, the caption read, with Valued Friend in the same crude carving underneath. Karen looked at it closely. Why didn't she remember it? Her aunt hadn't allowed her to play in the cemetery out of respect for the dead. But she had helped to clear it of weeds once or twice. Bette had said the headstone had fallen and John had righted it. Still, she had no memory of it, either up or down.

"Nate Barlow...Valued Friend." Lee Parker's voice broke the stillness from close behind her.

She whirled around to glare at him. "Stop sneaking up on me! Either that or wear a bell!"

He had the audacity to grin. "I didn't mean to frighten you."

"Look where we are!" she complained, grasping at any straw to explain her reaction.

"Did you think I was one of them?" He seemed to find that prospect even more amusing.

"No! Just—" She turned back around, more willing to face any number of ghosts than this living, breathing man.

"It's the respect for the dead thing, right?" he ventured.

"I didn't know you comprehended that."

"Oh, yes. The Parkers have a cemetery very similar to this. Not far from ranch headquarters. Only everyone buried in it is family, one way or another."

"I don't care what you Parkers have on your ranch."

"You're the one who brought it up."

Karen tried to walk away. Why did he have to keep showing up? Did he have some kind of internal radar?

He caught her arm just outside the cemetery boundary. She broke contact as quickly as possible. "I don't want to talk to you," she said tightly.

"Because of what happened yesterday?"

"*Nothing* happened yesterday," she maintained.

"Now, that's a lie," he said softly.

"Just leave me alone!"

He sighed in frustration. "Look. Is there any possibility the two of us could just start over? You don't hold me responsible for what my brother did, and I won't—"

"What?" she asked suspiciously. "You won't what?"

"I won't hold you responsible for the fact that your parents didn't invite anyone from Twilight to your wedding."

Karen's breath caught audibly.

"I thought so," he murmured.

"They didn't—my parents—" she stumbled.

"Why was that?" he demanded. "Because they thought the people here were too much like rabble? Or because they thought *my* mother would think they were...and they didn't want that to reflect badly on you and them?"

CHAPTER TEN

KAREN FELT HER WORLD shift slightly. That her parents had refused to let her invite her friends from Twilight to the wedding had been a huge bone of contention between them.

"At least let me ask Bette and John!" she remembered saying.

"You can't invite them without inviting everyone else!" her mother had retorted. "And that I just will not allow! There are too many people coming as it is. Our friends, our relations, our colleagues...not to mention the people Jessica Parker wants to invite. The church will be packed already. Twelve more..." She'd shaken her head in complete vexation. "No. It's just out of the question."

"But they're *my* friends, Mother. And this is *my* wedding!"

"We can't afford another person! Now, if you want to retract the invitations to twelve of your friends from here or to twelve of our family members...or tell Jessica that she has to strike twelve people from her list..."

With that her mother had won, as she usually did back then. Karen knew she should have fought harder, but this had been before she'd learned to stand up for herself. At barely twenty-one, she'd seen only one avenue of escape. After she and Alex were married, maybe they could come to Twilight and see her old friends, introduce Alex to them. A trip that could easily be made during the visit Alex had said they'd soon be making to the Parker Ranch to introduce her to his other relations, who'd been unable to attend the wedding.

Karen blinked, moving from past to present. "I— I—" she stammered. Through Lee Parker's eyes she could see what she hadn't seen before. The real reason her mother, supported by her father, had refused to issue those invitations. They *did* think the people of Twilight rabble. Fit enough for their daughter to interact with during the summers, but not at any other time. Especially when they were on a campaign to impress someone as grandiose as Jessica Parker.

"This is news to you?" he asked incredulously.

It embarrassed Karen to have him be the person to point out this fact. Why hadn't she thought of it herself? In their own way her parents had acted with just as much snobbery as the Parkers had. *She* wasn't good enough for the Parkers and *the people of Twilight* weren't good enough for her parents.

Still she clambered for some kind of defense. "They— My parents— They were limited in what they could spend. The wedding cost so much. They—"

"I freely admit my mother's a snob," Lee said. "She's more impressed with being a Parker than most born Parkers. That doesn't mean I love her any less. I just weigh her actions on that scale. My dad is her complete opposite."

Karen had a vague memory of Alex and Lee's father. He had similar looks to theirs, of course, and was very quiet, staying mostly in the background.

"He took what Alex did pretty hard," Lee said. "He didn't talk to him for several years."

"Your mother didn't mind, though, did she?" Karen retorted, reliving the pain.

Lee's answer was honest. "She didn't approve of his method. But she was relieved the wedding didn't take place. Now I'm not sure how she feels. Alex has put her through a lot."

Karen couldn't muster much compassion for Jessica Parker. But knowledge of her own parents' complicity forced her to look at the entire affair in a different light. How could she continue to blame the Parkers for what her own parents had done, as well? She thought of Bette and John, of Carmelita and Juanita, of Hank and Pepper—all of the others. How would they feel if they knew? When they'd learned about the failed wedding, had they wondered why they hadn't been invited? Especially Bette and John, whom she'd been closest to?

"I don't want anyone here to know about this," she said emphatically. "I don't want them to think—"

"That *you're* a snob?" he asked softly, with a little half smile.

Karen met his gaze and couldn't look away. Without actually having said it, he was showing her what it felt like to be the accused when the act you were being blamed for wasn't your fault. Exactly what Bette had been trying to get her to see about him, and what Diane had attempted, as well!

"Yes, that," she admitted. "But mostly...I don't want them to be hurt."

"I won't say a word," he promised, and lightly tapped a finger to his lips.

Karen continued to look at him, caught in a sudden wave of intense feeling. The way he moved, the way he looked, that little half smile. She had an almost irresistible urge to lean forward and supplant his finger with her mouth. To once again taste those lips that had set her on fire, that had left a trail of liquid pleasure as they moved across her skin....

"Some people got nothin' better to do than stand around doin' a lot of nothin'!" a gruff voice grumbled from nearby.

"Pete!" Karen cried, startled out of her bewitchment. She jerked around to face him.

"Yeah, it's me," Pete said. He stomped closer, a pack over his shoulder, the black dog trailing tiredly behind. He gave them both an irascible look, his keen old eyes missing nothing.

Karen felt her cheeks grow hot, perturbed by thoughts of what he might have interrupted if his return had been delayed several seconds. "You're back!" she exclaimed. "I'm so relieved. I didn't want you to go, Pete. That wasn't what I was asking you to do."

Pete looked Lee up and down. "So you're that TV fella," he charged.

"Lee Parker," Lee said, extending a hand.

Pete ignored it. "You go around interviewin' people."

"Yes, I do."

"Then when you gonna interview me?"

"Whenever you like," Lee replied without missing a beat. "You're back to stay?"

"I s'pose. Dog got tired. Can't keep up like he used to."

All eyes moved to the dog, who'd gone to his favorite spot just off the shack's doorstep and had already curled up in a tight ball, ready to sleep.

Karen thought Pete, too, looked tired, but knew he wasn't about to admit it.

"How about tomorrow around noon?" Lee asked, seemingly careful to keep the moment casual.

"Sounds all right to me," Pete said, then without another word, he crossed to his shack and disappeared inside.

Karen wasn't about to remain where she was, standing in the lingering dusk with Lee. After everything that had happened—was happening—between them, she was afraid to trust herself. Her emotions were too unsettled.

He fell into step beside her as she walked away. "You mind if I come along?" he asked. "I'm heading for the saloon."

Karen shrugged. What else could she do? Say, No, I need you to walk ten paces behind me? What would that tell him? She wasn't going to make further conversation, though. They'd already done enough of that. She'd probably be awake for hours tonight thinking about it. About the way her parents—actually, her mother—had behaved. Her father, like Lee's, tended to stay in the background when Gemma was on a tear about something. Then there was that disturbing moment Pete had interrupted. That would be good for another couple of hours of restless thought. *Why did it keep happening?*

"Do you believe the dog story? He did look pretty tired." When she didn't answer, he said, "I guess they both did. Why did Pete come back so soon, do you think? To make more trouble?"

Karen shrugged again.

"John sure isn't going to like it," Lee persisted.

"No, he won't," she agreed shortly.

She sensed his smile. "You do still speak."

They were almost to the stairs outside the antique shop. Karen quickened her pace, and once she'd managed to mount the first step, she paused to say, "Don't push your luck, okay?"

"I thought we were going to start over."

"I let you walk with me, didn't I?"

"Well, that's something."

"Like I said…don't push your luck."

Then she ran upstairs, let herself into the apartment and assumed what had fast become her favored position since returning to Twilight—bracing herself against the door to keep Lee Parker outside.

Only, how did she keep thoughts of him from invading her mind?

EARLY THE NEXT MORNING Karen awakened to a loud, deep rumbling. The continuing vibrations seemed to permeate the air, dragging her from what little sleep she'd finally settled into late in the night.

Then the knocking started. Loud, rapid, unceasing. Karen slipped into her robe as she stumbled to the door.

Bette stood outside on the landing, her bright red hair in curlers, her face shiny with applied night oils. She, too, was in her robe. "They're here!" she cried excitedly. "The movie workers! In four big trucks—*huge* things—all on the near side of town. Most everyone's out there. I thought you might like to see, too."

Karen glanced at her attire. "Like this? I'll change."

"Almost everyone's dressed this way. No one expected them to come so early. John says they probably drove through the night, since it's cooler."

"Still, I'd—"

"Come *on!*" Bette said, grabbing her hand and pulling her downstairs. "We don't want to miss a thing!"

They hurried past the saloon and the empty buildings on its other side, until they were at the edge of town, where four massive eighteen-wheelers were lined up one after the other along the road. All were stopped but had their engines running. The noise would be ungodly at any hour.

Karen tried to cover her ears as Bette drew her into the assembled crowd. Most, as Bette had said, were in their nightwear. Some had robes, some didn't. John looked as if he'd leaped straight out of bed with just his pajama bottoms on. His thinning gray hair was every which way. Carmelita's robe barely covered her round body, Juanita sleepily held on to baby Jesse, while Diego had managed to pull on a pair of jeans. Hank and Pepper, Joe and Rhonda, Isaac Jacobs, even Mary and Benny were trying to take in what was happening. The only town member who wasn't there was Pete.

The driver of the lead truck climbed down to consult with John. Exaggerated hand motions accompanied shouted questions and answers as John suggested an area for them to park. While this happened, a large van, filled with some of the actual workers, drove up as well.

Karen was trying her best to at least tie her robe at the waist when the "Western Rambles" crew came into view outside the line of trucks, Manny, as usual, taping what was going on.

Howls of protest came from the crowd as the camera turned on them, but Lee, grinning, shouted for them not to worry. He wouldn't use the footage.

Somehow, the crew had managed to dress, or at least partially dress. Manny was barefoot but had on jeans and a T-shirt. Diane wore a pair of shorts, a wrinkled shirt and plastic thong sandals. And Lee— Karen wished she hadn't seen this!—was in his low-cut jeans and a check shirt. But the shirt was hanging loose and open, and as he worked, she had a full view of a nicely muscled chest, flat stomach, trim waist and a fine sprinkling of dark hair that started just beneath his throat to disappear beneath the button flap of his jeans.

Karen swallowed and tried to drag her eyes away. She was tingling at seeing him that intimately. Of wanting to see more. His body was like a beautiful work of art—strong and sensual and highly appealing.

Her heart thumped erratically, her breaths were shallow...this time, for all the *right* reasons.

No. No! *No!* she castigated herself. It was Martin she should be having these feelings for! Not—

She continued to feast on what was so freely given. Lee didn't seem to know that she was watching him. And if that was so, what did it hurt?

Then he turned to look straight at her.

Caught, she broke her gaze away. What was *wrong* with her? Had anyone else noticed? She was relieved to find that no one had.

Karen didn't want to look back but had to in order to see what he was doing, where he was. To ensure that he wasn't coming toward her. She wasn't sure what she'd do if he was—run to him or from him.

She didn't need to worry, though. Manny had stopped shooting and, of necessity, the crew members huddled together before hurrying to tape the workers exiting the van.

"I wish our shipment of souvenirs was here," Mary lamented loudly.

"I wonder where they'll sleep." Pepper also had to raise her voice to be heard.

"And eat!" Carmelita shouted.

The consultation about parking ended and the lead driver climbed back into his truck, used a radio to talk with the other drivers, then, after goosing the engine a few times, pushed into the proper gear. The truck rolled forward, swinging out to make a wide turn. As the other trucks mimicked the actions of the first, the crowd fell back into the town proper to allow the drivers all the space they needed to maneuver.

Little Jesse started to cry at the added noise and Benny protested loudly that he didn't like it, either, because it hurt his ears. Pepper and Rhonda declared they'd had enough, and echoing them, Karen told Bette she, too, was leaving.

She'd only managed a few steps before John caught up with her. He looked a new man, charged with excitement, completely oblivious to his state of undress or the fact that his hair was in wild disorder.

"It's all startin', Karen!" he said, leaning close. "I was beginnin' to wonder if it ever would—if it was all some kind of crazy dream—but here they are! It's no dream!"

Karen smiled at his happiness.

"There's only one problem." Some of the glow

left his face. "Pete's back. Would you mind goin' to talk to him again? I'm real worried that he'll start messin' things up again. Playin' his little tricks on us is one thing. Playin' 'em on this Hollywood crowd is somethin' else. They won't hesitate to call the law down on him. No two ways about it. So for his own sake... You got him to listen to you once. Surely you can do it again. Whatcha say? Will you do it?"

"I'll try," Karen promised, cupping her hand close to his ear so he would hear.

He grinned and nodded and patted her on the back.

WHEN THE DEAFENING ENGINE noises finally stopped, the resulting quiet was almost startling. With the return to normal levels of conversation, the "Western Rambles" crew came together to see what their next steps should be. They were accustomed to working on the run, to sudden bursts of opportunity, to being asleep one minute and up, dressed and moving speedily and efficiently the next. It wasn't remarked upon that Manny had no shoes or that Diane wasn't as well groomed as she normally was. Or that Lee's dark hair was rumpled and his customary T-shirt missing.

"They're going to set up their own place," Manny said. "So they'll be independent of Twilight. That's the way they usually do things, the guy I was talking to said. They try not to disrupt the status quo for the people in the area any more than they have to."

"Sounds reasonable," Diane said, finally getting a chance to run a comb through her hair.

"Might disappoint a few people," Lee murmured.

He was having a hard time getting Karen out of his mind. But then, it seemed he'd been having that trouble for years. Only it was worse now—when he could talk to her, when he could see her with little effort. God, she'd looked good earlier in that long T-shirt she'd obviously slept in and the silk robe she kept trying to tie. And the way he'd caught her looking at him. It made his blood course just to think about. Those big brown eyes, those wonderful curls that tumbled to her shoulders. The face of an angel, he'd decided last night as he lay awake, thinking. She hadn't looked at him like an angel this morning, though. Not an angel in the accepted sense of the word. This heavenly spirit could lift a man until he *thought* he was in heaven.

She seemed to be of two minds how to respond to him. One part of her was angry and hostile, the other...neither. And the possibilities that swirled around the latter prospect were intriguing.

"Lee...Lee?" Diane delivered a restrained thump to his arm. "Hey, you! Lee!" When she saw that she'd finally gained his attention, she repeated her question. "Did you talk with Shannon last night? To ask about Nate Barlow's story and the mysterious Parker reference?"

"I talked with her," Lee said. "She doesn't know any more about it than we do. There's nothing in the family history. But there's a lot of material she said Mae didn't feel was necessary to include in the history. She promised to look through it again. Keep her eye out. She'll let us know."

"Well, that's something," Diane murmured...an exact repetition of his response to Karen last evening when she was on the stairs and challenging him by saying that she'd allowed him to walk with her.

Lee frowned, uncomfortable with what was happening. It was one thing to devote his resting thoughts to Karen, and another entirely to allow them to intrude on his work. "Western Rambles" came first in his life. It had since its inception. He wasn't going to let that change.

To aid in maintaining their professionalism, Lee called a break so they could dress properly and eat breakfast before once again returning to work.

DIANE HAD LEFT for Del Norte by the time Lee's noontime interview with Old Pete Tunny arrived. Originally the crew had planned to have several additional resident interviews taped by midday, but events of the morning had shoved everything else aside and the interviews had been postponed. No one objected. But Lee knew better than to chance letting this opportunity with Pete slip away. The old man could change his mind as easily as the wind could change directions.

Pete saw Lee and Manny into his one-room shack and with great dignity offered them some of his strongly brewed coffee.

As they sat around, steaming cups in hand, Pete rubbed his whiskered chin and said, "The first of the crazies are here, I guess. Couldn't come into town nice and quietlike. N-o-o-o! They had to sound like a bunch of banshees, wailin' and carryin' on."

"It's hard to arrive quietlike in four large trucks," Lee said, smiling at Pete's description.

Pete's bright eyes narrowed. "Four of 'em, huh. I thought there was more."

"That and a van."

"A van!" Pete repeated.

The way he said it, Lee wasn't sure he understood

the meaning of the word. "A big car," he explained.
"Carries eight or ten people."

"Next you're gonna be tellin' me what a car is!"
Pete snapped. "I know what a car is…and a van! I
just think they're awful. If God'd meant for us to ride
around all the time, he'da given us wheels, not feet!"

Lee wished the tape was rolling. He tapped
Manny's shoe with his boot.

Manny, who'd been staring at Pete as if he were
some kind of anachronism, readied the equipment.

"You don't mind if we start taping our talk, do
you?" Lee asked.

"Not if you don't mind me sayin' what I think."

"That's what we're here for."

"I don't like that," Pete complained, squinting
when the auxiliary light was switched on.

"We can go outside."

"Nope," he said, "let's get this over with." Then
he positioned himself as stiffly as if he were standing
before a firing squad.

It took a full hour for them to finish. Instead of
being cantankerous, as Lee had expected, Pete had
continued on his best behavior. He'd slowly relaxed
and talked about Twilight and its past, including his
own past. He'd told stories. He'd laughed and poked
fun. It was an amazing interview.

Manny had managed to wrangle an invitation to
lunch with the studio workers, so he hurried off. But
Lee stayed a little longer to visit with Pete.

"You remember the first time I saw you?" Pete
asked after an extended pause.

"Your…salute?" Lee murmured.

"I meant it!"

"I know you did. Why'd you give us the interview?"

"I got a question, too," Pete said instead of answering. "Just what are you plannin' for that little gal of ours?"

"Little gal?"

"I saw the way things was between you last night. Don't think I didn't!"

"I don't have any plan," Lee denied.

Pete snorted. "Yeah, and pigs don't have snouts! She said it was your brother that hurt her before. You better not let me catch you doin' the same thing."

"I don't intend to hurt Karen, Pete."

Pete scooted forward in his threadbare chair. "Funny thing about intentions…they have a way of goin' wrong. That's what these people in town don't understand. They don't *intend* for things to get outta hand. But it happens. Without you meanin' for it to. You start off with one thing, it turns into somethin' else, then all heck breaks loose. You understand what I'm sayin', son?"

"Why did you come back, Pete, if you still feel the same way?"

Pete didn't appreciate being pressed. His answer was irritable. "I know it ain't much, but this place is my home."

"I thought your home was on the land, in the hills."

"It was! It is! But—" He bent to pull off a worn boot, dropped it on the rough wood floor, then peeled away a holey sock to reveal a terrible-looking bunion. "Other foot's got one just like it," he said matter-of-factly.

"You should have that seen to," Lee said quickly.

It was hard for him to believe the man could walk at all!

"I ain't been to a doctor in my life and I'm not startin' now!"

"Pete, if it's money—"

A light knock sounded on Pete's door, followed by Karen's voice. "Pete? Are you in there? Answer me if you are, Pete. Please."

The old man hurriedly thrust his foot back into the sock and redonned the boot, not wanting her to see. "Yeah…yeah…I'm here," he said gruffly. "Give me a minute."

"Would you like me to—" Lee had been going to say "get the door," but Pete was already on his way, shuffling across the short space.

"Pete, I need to talk to you. It's really important," Karen said as she hurried inside, a frown marring her brow. Then she saw Lee and all movement stopped.

"I already got company," Pete grumbled. "We barely fit as it is."

Lee stood up. "I was on my way out."

"I—I can come another time," Karen said.

The pink in her cheeks made her look even more appealing. Her coloring was beautiful. She was beautiful.

She pushed a fall of chestnut curls away from her face, a nervous movement. "Truly, I can come back."

Lee didn't want to go, but he could see that she wouldn't be comfortable with him around. "I've been here over an hour. Now it's your turn."

"An hour…for Pete's interview? I—I thought you'd be gone long before this."

"Pete was great," Lee said. "He'd make a wonderful ambassador for the town if he'd let himself. Our audience will love him.''

Pete crossed his arms. "It's still crowded in here."

Lee laughed. "I'm going." Then at the door he said, "Thanks, Pete," and gave Karen a little nod.

KAREN COULDN'T SETTLE. She moved around Pete's small room as she had when a child, examining the numerous mementos from his desert treks. Tiny animal bones bleached white by the sun, interesting rocks, pieces of dried wood.

There was no getting around it. She had to acknowledge it and not take it back later. Lee Parker bothered her. Bothered her in a way she shouldn't let him. She could still feel the vibrations of his presence in this room and from earlier this morning at the trucks.

"You have somethin' you wanna say?" Pete demanded after a brief observation of her jerky movements.

"Uh, yes. Yes, I do." Karen forced herself to concentrate. She had to stop thinking about Lee, at least for the moment. "It's—it's about you coming back."

"I got somethin' to say about that, too," Pete declared, and he said it with such conviction that Karen looked at him fully. "I decided you was right about Augusta," Pete said. "If she was here, she'd be kickin' my butt all over the place for not helpin' out. I still don't think she'd want Twilight to change, but it's gonna change either way. Like you said—be a real ghost town or a pretend one with lots of visitors." He paused. "I guess the pretend one's best."

Karen absorbed what he said. In effect, he was telling her that he was going to stop making trouble. That he wasn't going to continue upsetting everyone with his pronouncements and his high jinks. And he'd already made a start by giving Lee a "great" interview.

"Oh, Pete!" she cried, and hurried to hug him whether he liked it or not. "Pete, you've made me so happy. Everyone will be happy!"

Pete wiggled free. "Hey, little girl. Don't do that. That's enough," he protested.

She looked at him with glowing eyes. "Everyone's going to want to do that, Pete. Better get used to it."

"Maybe I should get outta town again."

"Don't you dare!" she said, grinning. "I'll come find you this time. And I mean it!"

Pete grumbled and fussed some more, but Karen could see that, for the first time since she'd known him, he was deeply touched.

CHAPTER ELEVEN

THE NEWS of Pete's capitulation spread around town like wildfire. It wasn't widely accepted at first, but with Lee and Manny's concurrence about the interview—even to the point of playing some of the raw footage back for them—everyone became believers.

Typically, Pete hid himself away. And unwilling to give him any excuse to change his mind, no one insisted on him joining the merriment. As a result, so much gratitude was extended to Karen that she began to sympathize with Pete's reclusiveness. She was barely able to get any work done at all, for people stopping by to talk.

Excitement reigned for the whole day, even after Carmelita and Mary, who'd envisioned setting up a small café, learned that the movie studio had made full provisions for their workers in the tiny toadstool of a town that had suddenly sprung up adjacent to Twilight.

"I bet we'll get 'em into the saloon later on, once they settle in," John consoled everyone. "We'll make sure they have an invite, that's for sure!"

"And when the souvenirs show up, they'll want some of those, too, I bet," Mary had proclaimed.

The general outlook was rosy as it began to dawn on each of them that their project stood a good chance of success.

"Wow," MANNY SAID at what had become almost a nightly meeting for the crew in the Cruzes' bedroom. "These people are really excited."

"I have to confess," Diane said, "I'm getting excited, too. I'm looking forward to Twilight's big show." She glanced at Lee. "What did that Melanie Taylor person have to say? Did we get the okay to tape?"

"She's talking to her boss, who'll talk to his boss, but she says it's only a formality. She knows 'Western Rambles.' Says they'll cooperate in every way they can. Even ensure interviews with the appropriate participants during the junket. She's smart. She sees it as free PR for the film."

"You scratch my back, I'll scratch yours," Diane murmured.

"Exactly." Lee paused. "What about your trip into Del Norte? Did you have any luck?"

"I didn't find a thing."

Lee tapped his bent knee. "I haven't heard from Shannon, either."

"What would it mean if we did find something?" Diane asked. "I mean, found something that contradicted... What would we do?"

"I don't even want to *think* about it," Manny moaned.

"Then why are we looking?"

"You're asking that?" Manny challenged. "Ms. Accuracy in Reporting?"

Diane examined her hands. "Yeah, well, I don't want to do anything that will hurt these people."

"The truth is the truth, Diane," Lee said.

"Yes...but they're so happy."

"And may continue to be that way. We haven't

found anything contradictory yet. Just information that's not there. All we're trying to do is fill in the blanks.''

"Like always," she agreed, but it was easy to tell that her heart wasn't in it.

KAREN SAT at her bedroom window, looking out into the night. There was something so lonely and yet so reassuring about the vast emptiness of the land. A coyote called, another coyote answered. Distant, haunting. She'd loved to listen to them as a young girl, their wild natures speaking to something buried deep within her.

Was it the evolution from city girl to country girl that was again causing her problems? Was that why, at times, she felt as if the world in which she'd existed previously were somehow slipping away?

She knew she had to make some decisions. Decisions that would have long-range effects. Whether or not she cared enough for Martin to accept his proposal. Whether she wanted to open her own shop. And if she did, where it would be. In Twilight or elsewhere.

Her most vexing problem was something else, though. Or rather, someone else. She couldn't believe it, but Lee Parker was starting to consume her every waking thought, and sometimes her dreams! She didn't want it to be that way, but—

The coyote yipped again, his elongated cry a plea to the universe surrounding him.

Once again she felt a kinship to that distant desert wolf and silently echoed his cry in her spirit.

KAREN WAS AT WORK the next morning, nearing completion of her first inventory of the articles in the shop

proper. By now she'd done a full-scale sweep from
one side to the other, assigning numbers to most of
the furniture and larger objects that also corresponded
to notations in her notebook. As before, she wasn't
taking time to look anything up, just continuing the
list she could refer to later. Next, she would start on
the storage shed and do the same thing. Once that
was accomplished, she would take up where she'd left
off several days ago—trying to make some sense of
it all by studying the reference books, and possibly,
this time, even making a few calls to people with
greater expertise than she had.

She was on her hands and knees, peering under a
table, when Bette came rushing into the shop.

"Oh my heaven! You are not going to believe it!"
Bette's eyes were wide, her expression slightly
shocked as Karen looked at her. "You'll never guess
who's sitting in my living room right this very minute! I told them I was slipping out to get some coffee
from downstairs, but it was really to come over here
to tell you—to warn you, I suppose."

"You're not making any sense, Bette," Karen said,
straightening.

"*The Parkers!* The Parkers are in my living room!
Mae Parker and a younger woman she calls Shannon.
Doesn't look like a Parker at all, though. Got blond
hair and blue eyes. Maybe she's one of the in-
laws—"

"Mae Parker?" Karen repeated as memories of the
aborted wedding burst into her mind. Mae Parker saying in her imperious way, *This is a travesty…a complete and total travesty!* In one of her bitterer moments, Karen had determined that if she ever met the

woman again, she'd tell her straight to her face what she thought of her. That *her* behavior had been even more atrocious than that of other members of her family.

"They've come to visit Twilight," Bette said, rushing on, "and Lee, of course."

Lee! Karen remembered what she and Lee had talked about concerning her parents. But even though they were guilty of elitism themselves, her parents hadn't gone out of their way to cause pain, as Mae had with her words.

"I've got to get back," Bette said. "They'll notice if I'm gone too long."

"They're visiting Twilight?" Karen called after her, seeking to confirm what she thought she'd heard. "They plan to look around?"

Bette paused at the back door. "That's what I'm trying to tell you! Mae says she wants to see *everything*. And believe me, she's the kind of person who means what she says!"

BY NOW LEE WAS as competent as a native when it came to guiding his relations around Twilight. He introduced them to the citizenry they came upon, showed off the well, told the story of the outlaw as legend had it, showed what the studio workers had started doing first thing this morning in the music hall, ushered them through the saloon, the mercantile, the hotel still under renovation.

Mae's hawklike eyes missed nothing. "More here than I remembered," she said. "Why don't they put a coat of paint on the place? It'd look a lot better."

"The movie studio wants it as it is, Mae. They like it looking old."

Mae stopped to lean on her cane. She was dressed neatly in a conservative tan skirt and a white blouse with a black belt that matched her shoes. Her snowy white hair was in its accustomed knot on top her head. Few would believe she was eighty-eight.

"Wait'll they get old. They might not like it so much!" she grumbled.

Shannon laughed. "Mae!"

"Well, it's the truth. Place probably wouldn't mind bein' spiffed up a bit."

They stood on the sidewalk outside the saloon's front doors.

"What's that?" Mae asked, pointing to a storefront down the way. "Sign says Antiques. Aren't we goin' to look there?"

Lee had been dreading this moment. "Uh, Mae? Before we go in—"

"I know the place belongs to Augusta Lamb," Mae cut in. "You don't have to pussyfoot around. Might think you do, but you don't!"

"Belonged," Lee corrected. "Augusta died earlier this summer. It's…Karen who's here now, sorting through her inheritance."

Mae gave him a sharp look. "Karen's here?"

"I knew she might be. It's one of the reasons I came—to apologize."

"Who's Karen? Who's Augusta?" Shannon asked.

Shannon hadn't been a member of the Parker family seven years ago. If later she'd heard about the embarrassment—which Lee imagined she had, being around Mae—there was no reason she'd remember the names.

"Karen Latham," Lee explained. "The girl my brother, Alex—"

"Left standing at the altar!" Mae completed. "It was terrible! Worse thing a Parker's ever done! If I coulda got my hands on him afterward, he wouldn't've had enough left in him to humiliate us again like he has!" Her shoulders jerked spasmodically. Finally she demanded, "Did she? Did she accept your apology?"

Lee grimaced. "Let's just say things are at a rather...delicate stage."

"Maybe I should talk to her," Mae declared, and started forward.

Lee reached to stop her—that was exactly what he *didn't* want—but a hand slipped inside his elbow to restrain him.

"Maybe it's like a saddle bur," Shannon said softly. "Better to get it out in the open. I remember now. Mae was still upset when she told me." She glanced at Mae, who was already disappearing into the shop's open doorway. "Why not let the two of them have their talk? Then we can talk, too. I have something to show you."

KAREN KNEW INSTANTLY that she was no longer alone. She also knew who the visitor was without looking. Mae Parker had a force about her. A presence that set her apart.

She sensed the older woman glance around the shop, at the still-too-crowded conditions, then her penetrating gaze settled on her.

This time Karen was ready. She stood—her back straight, her chin high—on her own ground now. She would not be intimidated. She stepped away from the cheval mirror she'd been about to move and spoke first. "I heard you were in town."

"I just learned you were."

Mae looked only a little older than the last time Karen had seen her, and even though she now relied on a cane, Karen wasn't fooled into thinking the intervening years had softened her in any way. "So you just had to drop by," Karen said.

"I would have considered it rude not to."

Karen's smile was quick, sardonic. "And heaven forbid, you mustn't be rude."

Mae tapped a wicker planter with the tip of her cane. "I understand your aunt has died. The Parkers extend our condolences."

"Why?" Karen demanded.

"Because it's the right thing to do."

"You didn't care about her when she was alive. Why should you now?"

"Lee tells me he's apologized."

Again Karen didn't respond.

Mae smiled tautly. "Would it help if I apologized, too?"

Karen found facing Mae difficult, but continuing to stand up for herself was important. She had to, to compensate for when she hadn't. "Are you apologizing for your behavior or for Alex's?"

"My behavior?" Mae repeated, surprised.

"Oh, yes. You made it very clear you didn't want me in your family. Which is fine. Because I'd rather be where I am than owing anything to you."

"You're a very bitter young woman," Mae decreed.

"And I shouldn't be?"

Mae moved past Karen to a straight-back chair, where she sat down slowly and carefully. Then, leveling her gaze on Karen, she said, "I've dealt with

stubborn people all my life. Hell, I'm the most stubborn person I know. You say I didn't want you in the
family...I didn't even *know* you, girl. How could I
make a decision like that? And as far as Alex
goes—'' she laughed ''—I should think you'd count
yourself lucky! That boy never was any good for any-
thin'. Spoiled rotten. Used to havin' his own way.
What kinda husband does that make? If all men were
like him, I'd rather be the old maid I am than married
to one of 'em! Now, wouldn't you, too? Truthfully?''

Karen tried to steel herself against Mae's logic.
Years ago Alex had told her the way the family matriarch liked to bend and maneuver people to achieve
her own ends. That she liked to rule other people's
lives. ''I don't believe you,'' Karen said. ''I heard
you myself.''

''Heard me?'' Mae echoed once again.

Karen picked up a Hummel figurine she'd missed
putting away and rubbed at a spot of dirt on its base.
''Look, I'm very busy. If it means so much to you, I
accept your apology. It's what Aunt Augusta would
want, so I'll do it.''

''I liked your aunt Augusta.''

Karen's cleaning stopped. She looked at Mae in
surprise. ''I didn't know you knew her.''

''I didn't, not really, but I'd like to have. I invited
her to tea at the ranch once. She said it wouldn't be
right without you. We came to an understandin',
though, about what a terrible thing it was that happened to you. I told her I considered it a travesty.
That boy wasn't ready to marry anybody. His momma
shoulda put her foot down and stopped it right when
he first told her what he planned to do. He humiliated
you, your parents. He humiliated himself, his parents,

his brother. But worst of all, he brought disgrace to the Parker name.''

"I'm glad you think your name is more important than living, breathing human beings.''

"The Parker name *is* living, breathing human beings,'' Mae retorted. "What do you think we all are out at the ranch? What Lee is…and his daddy? And there's lots more scattered throughout the state. It's not just a *name*. It's a symbol of all the principles we live by. And leaving a young woman stranded at the altar on her wedding day breaks every single one of those! That's why Lee and I tried to talk to you and your parents right away, to do what we could to make things right.'' She stopped, her lips thinning. "But they wouldn't listen, and they wouldn't let you listen, either.''

Travesty…principles…disgrace. Had *that* been what Mae was referring to when Karen heard her making pronouncements all those years ago? Not that she, Karen, was unworthy, but that Alex was too irresponsible to be contemplating marriage! Mae had thought *he* was wrong. That Jessica Parker was wrong in not doing more to stop it.

Realization of another mistaken perception flooded through her, and in its aftermath came deep embarrassment. It had been so easy for her to jump to conclusions back then. She'd been predisposed from the way her parents had reacted to the Parkers, in their attempts to prove themselves— No. Karen pulled her thoughts back. She could see it all now. For her *mother* to prove herself good enough for Jessica Parker. It had injured her mother's pride to be thought of as wanting—for her daughter to be. That's why she'd done everything she had for the wedding, spent so much money, reacted beyond reason when it was canceled. Still reacted beyond reason.

Even after Lee's attempts at clarification, Karen had held on to her anger at Mae. She'd heard Mae with her own ears! Now, if Mae was telling the truth—

The older woman exited the chair as quickly as she could and saw Karen into it. Mae also removed the figurine from her hand and put it safely on a nearby shelf.

"You look like you've seen a ghost, girl," Mae murmured anxiously, seemingly out of character for her. "You're all pale." She hissed at herself, "I shouldn't've said everything I did. Sometimes I forget other people have a different way of dealin' with things than I do. Can I get you somethin'? Some water, maybe?"

Karen strove to collect herself. To startle someone as tough as Mae, she must look pretty terrible. "No, I— I'm all right. I just—"

"How about that lady at the saloon? Bette, that's her name, isn't it? Maybe she can—"

"No, really, please." Karen got back to her feet and shook her head, trying to clear it.

Mae gave her a long, hard look before, apparently satisfied, she relaxed a degree. "You had me goin' there for a minute. I didn't want to have to explain to Lee and the others that somehow I'd managed to fuss you to death!"

Unbelievably, considering the hostile way this confrontation had started, Karen found herself smiling at Mae's little jest. "I'm a lot stronger than that," she murmured.

"That's what I always thought," Mae retorted, giving a wisp of a smile. Then, more seriously, she added, "Actually, I always thought you were pretty strong. Your aunt thought so, too."

"The two of you…Aunt Augusta and you. You certainly seem to have covered a lot of ground when you talked."

"Anybody can when they don't dillydally around." Mae paused. "I truly am sorry to see Augusta go."

"Thank you," Karen said simply.

With a nod of understanding Mae left the shop, her cane tapping lightly on the plank floor.

LEE AND SHANNON SAT in the deserted saloon. The whole town seemed busy with one project or another, rejuvenated by the arrival of the studio workers and Pete's declaration of cooperation. Some of the women were now toiling inside the hotel, painting and wallpapering and helping with the finishing work whenever construction got to that point. Lee, Diane and Manny had been taping their progress when word reached Lee that his relatives had arrived. Diane and Manny continued without him.

At first Lee couldn't concentrate on what Shannon was saying, his thoughts on the two strong-willed women together in the antique shop. But her information became so engrossing, Shannon soon gained his full attention.

"I didn't make anything of it at first," she said, continuing. "Then I read it again and there it was—Byron Parker's account of rescuing a child from what he called 'the spring.' I searched further and found that he'd have been twenty-two at the time. Old enough to have been a member of the posse chasing

Nate Barlow, like he claimed in his other account. I also looked at his gravestone in the Parker cemetery, and his birthdate corresponds. He didn't die until 1944, at the age of seventy-four. Read it. All of it,'' she urged, passing Lee the loose sheets of paper that had been taken from two different writing tablets.

For whatever reason, whether to set the record straight by request of local law enforcement or for his own satisfaction, Byron Parker had filled six pages with his old-fashioned script.

Lee found the writing difficult to decipher at first but soon grew comfortable with the style. He quickly became absorbed. Minutes later his head jerked up. ''He says here Nate Barlow was hanged in Del Norte, after due process of law...and that the posse caught him in Twilight, not because Nate had stopped to rescue a child but because he was up there—'' he pointed to the ceiling ''—taking a little siesta in one of the bedrooms with the saloon owner's daughter!''

Shannon nodded.

Lee finished the last two sheets. This time when he looked up, all he could do was shake his head and say softly, ''My God, he does claim to have rescued a child. The spring must be the well. He says he and his buddy did it during all the excitement following the capture of Nate Barlow. There were only two families in Twilight at the time. The saloon owner and his daughter and the Ramerizes—a husband, wife and their two young kids. The oldest kid hid out in the well when the posse members started yipping and shooting their guns off in the air to celebrate. Then he couldn't get out. Byron and his friend heard the kid yell, Byron dropped a rope down to him and pulled the kid out.''

"Do you think it's true?" Shannon asked.

"I don't know what to think," Lee said frankly.

"It is what you wanted, right?"

Lee still felt stunned. He hadn't expected anything like this! In fact, he'd hoped deep down that they wouldn't find any documentation to question the Twilight legend. "Uh—yeah. It is. Thanks."

Shannon was perceptive. "But it's going to cause complications, isn't it?"

Lee was having a hard time taking it all in. "Yeah. Listen," he said, leaning forward to gather the papers. "Can I have these for a bit? I'll take good care of them. But I think, since the information could cause such mischief, we need to check it out properly before we do anything. Just because old Byron said it—"

Shannon grinned. "Are you intimating a Parker might exaggerate?"

"I'm saying a Parker is subject to the same flights of fancy as anyone else. And look at the dates—these accounts were written in 1922. Thirty years after the fact. Memories can get pretty fuzzy."

"I haven't said anything to anyone. Not even Rafe or Mae."

"Good idea. Let me—let me have it for a while first."

"I'm sure Mae already knows about it. She's been through all this material numerous times. The sheets were folded together in the pages of a book, but if I found them—"

"What is it Mae already knows about?" Mae demanded from the saloon's front doorway.

Lee spun around. "How did it go?" he asked, hoping to divert her.

"Fine," Mae said. She waited pointedly for her answer.

Shannon sighed. "Mae, do you know anything about Byron Parker and the spring here in Twilight?"

"About him rescuing that child, you mean? Of course I do."

"And about Nate Barlow's capture?" Shannon pressed.

"That, too."

"Then why didn't you say anything? You knew why Lee was coming here. And you know what people think."

Mae shrugged. "What difference does it make? Byron knew he did it and that's all that matters."

Lee gazed at the oldest living Parker. "What about earlier? At the well…when I was telling you the story?"

"You were havin' such a good time I didn't want to burst your bubble. And what does it hurt, anyway? People are gonna believe what they want to believe. Haven't you learned that yet?"

Lee was fascinated by her attitude. "Mae, you're a wonder. But if you don't mind, would you keep this to yourself? Other people might find the news more than a little…distressing."

"Like the movie studio and this town," Shannon murmured.

Lee patted the papers. "I'll put these away in a safe place."

"You do that," Mae said. "We don't want 'em lost. They're part of Parker history, even if they're not in the official book."

LEE DIDN'T GO BACK to the hotel after seeing Mae and Shannon off in Mae's beautifully preserved black

Cadillac. He had a lot to think about. What if the
accounts Shannon had found turned out to be true?
Or...if they were true, could never be proved, other
than on the merit of Byron Parker's word? Did the
lack of any backup records at the courthouses pre-
clude the accuracy of the accounts? Or did that make
them all the more valuable? And if any of that was
the case, what should his next step be? As Shannon
had intimated, these findings would hit the movie studio hard, calling into question the facts supporting
both the original movie and the remake. Audiences
had been led to believe both versions of *Justice at
Sundown* were based on a true story. Cryer Studios
had spent millions on the marketing campaign, even
to the point of creating this press junket in the town
where the supposed rescue had happened, not to mention the bigger, more ballyhooed premiere scheduled
to be held two weeks later in Los Angeles. Lee could
just imagine the chaos his six little sheets of old-
fashioned tablet paper could cause.

His reporter's instincts were tweaked. If he and
Manny and Diane practically killed themselves putting together the "Western Rambles" special, he
could bully Jim Hinley and the powers-that-be into
airing it a few days before the Hollywood premiere.
And they could break the news to the world. They
could publicize it on their own, alerting the other arms
of the media that there was a problem with the facts.
That would certainly whip up interest, both with the
media and the viewing public. The numbers for the
special would be spectacular. Everyone would know
"Western Rambles" after that.

As a human being, though, where did his responsibilities lie?

He looked around at all the activity humming through the little town. People were working their hearts out. The studio workers, because the studio paid them. But most important, the townspeople, who wanted to use the movie's popularity as a way to better themselves and to keep the town alive. What would happen to them if the Twilight legend turned out to be false?

Accountability fell on Lee like a huge weight.

What should he do?

CHAPTER TWELVE

LEE WANTED TO SLEEP on the information he'd received—reread Byron Parker's personal account, think about it—before telling the Cruzes. But sleep was a long time coming and worry wasn't. He tossed restlessly and stared at the darkened ceiling, trying to thrash his way out of the perplexing maze. Without much luck he tried to convince himself that the ripples caused by his stone of truth wouldn't radiate out and swamp everything in their path. He tried to convince himself that *he* wouldn't be the person responsible. He knew something very few others did, and his responsibility was to that possible truth. Not to mention to his show. When finally he did sleep, it wasn't for long, and he awakened at dawn to another replay of his earlier thoughts.

The building was still quiet when Lee tapped on the Cruzes' door. A sleepy Manny answered.

"What's up?" Manny asked, yawning. He did a double take when he saw Lee's expression.

Lee knew he must look grim but could do nothing to change it. "We need to talk," he said. "Is five minutes okay?"

Manny looked over his shoulder at the unmoving lump in the bed. "It's fine," he said, then he shut the door.

Lee waited in the hall, his head tipped back as he

leaned against the wall. He overheard the low buzz of his cameraman's voice and Diane's protesting moan. It took considerably less than five minutes for the door to open, though—Diane blinking out at him and motioning for him to enter.

Instead of staying up she crawled back under the covers. Not to lie down but, like a child, to sit and rub her eyes with her fists. Manny, now in a pair of jeans, ran a comb through the dark spikes of his hair as he stood in front of the room's lone mirror.

"What is it?" Diane asked, her words muzzy. "Manny said you're—" She looked at him closely for the first time, and all signs of sleepiness vanished. "What is it?" she repeated shortly. "Tell us."

Lee handed the tablet sheets to them as the two separate documents they were. "Read this," he said.

His friends frowned at each other as they cautiously took the papers. Moments later, Diane's head snapped up. "Is this true?" she demanded.

Manny, with the longer account, whistled at the end.

"Exchange them," Lee directed.

Once they had finished, Manny sank onto the bed at his wife's side and Diane stared blankly at Lee.

"Did Mae bring this to you?" she asked sharply.

"Shannon did," Lee replied.

"And you didn't tell us right away?"

"I wanted to think about it. There's a lot to consider."

"You believe it?" she demanded.

"I believe *he* believed it."

Manny pointed to the signature. "Who's this Byron Parker? A relative of yours?"

Lee smiled tightly. "Oh, yes. He's a son of Virgil

Parker, one of the two brothers who started the Parker Ranch. Everything checks out about him. His age, the dates.''

"These were written in the early twenties," Manny pointed out.

"His recollections."

"'Nate Barlow was captured and taken to Del Norte,'" Diane read aloud. "So who's the person out in the cemetery?"

"That's a good question."

"It could be Nate Barlow." She supplied her own answer. "These might be fakes."

Manny elbowed his wife to remind her that she was disparaging a Parker to a Parker.

"Could be," Lee said quietly. "That's what we have to find out before we do anything with them."

"*Do* anything?" Diane echoed, then she quickly realized the potential of his proposal. "Oh my God, Lee! We can't do that! I know we talked about it. But these people—"

Lee explained as clearly as he could. "If everything here is based on a lie, isn't it our obligation to show that lie for what it is?"

"And in the process ruin all the townspeople's lives?" Diane was shaking her head before she finished speaking. "Uh-uh, no, I don't think so."

"It sure would put the special over the top," Manny said quietly.

Diane looked at him as if he were a striking cobra. "Oh, Manny, not you, too."

"I like these people," Lee said. "I don't wish them harm or the movie studio harm. But what do we do about this?" He retrieved the accounts from on top the bedcover and wagged them in the air.

"We burn them!" Diane retorted.

"What about Byron Parker?" Manny asked his wife. "Should Nate Barlow get the credit for what he did? Isn't there something essentially wrong about that? People all over the world think Nate's a hero—"

"That happened a lot in the Old West!" Diane maintained. "Truly rotten people were turned into heroes by the storytellers. They kept order by shooting people in the back or when they slept. And now we have this inflated opinion of—" She realized she was overturning her own argument and shut up. Finally, with an irritated sigh, she admitted. "All right. I concede your point. But I don't have to like it."

Lee smiled slightly, approving of her spirit. "I think what we need is to check this out more. See if we can find anything to confirm it. You weren't looking at old trial records before. Unless they were burned in the fire, there should be some kind of notation or something."

"Do you mind if I hope I don't find anything?" Diane asked.

"Not at all. I hope you don't, either. But either way, we still have to deal with the significance of these papers."

"It would really make a big splash for the show," Manny maintained.

All three of them nodded, none enthusiastically.

KAREN SPENT a good portion of the night at her window, thinking about everything that had happened since she'd returned to Twilight. What she'd learned about herself, about others. The fallacy of the assumptions she'd been harboring for the past seven years. *Seven years!* Had she wasted that much time blaming the Parkers as a whole, when in fact she should have been blaming only one of them—Alex? And maybe herself for having allowed her parents such great influence on her? And why should she blame anyone? It had happened. She should've gotten over it. Gone on with her life…not buried everything and *pretended* to have gone on with it.

She thought about her existence in Kerrville. It seemed as far away as the moon right now. Her work for Mr. Griffin in his antique shop, her almost engagement to Martin. Only her friendship with Rachel provided a slender thread of connection.

She didn't know what she wanted, but she was certainly beginning to get an idea of what she *didn't* want. She didn't want to settle…not for anything, not for anyone. The Karen she became when existing freely in Twilight was the true Karen and always had been. It was the person she felt most comfortable with. The person with the clearest vision. And it was to this Karen that she should listen.

This Karen actually had liked Mae Parker. She hadn't wanted to, but she had. This Karen was ready to slough off the past, to head in new directions. This Karen wasn't even averse to being with Lee Parker.

She was comfortable in Twilight…maybe she would stay here! But she wasn't going to rush herself. When the time came, she would make a decision. A considered, reflective decision about what she truly wanted.

In the midst of everything she was finally gaining an inkling as to why her aunt Augusta had stayed in Twilight when she could have gone anywhere else. Maybe Augusta had liked the person she was when she was here, too. Or maybe, more likely, Augusta

had always known who she was but had found a kin-
dred spirit within the soul of this town.

KAREN SOUGHT OUT BETTE the next morning instead
of the other way around. She was ready to begin
again. Only instead of Bette, she found Lee in the
kitchen, scrambling eggs.

"Oh! I thought—" She stopped in the doorway.
The saloon apartment's door had been ajar, and when
she'd tapped on it and called Bette's name, the response she'd received was cooking noises from this
quarter.

"They're all out," Lee said. "Bette went to the
hotel with John. Diane's doing some research, and
Manny...Manny's doing what Manny does best, taking pictures. So you'll have to make do with me if
you're looking for company, unless you find the idea
too repulsive." He lifted the skillet. "Want some?"

The other Karen would have declined immediately.
"Sure," she said. "Would you like me to butter the
toast?"

He lifted a skeptical eyebrow. "What did Mae say
or do to you? Did she give you a concussion that
wiped away your memory?"

"I don't *have* to butter the toast," she reminded
him.

He shrugged his acquiescence.

Moments later they were sharing the tiny table for
two in the kitchen that Bette and John used for most
of their meals when they were alone.

"Why are you still here when the others aren't?"
she asked.

"I couldn't face the thought of food earlier."

"Why not?"

He gave a half smile that she found extremely sexy. "Is this some kind of trap?"

"It's no trap."

"I'm afraid you're going to have to explain before I believe you."

Karen set aside her fork. She'd known this moment was inevitable—that matters couldn't stand as they were between them. She'd been mistaken about so many things and needed to acknowledge it.

"I've learned something," she announced quietly, and noticed that he stiffened. As she continued, though, he slowly relaxed. "For years I thought Mae—all the Parkers, really—hadn't wanted me in the family. My strongest proof was something I heard Mae say. To you, actually, but also to anyone who'd listen."

He frowned. "To me?"

Karen nodded. "She said Alex marrying me was a travesty. I remember it perfectly. It's been a part of my life for all these years."

"I don't remember her saying that," Lee said.

"That's because she didn't. Oh, she used the phrase, but it wasn't directed at me. She was talking about Alex. She didn't think he was responsible enough to marry anyone!"

"A fact he's proven repeatedly."

Karen spread her hands, smiling.

"So you *can* smile," he murmured.

"Of course."

"You've never smiled at me before."

"Oh, I must have! When we first met, surely? Right before the wedding?"

"No, I'd have remembered."

"Well, if I didn't, it was because I didn't think you

liked me, either.'' She leaned forward to look into his eyes. ''I need to explain something about that, too. Actually, about my parents. Everything seemed to change for them after I became engaged to Alex. Particularly for my mother. It was as if she saw the wedding as a contest. Everything was meant to impress your family—your mother. 'The Parkers' this. 'The Parkers' that. She said it so many times I wanted to scream. The Parker name meant nothing to me. It still—''

''Doesn't,'' he cut in, smiling.

She shrugged. ''Well, obviously not as much as it does to all of you.''

''My mother would have a heart attack.''

''My mother thought your mother was slighting me…us.''

''I told you my mother's a snob.''

''Now I know my mother is, too. In her own special way, as you so kindly pointed out.''

''I didn't mean to hurt you.''

''I know that. So I've decided to do what you said before. I won't hold your family against you if you won't hold mine against me.''

''It's a deal,'' Lee agreed, and they shook hands over the table.

A spark of awareness caused Karen to draw back. She wasn't ready for more at this moment. A declaration of peace was a huge step. Later on…

She stood up. ''I have to go. Thanks for breakfast.''

He glanced at her plate. ''You didn't eat much of it.''

''It's the sentiment that counts, isn't it?''

Again, he smiled. Which did amazing things to Karen's heart rate.

"I won't complain," he returned softly.

Karen had to get herself out of there. Either that or surprise him even more by pouncing.

LEE STOPPED by the music hall to see what the studio workers were doing and was amazed to find that in just two short days they'd stripped off the near psychedelic finish someone had applied to the floor in the sixties, almost completely redone the wiring, removed the huge velvet curtain that had been in tatters and were now busily repainting every walled surface. The large room was going to be beautiful when they finished. It was something like watching a battalion of army ants attack an objective and overcome it. And Manny was recording each event as it unfolded. Lee could see the scene played out in quick time for the special—the music hall's reconstruction from beginning to end in the space of a minute.

He then dropped by the hotel to check the progress there. Some of the men had moved upstairs to begin on the three bedrooms they hoped to have open for business after Twilight's big night, while others did finishing work downstairs.

Bette, applying wallpaper in the lobby, asked him what he thought.

"It looks great!" he said, meaning it.

"It sure does," Pepper, her assistant, agreed with a grin. "I just might wanna come spend a night or two here myself when we're done!"

Lee left by the back door, going through the kitchen, which also was nearing completion. Once outside, he nodded to Benny, who paused long enough from stacking used lumber to smile hugely and wave.

Rather than turn toward the saloon to complete his circuit, Lee swung onto the path that led to the cemetery—his foremost destination all along. He wanted another look at Nate Barlow's grave. But he hadn't wanted his interest to be obvious.

Along the way he saw Pete sitting under a scraggly tree in what passed as his yard. The old man was peering into a hand mirror, grooming his beard.

The sight was enough to draw Lee off course.

"Mornin', Pete," he murmured, slipping into his comfortable cowboy drawl. How many times had he seen scenes like this, with grizzled old cowboys performing their ablutions after a long week's work wrangling cattle? "You decide to comb the stickers out?"

Pete leveled his bright eyes on him. "Is there a law agin' it?"

Lee laughed. "Not that I know of."

"Then that's what I'm doin'." Pete snipped at an occasional stray hair with a tiny pair of scissors.

As far as Lee could see, he wasn't accomplishing all that much. His beard, like his hair, was still a flyaway snowstorm. Only it had been washed and combed.

Pete snipped another hair or two, then, satisfied with the result, stood up and crammed the same dirty old hat on his head. Which matched the same ragged old clothes.

When Lee saw him start to hobble off, he remembered the sad state of the man's feet. "Hey, Pete," he called. "I've got a proposition for you. How about you get those feet checked out and 'Western Rambles' will take care of the bill?"

Pete turned to look at him. "I told you. I don't like doctors."

"You said you've never been to one before," Lee countered. "But what if a doctor could make your feet feel better? Let you walk easier."

Pete screwed up his face. "'Western Rambles,' you say? That's that show of yours, right?" When Lee nodded, Pete continued, "That's what I thought. I don't take charity. But thanks for offerin'."

"It's not charity, Pete. It's…a payment for your service."

"I know exactly how the cow ate the cabbage, son. It's charity." Then, before Lee could say anything more, Pete called for his dog.

The dog, who'd been asleep near the chair, instantly responded. But after getting up and shaking himself, he looked curiously at Lee, who immediately squatted down and extended his hand. Moving cautiously, the dog came nearer, and after a sniff, he let Lee pet him on the head and neck. His tail wagged slowly.

"What's his name?" Lee asked, smiling.

"Tex," Pete said gruffly. "Come on, boy," he called, and seconds later both the dog and the old man disappeared inside the shack.

Lee returned to his appointed task. As Diane said, if Nate Barlow had been tried and hung in Del Norte, just who was taking up space in the Twilight cemetery? It didn't make sense for the outlaw's body to have been transported back to the little town, not in the early 1890s, and not when there didn't seem to be any connection other than the fact that he'd been caught in bed here with the saloon keeper's daughter.

He hunkered down for a closer look at the headstone. Nate Barlow, the rather primitive carving read, as it had before, with Valued Friend underneath. After a quick check for witnesses, Lee took out the tiny flashlight he'd brought along with him and shone it on the carving. That was when he saw it. The *B* and the *W* in Barlow had been altered, much the way rustlers modified brands on stolen cattle. A new mark here, the obliteration of another mark there.

Lee pulled back. What did it mean? The lettering was so crudely done, could it have been a mistake from the onset? The Nate looked proper, so did the middle letters on the last name. Could the original carver have misspelled the outlaw's last name and needed to correct it?

He took another close look. There definitely was something wrong with the *B* and the *W*.

Just for the heck of it he strolled through the rest of the cemetery, moving from row to row, looking at other plaques, crosses and headstones. In the middle row a family name caught his eye—Harlon. A wife, a child—both with that name. And, next to them, an unmarked grave. It would take only a little effort to change Harlon to Barlow by adjusting the *H* and the *N*. Then, *presto…change-o,* Nate Barlow had himself a headstone.

As a prank it might be amusing. But in a serious investigation it lent credence to Byron Parker's account that Nate Barlow had not been buried in this cemetery. Someone was playing a little game, moving headstones, altering letters.

Lee knew he should be excited by the discovery. Instead, he was disheartened. He wanted everything to be aboveboard for the people of Twilight. He wanted the good things they hoped for to become reality. He wanted Karen not to think ill of him again.

She'd been so very different this morning. Whatever Mae said had acted as a release for her. She was no longer a prisoner of the past. She'd been friendly to him, even smiled! He didn't want her to hate him again—this time by his own action, because he'd used Parker family records to debunk Twilight's outlaw legend.

He searched for additional explanations. Possibly the stonecutter had used Mr. Harlon's headstone himself, saving the time and effort of making a new one. The men's first names being the same, the adjustments to the last were easy. And if the Harlon family had no living relations in Twilight to protest, and if the few remaining townspeople were in a hurry to honor the outlaw for saving the child, the stonecutter might have taken a shortcut. A shortcut no one had noticed until now.

Lee shook his head as he started back up the pathway into the town proper. *Possibly...if...if....* Not very likely.

He wished he'd never seen Byron Parker's accounts. He wished he'd never asked Shannon to check the family history. *Why* was he trying to complicate everything? The team had come to Twilight to do a simple little story of a town's response to a reawakening of interest in its history. Where did it say he needed to investigate that history? To be sure that every *i* was dotted and every *t* crossed? Wasn't that the reason he'd left TV news? His revulsion at the value of sensation over humanity?

As he crossed through the antique shop's backyard, he wanted to stop to see Karen. Not to tell her what he'd learned. Just…to be with her. But he decided against it. He didn't want to tarnish the memory of that morning. It might be something he'd have to hold on to for a long, long time.

WITH EVERYONE IN TOWN being so industrious—the townspeople, the movie workers, the "Western Rambles" crew—Karen had offered to help, as well. She could paint and wallpaper, she said, and do her part to help improve the town. But her proposal had been turned down. Everyone knew how hard she'd been working in the antique shop and the massive job she yet had ahead of her.

"You just keep doing what you're doing," Bette insisted, acting as spokesperson for the rest of the citizenry. "We have everything under control. It'll all be done in time for next weekend. Anyway, you helped most where none of us could do any good—with Pete."

That afternoon Karen started on the storage shed. Bette, bless her, had offered the use of part of their garage to put things in while she sorted. It wasn't an hour later that Karen gained an even greater appreciation for the offer. There was no way she'd have found room in either the shop or the upstairs apartment for the large pieces of furniture she discovered inside. And, as before, they blocked the way to everything else.

"Your aunt bought many things," Diego had commented when he'd hurried over to help. He must have been working in the rear of the hotel and seen her struggling with a large chest. He'd pressed Benny into service and the two men made quick work of removing the larger pieces. "She told us to fit them in as best we could," he said.

"Best we could!" Benny agreed.

The pair had already gone back to the hotel when Pete turned up.

"Can't imagine why a person'd want all this stuff," he grumbled in the doorway as Karen stood on tiptoe to remove a child's wagon from on top of a crate.

Once she had the wagon safely down, she turned to smile at him. "You sound just like Bette," she teased.

"Never could figure it out," he said, shaking his woolly head.

Karen looked at the toy. It was in good condition for its years. Probably from the late forties, early fifties. She said, "Pete, people are willing to pay a lot of money to be able to hold a memory again. See this? Some adult who had a wagon like it as a child would love to own it now. For their child, for their grandchild or just to look at themselves. Like I said, memories."

"What about that?" Pete said, motioning to an old-fashioned washboard hanging from a nail. "I got one a them. Who'd be crazy enough to pay money for it? I found mine on a trash heap. Still use it, too. On occasion."

She grinned. "It depends. Some of them are worth hundreds of dollars."

"You're joshin' me!"

"No. Almost anything from the past is of value to someone. Sometimes great value."

All Pete could do was shake his head.

She expected him to leave. Pete didn't usually stay

around long to converse. But when he didn't leave, she inquired carefully, "Is something bothering you, Pete?" and braced for his reply.

What he said surprised her. "That Lee Parker...he'll do."

For Pete this was high praise. She wasn't sure what she was supposed to say, but inside she felt ridiculously pleased. Which really made no sense. She had no claim on Lee Parker and shouldn't bask in any way in his reflected glory. Still...

"Tex likes him," Pete added.

"Who's Tex?" Karen asked.

Pete glanced at his black dog.

"Oh," she murmured.

"He was doin' somethin' kinda strange earlier. Out in the cemetery."

For a moment Karen thought Pete meant the dog, then realized he was referring to Lee.

"Lookin' real close at a marker...had a flashlight. Then he walked around some more, lookin' at others. Then he stopped and thought for a long spell before he went away. I thought that was kinda strange, like I said, so I went out to where he was before and had a look-see for myself."

"And?" Karen urged him to finish. Pete loved to drag out a story.

"First thing he was lookin' at was somethin' I never seen in that cemetery before—a marker for Nate Barlow. Next thing, as best I could tell, was somethin' toward the middle. But I never saw nothin' that could make him think for so long."

Nate Barlow. She frowned. "Pete? You don't remember Nate Barlow's grave being in the cemetery, either? I thought it was just me. That I might have missed it.''

"Weren't there a few weeks ago. I can tell you that for a fact.''

"Then how—''

"There's somethin' funny goin' on around here. And it ain't just Tex chasin' his tail. I thought you should know about it. That's all.''

With that said, Pete shuffled away after making sure his loyal dog was trailing after him.

The storage shed was a step up off the ground, and shaking her hair free of its restraining band, Karen used the doorway as a seat. It was hot working in the tiny room with little to no air circulation. She should probably have waited until later in the afternoon or evening for this but had been impatient to get started.

While she rested, she thought about what Pete had said—"somethin' funny goin' on around here.'' The mysterious appearance of Nate Barlow's headstone and Lee's close examination of it. What did it mean? John had found the headstone and righted it again, or so Bette had said. Had John done something he shouldn't? And had Lee found out?

A little of the gloss wore off the day for Karen, and a niggle of unease was triggered.

"IT'S TRUE,'' DIANE SAID dispiritedly, slumped on the foot of her bed. She'd spent the whole day visiting both the local county courthouse in Davisville and the Briggs County courthouse in Del Norte. "It was just a little squib in Briggs County's earliest records, but I made a copy. Here.''

She handed the paper to Lee. Manny, looking on, was mournful.

Lee scanned the page filled with scratchy writing until he saw the spot Diane had circled lightly in pencil. "Barlow, tried and died. Good riddance," read the notation. Short, sweet and to the point. Just like old-time Texans.

Lee looked up. "Yep," he murmured.

Tears hovered in Diane's eyes. "We can't do it, Lee."

Lee nodded, but in acknowledgment, not agreement. "I have to think about it," he said. Then he looked at Manny, wanting his opinion.

Manny shrugged.

Lee took the paper to put with Byron Parker's accounts. "Good work," he told Diane. When she made no reply, it was only what he expected.

CHAPTER THIRTEEN

KAREN TRIED HARD not to let it, but Pete's warning continued to run through her mind. *There's somethin' funny goin' on.* In the end she knew she had to go to the cemetery herself. And since she didn't want anyone to know what she was doing, she had to go at night. This night. As soon as possible.

The saloon closed early, at ten o'clock. With people so hard at work, pushing to finish their jobs, sleep was essential. At ten-thirty Karen slipped outside. She crossed behind the hotel and onto the path leading to the cemetery, relieved that the waning moon still managed to cast enough light to guide her way.

Tex barked once as she passed Pete's shack, but he didn't bark again. Maybe he sensed the encroacher was someone he knew. Or maybe it was Pete who guessed and had hushed him. Either way, she continued undisturbed.

Karen knew exactly where she was going and didn't stop until she got there: Nate Barlow's grave. Crickets chirped in the high grass, a thin cloud passed across the face of the moon. The moment could have been spooky, but Karen didn't have time for imagined specters. Her dread was more substantive—a fraud surrounding the claim of Nate Barlow's burial in this cemetery.

She switched on her flashlight and bent to examine

the carving in more detail. N...A...T...E B—the *B* looked funny. A...R...L...O—the *W* looked funny, too! She made a small noise in the back of her throat, then almost screamed when a boot scraped on loose rock directly beside her.

Of course it was him. Ludicrously, like a child caught doing something she shouldn't, Karen straightened and switched off the flashlight, as if that could somehow hide her previous movements.

"Wh—what are you doing here?" she demanded tightly.

"I could ask the same of you."

She looked around. "I—I like to come here."

"At night?"

She raised her chin. "Of course. What better time?"

He shone his flashlight on the outlaw's headstone. "You see the difference, too, don't you?"

Karen didn't want to get John in trouble. She had no idea if altering a headstone broke any kind of law, or if "Western Rambles" would stop taping...or worse, televise to the nation what he'd done. Rather, what she *suspected* he'd done, she amended.

"I don't see a difference," she maintained.

"C'mere," he invited, pulling her down beside him—too close beside him! He made her look where he was pointing the light beam. "It's the *B* and the *W*. Now come over here." He took her to the middle of the cemetery and again pulled her down. "Look here. Harlon. See that? A woman, a child...then a missing headstone from the next grave. Does it tell you anything?"

"It tells me—" she started to contend, but wasn't given the chance to finish. He reached out to touch her hair, her cheek, his fingers trailing lightly over her mouth, parting her lips. Karen's breath was cut off.

"Forget what it tells you," he murmured huskily as he stood up, drawing her with him. Then slowly, every so slowly, he lowered his head.

Karen could feel the heat of his body, the strong contractions of his heart, sense his strength, his determination, yet she found courage enough to whisper, "Here?" as his lips hovered just above hers.

"Why not here? Don't you think these people would rather see kisses than tears?"

Karen had no answer. No matter what he said, it would make sense when uttered with such impassioned reason.

The kiss lasted for an eternity. She had no idea of the passage of time. She wouldn't have been surprised if, when she opened her eyes, the sun had broken the horizon.

She needed support when their mouths finally parted.

"My brother was insane to walk away from you," he said softly. "But I'm glad he did, because I just might have had to steal you away."

"You'd do that?" she breathed.

He looked at her, long and deep. "In a heartbeat." Then something in his expression changed, and his hold on her became more urgent, more intense. When he kissed her again it was with fire, with need...almost with desperation.

Karen was breathing hard when once again they parted. This couldn't continue. They had to stop or the spirits here were going to see far more than a mere kiss!

"We have to—" she began, trying to give voice to her thought.

"You're right. We do. Either that or—"

Her laugh was shaky.

"Then again," he murmured, tugging her closer.

She took a couple of steps back. "I—I think we need to talk."

He glanced at the three graves and the two Harlon headstones. A muscle jerked in his cheek. "Once again, you're right."

For a moment Karen wished she wasn't. There was something about the way he'd looked in that last second that told her everything she needed to know. He, too, thought the headstone was false.

"There could be any number of reasons why this happened," she said in excuse. "There—there could be—" She couldn't think of one. Not one!

He watched her steadily.

Karen cast about, trying to come up with something...*anything*. Then she gave up all pretense. Sighing in defeat, she asked, "What are you going to do about it?"

"Who do you think did it?" he asked. "John?"

Karen's start gave him his answer.

"He's my choice, too. He's the first I heard talking about it. And he brought us out here to see it."

"He won't get into trouble, will he?" Karen asked anxiously. "I mean—whoever did it won't get into trouble? We can't be sure it's John, you know. It could just be...circumstance. And anyway, it's—it's not that bad. All he was trying to do was create a little more interest, give the tourists a treat."

The longer she talked, the grimmer Lee looked. Unless it was a trick of the moonlight. Shadows sometimes did strange things to people's expressions, she reassured herself.

But when he spoke his tone was somber. "There's more to it than that."

"I don't understand." She trembled lightly, more in fear of what he was about to say than in actual chilliness.

"You're cool. You should go inside."

"I'm fine."

He was wearing a light jacket against the briskness of the desert night, something she'd neglected to bring with her. He peeled it off and wrapped it around her shoulders.

The warmth left from his body washed over Karen and once again she trembled.

"Let's go in. I'll tell you there."

"Please," she appealed to him, not moving.

He didn't want to tell her. She could see it in his eyes. In the set of his shoulders. She touched his arm, held on to it.

After a moment he said, "Nate Barlow didn't die in Twilight. He didn't rescue a child from the well. He was caught here having sex with the saloon keeper's daughter, taken to Del Norte, tried and hung. I don't know who's buried in that grave over there, but I have serious reservations that it's him."

Karen felt as if he'd punched her in the stomach. She stared at him, barely comprehending. "How do you know this?" she asked huskily.

"Diane found a notation in the Briggs County trial records."

"Maybe—maybe the records are wrong."

"She looked in the trial records because of some-thing else we have." He hesitated. "An accounting by someone who claims that he and another man helped the child out of the well. They were members of the posse that caught Nate Barlow.''

''Who?'' Karen breathed. ''Can he be trusted? Maybe—maybe it's all wrong.'' She shook her head. ''No, this can't be happening. I don't believe it. This is just someone trying to cause trouble. The movie...the movies! They both say that Nate Barlow found the child, rescued him and was hung...*here!*''

''That's the legend. Facts are something else again.''

Karen released his arm. She'd almost forgotten that she'd been holding it. He took a step toward her but she backed away. She didn't want him touching her again, confusing her thoughts. She needed to try to work this out.

Finally, looking at him in growing horror, she questioned, ''What are you going to do? You can't destroy all these people's hope. They want so little. Just to have a decent life. They're working so hard.'' Her thoughts crystallized on one point. ''Have you told anyone else?''

''Manny knows.''

''You can ask Diane and him not to tell anyone and they won't.''

''You want the legend to continue, even though it's a lie?''

''I want the *town* to continue. I want Twilight to live!'' She looked at him. ''Why would you do this? What would you gain?'' Her mind worked. ''Ratings? Is that it? You're willing to trade the last remaining drop of Twilight's lifeblood for points on a popularity scale? Oh, and more money. High ratings would mean that, too, wouldn't it?''

"There's something to be said for telling the truth," Lee returned tightly.

"Huh!" she exclaimed in disbelief. Then she thought of something else. "You never answered me before. Who is it? Who is it you believe over everyone else? The person whose word you're willing to take over—"

"Byron Parker." His declaration interrupted her harangue.

The silence that followed was electric.

In the interval the wound that had been healing between them ripped open again. "A Parker," she breathed with renewed loathing.

"Karen—"

She twisted away when he reached for her and sloughed off his jacket from her shoulders. She couldn't believe she'd been in his arms only moments before, letting him kiss her, touch her—

He caught his jacket as it fell. "Karen, please—"

"I should have known, shouldn't I?" she demanded tightly. "Somehow, it all comes together. A *Parker* rescued the child from the well. A *Parker* caught the terrible outlaw Nate Barlow. Now a *Parker* is going to give this tiny town its final wound. I don't know what happened to me over these past twenty-four hours. I was actually starting to think that—" She clasped a hand over her mouth and, unable to continue, ran away from the cemetery and the man she now knew she loved.

That was why it hurt so much. Why it was far worse than merely another betrayal. What Alex had done all those years ago had caused chaos in her life. What Lee was doing now—

She didn't want to think about it. She didn't want to think about him. She couldn't!

LEE HELD THE JACKET in his hand. He moved calmly to put it back on. Calmly to exit the fenced-in cemetery plot. Calmly to trace Karen's footsteps back into town. Only instead of returning to the saloon, he continued walking down the road into the arid land his people, the Parkers, had played such a prominent role in settling.

Hours passed before he returned. Hours that had done him little good in reconciling his future actions. It would be easy to follow his first instinct. Put Byron Parker's accounts away and let everything proceed as planned, perpetuating the myth. Make Diane happy. Make *Karen* happy.

The way she'd looked at him...more wounded than she'd looked at him at the failed wedding.

He'd known this could happen. That was why he'd had to take what sustenance he could from her before she learned the truth. One kiss had been so sweet and natural, as if they were long-ago lovers at last together. And the other—ardent, intense.

He loved her. There was no longer any doubt in his mind. He loved her fully and completely, and he had all along. He wanted nothing more than to please her.

But like this? If the truth needed to be told, how could he turn away from it?

He was on his way to his room a short time later— he thought without making a sound—when Diane cracked her bedroom door and popped out a tousled blond head.

"Are you all right?" she asked, concerned.

"Manny's buzzing away, but I couldn't sleep. Neither can you, I see." She arched a brow at his jacket and day clothes.

"I told Karen," Lee said simply.

"How did she take it?"

"Badly."

"Did she blame you?"

"Doesn't she always?"

"Lee—"

"I know…I know. I'm being unfair. I'm being selfish. I'm being greedy—"

"Is that what she said?" Diane asked, compassion in her tone.

"Isn't that what you think, too?"

"No, I know you better. And she would, too, if—"

"She's never going to know me better. She won't let herself." He paused. "Why don't you go get some sleep? I'm a big boy. I can take care of myself."

"Sometimes I wonder about that," Diane muttered.

Lee, tired as he was, disheartened as he was, found a smile. "You and Manny need to do something about making that baby you keep talking about. Then you'll have someone to mother."

"Well, if you didn't work us so hard," she sniped gently, "we might have a little time to— You know? I've almost forgotten what!"

"I'll have a little talk with Manny," Lee teased back.

"Don't you dare!" she retorted. Then, grinning, she shut the door.

THE PRESSURE ON KAREN to talk to Lee again was almost overwhelming. She felt she hadn't pleaded the town's case with nearly as much force as she could have if she hadn't been reacting to another instance of Parker treachery. This time, Lee's treachery. Yet even as she thought that, she could see his dilemma. He said he had proof, outside the Parker papers.

But couldn't he see the damage he was about to inflict? What did it matter whether Nate Barlow was the true hero or someone else? Even if that person was a Parker. Both men were long dead and buried— Nate Barlow in Del Norte, if not Twilight, and Byron Parker in all probability on the Parker Ranch. The people of Twilight were very much alive, though. Didn't the living take precedence over the dead?

Karen couldn't just sit and watch it happen. Watch Lee destroy the myth, if that was what the Twilight outlaw story was. Surely there was something to be said for keeping a secret.

She had to ignore her feelings for him. She had to ignore her pain. Augusta had loved this town and its people, and she did, too.

She sought Lee out the next morning, her argument ready, but the only member of the "Western Rambles" crew she found in the saloon's apartment was Diane Cruz. The others were off working.

If Diane was surprised to see her, she didn't show it. Instead, she smiled in a friendly way and asked if she'd like a cup of coffee.

Karen wanted to talk to Lee, but maybe, everything considered, Diane would be a better bet. She knew the problem, Lee had said, and Karen wouldn't have to fight so hard to maintain her detachment.

She accepted the invitation and soon found herself at the same small table in Bette's kitchen that she'd so recently shared with Lee.

"I know you know about Nate Barlow," she stated

clearly, without hesitation. "Well...you have to stop Lee. You can't let him use the information he has. I know you've talked with the people here, been present at most of their interviews. That should show you how badly—" Her throat tightened, but she made herself go on. "John has to feel needed. He's a new person when he talks about taking Twilight forward, energizing it. Mary—you know the trouble Mary's had in her life, the way she worries about Benny, about his future. And Diego—you've seen his mouth. Hank wants a new truck, Pepper a living room set, Joe and Rhonda...Isaac. I don't know what they want, but I know it's not any more than the others. It's not as if they're asking for millions of dollars. They just want what so many other people take for granted. A chance to live life with a little dignity. And to live it in Twilight. If Lee exposes Nate Barlow's story, not only will the people not get what they're hoping for, but Twilight will die, too. The people aren't going to be able to afford to continue living here. One by one they'll leave. And without people, Twilight will become a real ghost town." She paused to be sure that she still had Diane's attention.

"Go on," Diane urged.

"I'm the first to know that there are things of value here. I work with antiques—I'm sure you're aware of that. The Lady Slipper's furnishings would bring in a nice price, and so would the mercantile's. Country-store-type things have a huge market right now. My boss would have a fit to sell some of them. But it would be a quick fix with no lasting benefit. I'd be glad to share what my aunt left me, too, but no one here would accept it. They turned her down when she offered help. For good or bad, they won't take what they consider charity. But they're willing to work for what they want.'' She paused again, tears welling unexpectedly. "How can you do this to them?" she demanded, then had to stop.

Diane covered her hands on the table and squeezed them. Karen wasn't sure, but she thought she saw moisture in her eyes, as well.

"You, uh, make a good case,'' Diane said.

"So you'll help?" Karen asked hopefully.

"I'm only one part of the team."

"That means you won't."

Diane shook her head. "That's not what I said. I said I can't make any decisions on my own. I can give my view, but that's it."

"And your view is?" Karen questioned.

Diane sighed and said levelly, "None of us want to hurt this town or these people. It was the furthest thing from any of our minds when we came here. But we've discovered a fallacy. Now we have to decide what to do about it."

"You said you don't want to hurt the town."

"We don't."

"Then leave it alone. Don't say anything. Who's it going to bother if everything stays as it is?"

"Who changed the headstone? That person knows something."

"It was probably only done as insurance."

"Do you know who did it?"

"Lee hasn't said?"

"Lee keeps a lot of things to himself."

Karen laughed shortly. "Too bad he can't keep *everything* to himself."

"He has an added worry."

"I'm sure he does—the Parker name."

Diane smiled dryly. "I was thinking of you."

Karen became still.

"You two have a history, I know that," Diane continued. "His brother—you. But I've never seen him this way with a woman before. He's...off track. Manny and I—" She stopped. "I'm saying too much. Something I do a lot, I'm afraid. But I worry about him."

"I doubt seriously he needs you to worry."

Diane had forgotten about the coffee and went to pour two cups. She brought them back to the table, sliding one over to Karen. Karen pushed hers away.

"Would you mind if I tell you a little story?" Diane asked as she resumed her seat. "Lee had a promising career going for him when he left broadcast news. One of the major cable networks was starting to nibble. But do you know why he left? Because he couldn't stomach the way news was being handled. There's a tragedy and those who're grieving immediately have microphones stuck in their faces and are asked how they feel. How does anyone *think* they feel?" She took a breath. "There were two little boys killed by their father in a particularly gruesome way. The news director knew where the mother worked and sent Lee to interview her. She didn't know her children were dead. No one had told her. When Lee learned this, he threw down his microphone, went back to the station and punched out the news director after telling him exactly what he thought of him. He was fired, of course. But he didn't care. Manny was his cameraman on that outing and walked away with him."

Karen said nothing.

Diane went on, "After that, Lee did a lot of other

things in the business, but never again the news. And he made sure that Manny always had a place with him. I came along later—when Lee finally got 'Western Rambles' off the ground. You'll never find anyone who's worked harder than Lee to make something a success. This show's been his life.''

Karen twitched in her chair. ''You're trying to say he has integrity.''

''By the boatload. I truly respect him.''

''Yet he's willing to do this to Twilight. How do you reconcile it?''

''This whole outlaw thing has turned out to be a sham. If we go along with it, we continue the lie. Become part of the conspiracy. Now do you understand?''

''That's a little strong.''

''Not at all. That's Lee's dilemma.''

''And if you don't…go along?''

''We have to be able to live with ourselves afterward.''

''Isn't that the case either way?''

''Lee will do the right thing—whatever he decides.''

Karen was quiet for a moment. ''Lee said you have evidence.''

''Two accounts written by Byron Parker. We weren't sure whether to believe them or not, until I found the court record.''

''Who gave you this evidence?''

''It's part of the Parkers' family history.''

''Mae Parker gave it to you?''

''Actually, Shannon Parker did.''

Karen barely remembered who Shannon Parker was and didn't much care. She had all the information she needed for her next move. A move that had just occurred to her.

She stood up. "I have to go."

Diane got slowly to her feet. She was frowning, as if she sensed that once again she might have said too much. "None of us want to hurt the people of this town," she repeated.

"Do you actually think that's good enough?" Karen challenged. "Especially when you continue to pretend to be their friends?"

"We're not pretending. And either way, we have to put a show together."

"Either way," Karen repeated tautly, and shaking her head, left the room.

Diane caught up with her at the apartment's front door. "I don't want to hurt them," she claimed.

Karen returned the researcher's sober look. "Maybe you'd better tell that to Lee."

KAREN WENT BACK to her aunt's apartment, bathed and dressed in fresh clothes. It was important that she look her best, even if her best was the one light summery dress she'd brought with her. At the time she hadn't planned to be here more than a week. Or expected to pay a call to a personage and a place that on the way here she remembered being afraid to even think about. A lot had changed in a very short time. And one of those changes, Karen acknowledged, was that she had finally found her backbone.

If it took going to see Mae Parker on the Parker Ranch to save Twilight, she would do it.

"Oh my, don't you look nice!" Bette exclaimed as she caught Karen opening her car door, about to slip in. "Are you going into town?" she asked.

"I thought I might go into Del Norte. I, uh, need a few more boxes."

"John will probably start to have a few extras around soon. He'll be glad to save 'em for you. Business is picking up since the studio workers discovered the Lady Slipper."

"Tell him thanks," Karen said, "but I still have to—" She patted the rim of the open car door.

"Oh, sure...sure."

Karen wondered if Bette wanted to go along, and was trying to decide how best to get out of it when her friend snapped her fingers.

"That's it! I was trying to remember what I needed. Could you get me some more of my favorite face cream? I'm running low. You know how it is out here—it's so dry your skin can whither up and blow away if you're not careful. I was in town not too long ago and forgot."

"Sure," Karen said, relieved. "What kind?"

"I'll go get my tube, then you can match it. It's sold everywhere. At any drugstore. I'd sure appreciate it."

Karen waited. A few minutes later Bette returned, laughing.

"Whew! A woman my age shouldn't hurry on a hot day. But then, that probably tells you how bad I need that face cream. I'd look like a hag in no time without it."

"That's not true and you know it," Karen returned, performing the ritual of one friend for another.

Bette was pleased. Then she said, "Work's really coming along. They're putting the new curtain up in the music hall today. They can't have much more left to do, I would think. And we're coming along great in the hotel, too. You should come see it. You wouldn't recognize the place." In a humorous aside she added, "You should see Pete now. Man's almost starting to make a pest of himself, being so accessible. He's turned up at each of the interviews Lee and Manny did today and is giving these helpful little suggestions. I've been told there's a couple of times when Lee looked like he wanted to tie him to a chair and leave him there. Oh! And something else. The souvenirs arrived. A big shipment of them. Made Mary extremely happy. She and Carmelita and Juanita are sorting through them right now. They can't wait to start trying to sell some to the studio people. I saw one of the T-shirts. Isaac's logo looks great! Really professional. Although that's what he is, isn't he? A professional artist. Maybe his work will get wider known after this. Wouldn't that be great?"

Karen nodded, aching to be off, and also not wanting to be burdened with yet another reason why this effort *had* to succeed.

Bette must have sensed her restiveness. "Well, I won't keep you. Don't you forget my face cream, okay? And have a safe trip."

"I won't. I will," Karen promised, answering the request and the directive individually. Then she waved to Bette, started the engine and, for the first time since she'd arrived in Twilight, left the town behind.

It felt as if she were leaving her home.

CHAPTER FOURTEEN

KAREN TRIED NOT TO BE impressed with what she saw of the Parker Ranch, just as she tried not to listen to her qualms. She drove right up the long U-shaped drive and pulled to a stop in front of the two-story stone house that dominated the others. It was also at the head, which meant it must belong to Mae.

A tall, leanly muscled man in his late thirties or early forties, dressed like a working cowboy, came out of the nearest house on the right. He strode off the porch toward her with a challenging air. As he drew near, she stepped out of the car to meet him. Obviously he was a Parker. With his strong, chiseled features, dark hair and smoldering dark eyes, he bore a striking resemblance to Alex and Lee. There were two exceptions, though—Lee's pale eyes and this man's dangerous edge. He seemed accustomed to dealing with trouble, a trait that demonstrated itself when he addressed her.

"Mind statin' your business?" he said curtly.

"Yes, I—I'd like to see Mae Parker."

His dark eyes burned into her. "Why?"

Karen lifted her chin. "I have business with her."

"Well, my name's Rafe Parker and I'm the ranch manager. You can talk to me."

Rafe Parker! She remembered Alex mentioning him with something like awe. She braced her determination and stated clearly, "My business is personal…with Mae."

A slight smile flickered at the corners of his mouth. He seemed to approve of the fact that she'd stood up to him. "And just who might you be?"

"My name is Karen Latham. I spoke to Mae the other day when she came to Twilight to visit Lee…your cousin."

"Karen Latham." He repeated her name as if trying to place it.

She cleared her throat nervously. "I was once engaged to Lee's brother, Alex. It…didn't work out."

Illumination dawned. "Ah, that Karen Latham."

The door on the big house opened and Mae stepped outside. Her frown deepened when she recognized Karen, yet she waved dismissal to Rafe. "It's fine, boy. She can see me, if that's what she came for."

"Would you like Shannon to come over?" Rafe asked.

"No, no. I can handle this."

Rafe moved away, but not before giving Karen another look. She had the feeling he was warning her not to make trouble or he wouldn't hesitate to act.

Mae saw her into a Spanish-style house, with white walls, black wrought-iron fixtures, gray stone floors and colorful rugs. She was shown to a seat in the living room on one of two couches, while Mae chose a straight-back chair.

When a plump, middle-aged woman stepped into the room, Mae requested, "Two lemonades, Marie. Unless you prefer iced tea?" She deferred to Karen.

"Lemonade will be fine," Karen said shortly.

Mae looked even more regal in her own home. The

queen of all she surveyed. "I doubt you're here to pay a friendly call," she said.

Karen tried not to feel intimidated. Thoughts of the danger to Twilight spurred her on. "Yes, actually, we do have something we need to discuss."

"You look flushed. Wait for your drink."

"I'm fine."

"Then wait until I have mine. It's a hot day. But then, this is the first of September. It's only to be expected."

Karen had an idea she was being manipulated, played with like a cat played with a mouse, but since she was here to request the family matriarch's help, it wouldn't do to react negatively. "Yes, it is hot," she agreed. "A friend of mine in Twilight was just saying that. Bette Danson…she and her husband own the saloon."

"The Lady Slipper. Yes, I like that name."

The housekeeper returned with two glasses. Karen accepted hers graciously, as did Mae. Karen even took a sip and found the cold lemonade refreshing after all. She hadn't noticed the fiery temperature outside, being too intent on what she would say to Mae Parker once she got here.

"Now," Mae directed, "talk."

Karen came straight to the point. "I'm here to ask you to help save Twilight. There's a threat to it and to everyone who lives there. I'm sure you're already familiar with it."

Mae frowned. "I have no idea what you're talking about."

"You and Shannon gave something to Lee when you visited."

"Are you talkin' about Byron Parker's personal accounts?"

"I am. And I've come to ask you to stop Lee from using them."

"Stop Lee! Why would I do that? If he thinks it's best to—"

Karen scooted to the front edge of the cushion, almost spilling her drink. She placed it on a side table for safekeeping. "But it's *not* for the best!" she argued. "If he tells people the Twilight legend isn't true, it will destroy the town. Tourists won't come. What reason would they have? Who'd want to see a place where something was supposed to have happened but didn't?"

"But if it didn't—"

"You saw how the people of Twilight are working to get ready for the movie preview. Their goal is to lure tourists—not just during the preview, but afterward, too. They want to take advantage of the studio's publicity for the new movie and combine it with a little publicity of their own to create something long-term. I'm sure they'll be asking permission soon to put up signs along the road bordering the ranch to guide the tourists. And with 'Western Rambles' doing a special—"

"I'm not sure I like the idea of a bunch of strangers driving by the ranch," Mae interrupted her.

"Then…then get the county to build another road! I'm sure you have the connections."

Mae smiled slightly. "Oh, yes, I have connections. But building another road…"

Karen saw the way Mae was looking at her, as if she were seriously delusional. She ran a hand through her hair and tried to calm herself. This wasn't going well. She should have known. But she'd thought Mae could be her strongest ally. If only she could make her care about the town!

"I'm sorry," she apologized, trying to back up a step. "I know this seems— But it means so much to me. And would to Aunt Augusta, too, if—"

"I don't see how Lee's telling the truth will bring an end to Twilight," Mae maintained.

"Because if tourists don't come, the people won't make any money, and they'll have to move away."

"They're living there now."

"They're barely hanging on! The cost of living has gone up everywhere, even in Twilight."

"Maybe I could get the place declared a historic site or somethin'," Mae said.

"That takes time, doesn't it? And time isn't something Twilight has very much of."

Mae thought for a moment. "I don't see how in good conscience I can ask Lee to go against what he thinks best."

Karen was losing the battle. She didn't know whether it was because she hadn't done a good enough job of making her plea or because she was up against the stubborn arrogance of the Parkers. She gave one last try, her voice rising. *"You Parkers have everything! Can't you let Twilight have something?"* Then she felt bad because she'd shouted at a very old woman in whose house she was visiting.

Marie hurried into the room, followed by a large, burly man with a round face and a nearly bald head. "You want us to get Rafe?" Marie asked gruffly, looking at Karen as if she were the enemy.

Mae waved them away as she had Rafe. "No, no. No need. I can handle it."

"But—"

"You and Axel go back to what you were doing. This little girl is just trying to make a point. That's all."

The pair didn't like it, but they did as Mae said.

Once again Karen felt the need to apologize. "I'm sorry. I didn't mean to shout."

"You feel strongly about that little town."

"And the people," Karen added.

"A town *is* its people," Mae declared, and Karen felt an optimistic spark. She wondered if she'd made more headway than she'd first thought. "Tell me," Mae continued. "Since you don't live there, why do you care?"

"I care because…I'm more a part of Twilight than I am anywhere else. I grew up in Austin, but Twilight is in my blood. I visited every summer when I was a child…did my aunt tell you? I love it." Her declaration was made with such simple conviction that Mae nodded.

"That's the way we Parkers feel about our land. It's a part of us. It's in our blood."

"Then you'll talk to Lee?" Karen pleaded.

"I'll talk to him," Mae agreed, "but I won't tell him what to do. 'Western Rambles' is his show, and it's a darn good one. A reflection of the man who makes it. Lee's one of us. He's a Parker. He stands for something. And I'm not goin' to try to make him go against what he thinks is right."

KAREN RETURNED to Twilight in a brighter mood than when she left it. She knew Mae had agreed only to talk to Lee, but that was better than refusing.

She parked her car behind the antique shop and

hopped out, remembering to bring with her the small bag of purchases from the drugstore. She would return later for the half-dozen moving boxes in the trunk.

She was halfway up the exterior stairs when she saw him. She almost dropped the bag when he unfolded his length from where he'd been sitting on the landing.

"We have to talk," he said quietly, and for a giddy moment he reminded her of his older cousin Rafe. The same dark menace, if a little more subtly held. The same steely determination. "In there," he added, motioning to her aunt's apartment.

Karen shook her head, remembering what had happened there once before. "I'd rather not," she murmured.

"We need to talk in private. Unless you'd rather have Nate's story—"

Karen pushed past him, leaving the door open for him to follow. She placed the bag on the kitchen counter and quickly positioned herself behind it.

"You went to see Mae," he said.

His knowledge startled her. She hadn't expected Mae to have called him so soon. "Yes," she said.

"You asked her to use her influence to quash the story."

"I did."

He came closer and she tensed. But he didn't try to move around the counter or touch her. "You went to the ranch to do this," he said evenly.

She lifted her chin instead of replying. She was tired of answering his questions.

"That must have been hard for you," he surprised her by saying. "Mae certainly admired you for it. She told me you were—her word—spunky."

His nearness and the positive spin he was putting on her visit to Mae was eroding her determined detachment. His voice, the way he looked... She had to do something! "And?" she challenged.

"From her, that's enough. She likes you. She approves."

"I mean, did she convince you? Are you going to quash it?"

"I haven't made up my mind yet."

Karen sighed. "It's a simple choice. Good things for you or good things for the town."

"If I choose the town, I'll be going along with a lie. The truth could easily come out one day. If we found it, someone else could, too."

"No one else has access to your family's records."

"They have access to that headstone and the county's records."

"Why would anyone care?"

"Some people like to make trouble."

"People like you?" she retorted. "Think about the harm you'll be doing. The studio's probably already out millions on publicity—playing up the legend."

"I've thought about that. Have you ever heard the saying, Any publicity is good publicity? They'd probably welcome the added notoriety. The more the picture's talked about, the more of an audience it'll draw."

"Then...your show. Is that the kind of program you want to put on the air? I thought you specialized in good things. Not—"

"Telling the truth *is* a good thing."

Karen curled her fists.

He smiled without enjoyment. "Not quite so simple, is it?"

"I'd like you to leave," she said tightly.

"Diane told me you'd talked to her, too. She thinks you hate her."

"I don't hate—"

"Don't take it out on her or Manny. They're part of the team, they get a say, but this one's mine to call."

"You're the one who'll have to live with it, then!" she retaliated. "Do you think you can do that?"

"I've lived with worse," he said quietly, and let himself out.

FOR THE NEXT FEW DAYS Karen existed in her own world. She'd done everything she could to convince Lee not to reveal Twilight's secret. There was nothing left to do but wait and see what he decided. She stayed to herself, working in the storage shed, working upstairs. But even as hidden away as she was, the excitement that was starting to grip Twilight's populace managed to work its way through to her.

She knew when the first set of movie workers departed and were replaced by a second group, whose specialty was to set up the preview. The original trucks having brought almost everything they needed, the transfer was accomplished smoothly and easily. What especially pleased the townspeople was that before the old crew left, they assembled in the Lady Slipper and wore their Twilight Texas T-shirts and sported their Twilight Texas caps. Drinks and goodwill were exchanged all around, along with wishes for luck.

Karen also knew that a couple of the townspeople had branched out in their construction to build the road signs, which would be put in place after this weekend's premiere, and that Isaac Jacobs had agreed to paint them. He'd done such a great job with the logo, he was the perfect candidate to repeat his success.

She knew all this, but she couldn't watch it. All she could think about was the power Lee Parker had to destroy everything.

THE "WESTERN RAMBLES" crew used their time to finish taping all the townspeople's interviews and to collect any other individual shots they thought they might need before the preview, particularly those of Lee, alone, delivering various segments of his copy. They knew that from the moment the media arrived on Saturday through the movie showing on Sunday afternoon, they wouldn't have many minutes to spare.

"I don't know...I feel like Judas or something every time we talk to any of these people," Diane complained from her position draped along the foot of the bed.

"Isn't that supposed to be me?" Lee asked. "Aren't I the one with the traitorous kiss?"

"You're not Judas."

"Then, for sure, you aren't, either."

"I am," Manny said while doing repetitive curls with his hand-size dumbbells. "I'm the guy everybody can point to and say, 'There he is, there's that Judas guy!'"

Diane tossed her pillow at him. "Still," she said, adjusting her position, "I do feel that way."

"Drop it, okay?" Lee was frowning. "I know what you're saying. I need to make a decision."

"Maybe it's best that you don't," Manny countered. "Not until after we leave the place."

Diane shook her head. "No, if he's going to do it, he has to tell them to their faces. Warn them. It's not their fault that the legend isn't true." She turned to Lee as if inspiration had struck her. "You know, if you're concerned about perpetuating the lie, we don't have to do it. Every time you mention the legend, you call it that. You say, 'The legend says this…the legend says that,' and then go on with it. Whaddya think?"

"It could work."

She pulled a face. "Gee, thanks for the enthusiasm."

Lee merely shrugged.

Diane caught the pillow that Manny tossed back at her and stuffed it under her elbow. "I've never felt this way about a shoot before. I'll be glad when this one's over."

"You want combat pay?" Lee asked dryly.

She looked at him. "Maybe." She sat up. "Okay. Cards on the table. I don't see anything wrong with believing in legends and myths. Think about Santa Claus and the Easter bunny and the tooth fairy. When you have a child one day, Lee, are you going to tell the little kiddie those things don't exist because it's not the complete and accurate truth? Manny and I aren't, I can guarantee you. I still like to believe and I'm an adult. Actually, I think adults need legends and myths as much as children do, maybe more. We all like to believe in heroes who are bigger than life. King Arthur, Robin Hood… Experts aren't sure if they ever truly existed, but the stories about them have been handed down through the ages. And that wouldn't have happened if people didn't *want* to believe in them. Belief in heroes speaks to something in the human soul."

Diane glanced from quiet man to quiet man and pulled another face. "Sorry," she murmured. "I'll step down off my soapbox now."

"No," Lee said. "You're right."

She drew another breath. "And believing that an outlaw like Nate Barlow sacrificed his life for a child—"

"You're right," Lee repeated, only this time a little more sharply.

Diane knew better than to press the issue further, and Lee gratefully got to his feet.

"I'm going to bed," he said. "I'm beat," Then, glancing at Manny, he teased Diane, "Don't let him drop one of those things on his foot. We don't need a cameraman who has to hop around."

Diane grinned, accepting his unspoken attempt at contrition. "All we need is a picture that goes up and down...up and down."

She was giggling at something Manny said when Lee closed the door.

His glimmering smile disappeared for good as he let himself into his room. He knew he couldn't continue to put off his decision. He'd been given several days' grace because nothing crucial had been in the works. Now it was all coming together in a rush. He was apprehensive about the media's impending arrival. Wary that with their twitching noses and curious minds they might catch on to the fact that something was indeed wrong. And the primary giveaway would be that headstone.

Lee hadn't spoken to John about it. He hadn't wanted to spook him, make him aware that they knew of the deception. He doubted that it went further than that. As Karen had speculated, in all probability the alteration had come about in order to tweak tourist interest.

Karen...

Lee fell back onto the bed fully clothed. Circumstance forced him to keep his love for her to himself. Look what she already thought of him! She wouldn't take kindly to hearing him say it. Not now. Not when Twilight's continued existence rested solely in his hands. That was exactly why it would be so easy for him to give in to his first instinct and drop his questions about the Twilight legend. But if he chose that path, was he doing it only to placate her? To get back in her good graces? To make her think well of him again? And if he did, where would his integrity and his honor fit into the equation?

He also had another problem. If he went through with exposing the truth on "Western Rambles," wasn't he doing what he'd once found so repulsive? Like his old news director, wouldn't he be laying himself open to accusations of callousness? Of giving priority to the sensation of a story over its cost to humanity?

His humanity told him to leave things alone. To follow Diane's suggestion and use her carefully crafted. "The legend says..." as a distancing tool between fact and fiction.

The legend says...

Lee got up, discarded his clothes and collapsed between the sheets.

There were times when he wanted very badly to believe in myths himself. Times, like now, when the correct course in life seemed hopelessly obscured.

A SLEEK BLACK LIMOUSINE pulled into Twilight the next afternoon. Inside it were Melanie Taylor and her two assistants from Hollywood. She made a show of getting out of the car and taking a quick inspection of the workers' temporary quarters. Both assistants had notebooks at the ready to jot down her impressions.

Karen, who happened to be talking with Bette on the sidewalk in front of the antique shop, watched the whole production.

"Oh, no," Bette moaned. "Not her again."

"It looks like," Karen said, smiling.

By this time Melanie had spotted them and hurried over. "The music hall...I can't remember. Where is it now?" she asked with a flash of her dazzlingly white teeth.

"Over there," Bette said, pointing to the large building across the street and to the far left of the well.

"Oh, that's right! Yes. Harry! Dwight!" she called to her two young assistants. "I'll meet you inside in just a moment. Yes, that building over there. I'll be with you as soon as I speak with my two friends." She rolled her eyes when they had trouble finding the correct building. "Honestly. I don't know how they make their way around LA, but they do. Quite well, as a matter of fact." She leaned close to kiss the air next to Bette's cheek, then did the same to Karen. "You're Karen Latham, aren't you? I'm remembering correctly, aren't I?"

Karen nodded.

"I'm Bette," Bette said. "John's wife."

Melanie grinned. "I know who you are! How could I forget? You and John have played such a large part in the success of this project. How is John? I definitely want to speak to him as soon as possible."

"He's at the hotel," Bette said levelly.

A light frown creased Melanie's brow. "The hotel?"

"At the end of the street. We're fixing it up for tourists."

"Fixing?" the studio representative repeated, a little hollowly.

"Yeah. Been working on it for the past ten days or so...ever since you left."

Karen glanced at Bette and saw the redheaded devilment in her expression. She was out to make trouble for this woman. To worry her.

"But...you weren't supposed to— Oh my God! Don't tell me that John's *changed* anything!" Panic had set into her blue eyes.

"Changed just about everything," Bette confirmed. "Looks really nice now. Doesn't it, Karen?"

Karen was having a hard time keeping a straight face. She had known Bette didn't like Melanie but had no idea just how deeply the feeling went. "Uh, yes. Yes, it looks very nice."

Melanie uttered a little squeal, something like a kitten caught in a tight space, then hurried down the street, the perfect little heels of her perfect little shoes tattooing against the old wooden sidewalk planks.

Bette doubled over with laughter and was joined by only a slightly more circumspect Karen.

"You are truly evil," Karen said, once she'd recovered enough to speak.

"She deserved it!" retorted an unrepentant Bette. "Trying to steal my man!"

Karen blinked. "You think—"

"I more than think—I know!" Bette said, no longer laughing. "And this time I'm ready for her. She pulls anything and she gets it, whether it causes problems with our movie premiere or not!"

"But John—"

"I told you before. John's not himself when she's around."

"Have you ever thought he might only be excited by the plans?"

"It's the plans I'm worried about. I'm just not sure which ones they are."

"Surely—"

"I think I'm going to see how things are progressing down at the hotel," she interrupted, returning to her devilment. "Wanna come along?"

Karen shook her head. She didn't want to get any more involved with Bette's war on Melanie, and she didn't want to meet Lee. So far over the past few days, she'd only seen him from a distance. And that had been more than enough. Even though she'd drawn her line and was holding out for the town, she wanted to be with him. She wanted to hear his voice, feel his touch.... She didn't think placing herself where she'd be close to him would be a good idea.

She watched as Bette left and wondered if he'd be there.

KAREN WAS IN THE STORAGE shed and had just finished filling a box with children's toys to take upstairs and compare with the ones in the reference books when she saw John walking desultorily across the backyard. He was headed away from the saloon toward the hotel, but there was no spring in his step.

"John?" she called.

John turned hurt and confused eyes on her. "Bette just told me to get out of my own place! I don't understand. All I did was tell her that Melanie said the media was set for sure to arrive on Saturday and she exploded. It's like she doesn't want Twilight to become well known. Like she'd just as soon see it wither away. And I can't understand that, neither!" His lament ended on a spurt of anger.

Karen motioned for him to follow her upstairs. She saw him in, sat him down and talked to him in a way that she hoped would help. "John, when did you notice Bette behaving like this last?" she asked.

John scratched his thinning gray head. "You mean her bein' irritable?"

"Uh-huh. The last time. It was about the time Melanie Taylor was here to secure the agreement for the preview, wasn't it?"

"Yeah, that's it. She got all testy, like she didn't give a darn. I thought she was mad 'cause I was so busy."

Karen smiled. "John, she's jealous."

"Jealous?" He repeated the word as if it were foreign to him.

"Of you. Of Melanie. She thinks something's going on between you. There isn't, is there?"

John almost leaped out of the chair. "Me? And Melanie? Gee whillikers, no! She's just twenty-six or seven, and I'm—" He stopped, stared at Karen, then said incredulously, "Bette really thinks that?"

"She says that every time Melanie comes around, you're different."

"That I'm— I like thinkin' I can do somethin' to help this place," he explained. "Make a difference, you know. That makes me feel good. An' I guess I do get carried away sometimes. Thinkin' of things. But me and that young girl?''

"Maybe you should include Bette a little more. She probably feels left out. What do you think?''

John still seemed stunned. "Yeah. Sure. I guess so. I can try.''

Karen smiled. "You do that." Then she thought of something else she'd wanted to talk to John about. "John, do you have another minute?" she asked.

"Sure. Is there somethin' else I'm not doin' right?''

"Only one thing, but it might be a biggie, too. John? Did you alter a headstone for Nate Barlow? Bette told me you found it and set it up again, but I don't remember one being there before and neither does Pete.''

John looked longingly at the door, as if he'd like to rush out of it. His wife had tossed him out in a fit of jealousy, and now Karen had caught him in an act of deception. It seemed more than his poor tired brain could deal with at the moment.

"Did you, John?" Karen persisted.

"Well...yeah. But it was only because I thought it would spice up the cemetery. Give people somethin' to talk about. Hank was in on it, too.''

"You took a headstone from another grave with a similar name?''

"Yeah....''

"Didn't you think someone might notice?''

"I did a pretty good job.''

"What about the Harlons?''

"The who?''

"The Harlons. If they have descendants, they

might notice. Didn't it bother you to steal that poor man's headstone?''

John shrugged. ''Well, he doesn't really need it anymore. An' I didn't think he'd mind if it'd help get Twilight famous. I wouldn't.''

Karen gave a long sigh.

''Are you mad at me, too?'' John asked, looking wounded.

''A little bit,'' she admitted.

''I'm sorry.''

She patted him on the shoulder. He hadn't meant anything terrible. He didn't know that by his simple act he'd added to the evidence condemning Twilight, rather than advancing its cause. And she wasn't about to tell him.

CHAPTER FIFTEEN

THE LADY SLIPPER WAS jumping with happy people on Friday night. Most of the hardest work had been completed. The interior of the hotel had only to pass a final inspection by John the next morning, and the setup by the studio workers was well ahead of schedule. Melanie, pleased, had reported their progress to her boss, Raymond Armstrong, who replied that he was looking forward to his visit to Twilight. He would arrive the next day, she told everyone, along with a fleet of small trucks and a flotilla of additional workers who would execute the final preparations for the preview. Probably near the same time as the media guests. Even Pete was in the Lady Slipper. Like many converts, he had become one of the town's most enthusiastic supporters. He'd created a nice niche for himself as the old sage, thereby ensuring an attentive audience for his stories.

Lee and Manny sat at the bar while Diane flitted from table to table, enjoying the chance to socialize.

One after another, singly or in small groups, the townspeople stopped by to clap them on the back or give them warm handshakes and hugs. It was as if they knew instinctively that this short lull would be the last they'd get until after the premiere. And they wanted to be sure the ''Western Rambles'' crew knew they were appreciated.

"You folks are like family now!" Pepper Douglas exclaimed. "Gonna make us stars, too!"

Rhonda Peterson grinned. "Those Hollywood people aren't going to have a thing on us!"

Hank pumped Lee's hand. "You know? When I first heard you was comin', I thought, 'They ain't gonna do us any good. They'll just get in the way with their cameras and their fancy ways.' But you're all great! I'm not sure we'da made it through with our renovations if you hadn't pitched in to help. Manny, you sling a good hammer. You, too, Lee. I'd be proud to have the both a ya on any reconstructin' job I do in the future."

"Maybe we can convince 'em to come back and help us with the museum," Joe proposed.

"What museum?" Manny asked.

"The one we're gonna put in the buildin' next to this. Right over there." He pointed behind the bar. "On the other side."

"What kind of museum?" Lee asked.

"Oh, this 'n that. Old Twilight stuff. Old ranch stuff."

"Maybe I can get my family to donate a few things to the cause," Lee offered, then realized what he'd said and glanced at Manny, who, for the moment, was studiously gazing at the bottom of his glass.

"Hey, that'd be great!" Joe said.

When they moved off, Mary came over. "Have you boys gotten your Twilight Texas T-shirts yet?" She handed them each a shirt. "Now, don't even think about paying for 'em. Your money's no good here. These are for you, with our compliments."

The player piano stopped suddenly as Benny hurried over. He hugged each man in turn, saying, "My momma's so happy!'' He looked around them, grinning. "Everybody's happy!'' Then he hurried over to Diane and gave her a surprise hug, before settling back at the piano to start working the foot pedals again, his shoulders bobbing and weaving with the effort.

"He's really enjoying himself,'' Mary said, her smile beaming proudly.

Minutes later Carmelita and her extended family offered their regards. Juanita was excited about the arrival of the stars, especially Johnny Mehan, Hollywood's latest bad-boy heartthrob, who'd taken the role of Nate Barlow.

"Have you ever met him before?'' she asked. "He's my favorite. I read where he and Andrea Wright fell in love when they were making the picture. Do you know if they're still together? I can't wait to see them here. Do you think we'll get to meet them…talk to them?''

Lee pointed to Melanie. "That's the lady you need to talk to. I bet she could set it up for you.''

"Oh…I couldn't talk to her.'' She shook her head shyly. "She's too—she's—she's busy all the time.''

Manny pushed off his stool. "C'mon. I'll bet she's not too busy now.''

"Oh!'' Juanita cried, and bounced as she kept up with him.

A half hour later Lee had all the merriment and well wishes he could take. He slipped, unnoticed, out the saloon's back door and walked into the night. With his hands stuffed deeply into his pockets, he wrestled with his predicament. What was he going to do? How could he let all these people down—turn their dreams to dust—when they considered him a friend? When they trusted him?

He glanced at the apartment over the antique shop. A light was on in a bedroom, from what he could remember of the floor plan. What he wanted more than anything at that moment was to go up those stairs and forget the weight of responsibility. Lose himself in the warm sweetness of Karen Latham's arms. Forget that he had to make a decision.

But the media was coming tomorrow. The media with its prying eyes.

As he continued to walk, Lee thought about his long-dead relation Byron Parker. Would Byron care that he hadn't received the credit for rescuing the child? If he'd wanted it, wouldn't he have done more than write a pair of accounts that, at most, had been seen by the local sheriff, then folded into the pages of a book to be forgotten by time? Mae's opinion was that it was enough that Byron knew. The Parkers didn't ask for attention or for gratitude or rewards. They did what needed to be done and never looked back. A code he'd always tried to be faithful to, as well, even if most of his time was spent off the ranch. What would the Parkers who'd come before him advise him to do?

One thing would be to stop concerning himself with matters that surrounded the problem and just concentrate on the problem itself. Not think about Karen. Not think about the film studio. Not think about either the good or the bad results for "Western Rambles." Maybe then he could sort it all out.

When he'd set out walking, Lee had had no clear idea where he was going, but it was no surprise that his subconscious had led him to the cemetery and the headstone that was symbolic of all his trouble.

He stared at it for a long time, barely able to make out the crude carving. Yet he knew the lettering by heart: Nate Barlow, Valued Friend.

Lee felt a tingling start in the soles of his boots, then spread throughout his body. Imaginary or real, it compelled him to action, and the next thing he knew he reared back and kicked the holy heck out of the headstone, knocking it flat. Then he grabbed hold of it, hefted its weight and flung it into the weeds.

Triumphant, he stood there as the reality of what he'd done washed over him. He'd made the decision. Relying not so much on intellect but on instinct to show him the way—and possibly with a little help from some Parkers of old and the unknown spirits of the Harlons—he'd come down on the side of the town.

The huge weight of responsibility lifted from his shoulders. The town would live. The people, he hoped, would prosper. At least, if they didn't, it wouldn't be because of him.

The truth of the Twilight legend would remain a secret.

SOMEONE KNOCKED on Karen's door the next morning. Not hard, but long—a knock meant to wake her. She stumbled into her robe, remembering the day the trucks had arrived. Pausing to listen, though, she heard nothing—except the rapid knocking.

"Who is it?" she called through the closed door. She could imagine what she looked like. Hair everywhere in a curly mass, eyes bleary from too little sleep, her face totally devoid of makeup. She had no idea what time it was, but judging by the brightness, she'd overslept.

"Open the door, Karen. It's me—Pete!"

This was a first. Pete never paid house calls. She stepped quickly out of the way and let him inside.

Pete looked as he always did, only this time, he was more excited than usual. He rushed into speech. "I waited as long as I could, until I couldn't wait no more! I hafta tell you what I saw last night. Darnedest thing! I heard somebody goin' by, so I looked outside, and who do you think it was? Lee! Walkin' along all sorry for himself. Hands in his pockets, head down. Like a whupped dog. Not like him at all. Anyways, I kept watchin' him, and he goes into the cemetery…just like before. He goes over to that grave that somebody's callin' Nate Barlow's, and he stares at the headstone for a while. Then pow! He kicks the darn thing over, picks it up and flings it out into the desert. Whaddaya think about that?"

Karen could scarcely follow. Lee had knocked over Nate Barlow's headstone and tossed it away? Why in the world—

"And that's not all," Pete continued. "About ten minutes later he came back with a wheelbarrow and a shovel, searched around in the grass until he found the headstone, then he put it in the wheelbarrow and took off for parts unknown."

"Have you been out there this morning? Are you sure it was Nate Barlow's headstone? Or at least—" She had been going to say the altered Nate Barlow, when Pete interrupted her.

"Sure did. First thing. It's gone. Spots kinda been swept around, too, so's the ground don't look like somethin' was taken away."

Karen's mind worked to play catch-up. Even though she'd gone to bed before ten last night, she hadn't gotten much sleep. From the noise emanating from the saloon, she decided she was probably the only person trying. Worry about Lee's decision and its aftermath wouldn't let her rest. Wouldn't let her—

Her thoughts stopped. Lee's decision! *Lee had decided!* Last night. He wouldn't have gotten rid of telltale evidence if he'd planned to use it. Use any of it! His family's papers, the court records! He had decided to let Twilight live!

Joy burst in her heart. She had to see him. Had to be sure that her assumption was correct. She looked down at herself, at the long T-shirt and silk robe. First she had to dress, then—

"Has Lee gone loco or what?" Pete demanded, frowning, and he was starting to look at her as if she were puzzling him a little herself.

"Oh, no!" she cried, unable to rein in her ecstatic feelings. "No, Pete, he's not one bit crazy! He's wonderful. He—"

"The whole place has gone loco," Pete pronounced, heading for the door.

"It's okay, Pete, really," she tried to reassure him. But all he did was grumble to himself as he went downstairs to join up with the waiting Tex.

Karen dressed as fast as she could, applied her makeup and brushed her hair. She was too thrilled to do more than think about breakfast. She wanted to talk to Lee. She *had* to talk to Lee.

She hurried downstairs and into the saloon.

Bette was behind the bar, finishing the morning cleanup. "If you're looking for John, he's down at the hotel,'' she said. "If you're looking for Lee, he's there t—''

She didn't finish. A tall blond man with a pleasant face and a nice smile stepped hesitantly through the saloon's front doors. "Ah—excuse me. I wonder if I might bother you. I'm looking for Karen Latham. I tried next door at the antique shop, but no one answers.''

Karen stepped out of what she knew would be the shadows from his perspective, amazed not only that Martin would come to Twilight, but that he'd picked this particular moment to present himself. "Martin?'' Her voice echoed her shock.

His smile grew. "Karen! I was beginning to think I wouldn't see you again. I was worried. You didn't call.''

Karen went to greet him under Bette's watchful eye. She let him hug her, kiss her, keep hold of her. She tried to act glad to see him. "Things have been...a little on the wild side here,'' she attempted to explain. "Did you see...on the way into town?''

His affection for her was clear. "Yes. What's going on? I thought you said this was a near ghost town. It looks more like a small city.''

"It's just temporary,'' she said, her voice shaky. She didn't want to be here talking to him, dealing with him. She wanted—

Bette came out from behind the bar, drying her hands on her apron. "And who might you be?'' she asked, glancing at the flushed Karen.

"Martin Frederick,'' Martin said, offering his hand.

Karen came alive to her manners. "This is Bette, Martin. Bette Danson, an old friend of mine.''

The two shook hands. "We're having a movie premiere, Mr. Frederick. Straight out of Hollywood. For the remake of *Justice at Sundown.* Have you heard of it?''

Martin frowned for a second, then said, ''Yes, yes I have, as a matter of fact. A customer in my restaurant was talking about it last week. It's about something that happened around here, isn't it?''

Bette nodded proudly. ''You bet it is. Why don't you get Karen to tell you about it? Show you the well. She knows the story.''

Martin grinned and tightened his arm around Karen. ''Sure. I'll do that.''

At that moment a group came in through the back door. John, Lee, Manny and Diane. They all stopped abruptly when they saw Karen enveloped by Martin's arm. But none so abruptly as Lee.

Karen's gaze flew to his. He stared back at her blankly.

Bette took charge. ''This here's Karen's friend Martin. I'm sorry, Martin, what was your last name?''

''Frederick,'' Martin supplied promptly.

''My husband, John Danson, Lee Parker, Manny and Diane Cruz. The last three are the crew for 'Western Rambles.' They've been covering the town for the last two weeks as we get ready for our big premiere.'' In an aside to the others, she added, ''We've already told him about our excitement.''

Karen felt Martin stiffen slightly when told that the crew had been there for two weeks. Still, he was politeness itself as he nodded. ''Good to meet you. 'Western Rambles'…is that a television show?''

Diane glanced at Lee, and when he didn't answer, she did. ''Yes. Public broadcasting.''

''Ah,'' Martin said.

There was a short, awkward pause. Then John said, "Hotel looks great. Can't see another thing needin' done." He delivered a quick kiss to Bette's cheek. "'Specially the wallpaper. You and Pepper did a great job."

Bette preened. "Thanks."

Karen felt Martin watching her. He wanted to talk to her alone. But she still wanted to talk to Lee. Now more than ever.

It wasn't going to happen, though. Martin would never countenance her telling him to wait. He'd come a long way to see how she was. And Lee didn't seem particularly pleased with the world in general. Was he regretting having removed the headstone? She groaned to herself. She didn't want anything to disturb the delicate balance. He could easily dig it back up again.

She forced a smile. "Well, uh, we'll see you all later," she said, then went out the front door with Martin.

Once outside, as subtly as she could, she separated herself from his hold. At the antique shop she took the key from around her neck—she'd started locking the place since so many strangers were in town—and let them inside.

"I knocked earlier," he said, "but I guess you weren't here."

"I'd only just left. The apartment's above, actually, but the stairs are out back. Come on, I'll show you."

He took in the shop's crowded conditions as he followed her. "Wow. No wonder you had to stay awhile."

"There's more in the storage shed out back."

Inside the apartment he tried to pull her into his

arms, but she evaded him. "What do you think of Twilight?" she asked, busying herself with clearing a second chair while filling the space between them with words. "It's not normally so busy. The population's probably tripled with the studio workers, and it's only going to get worse. The movie's having its first showing tomorrow. Of course, there'll be the bigger, official one out in Los Angeles in a couple of weeks." She sat down and motioned to the cleared chair next to hers, but he remained standing.

"Karen," he asked, "why didn't you call?"

"MARTIN." DIANE MURMURED the name, watching Lee out of the corner of her eye. "Martin Frederick. Very nice looking. Seems to know Karen pretty well. I wonder—"

"She called someone the first night she got here," Bette remembered. "To let him know she'd arrived safely. I wonder if it was him. I asked her if it was serious, but she didn't say."

"*He* looked serious," Manny said.

Lee listened to the conversation taking place around him but didn't participate. He'd been stunned to see Karen held by someone else. Shocked at his immediate and intense response. He'd wanted to go over, jerk her away and push the other guy's face into the wall.

"What do you think, Lee?" Diane asked.

"I think it's none of our business," Lee said tautly, then turned to John. "John, I need a minute."

His curt command was met with silence. He felt everyone's eyes on him. He knew he'd been rude, knew they were curious, but he couldn't deal with their questions right then. Or their speculations. It hadn't entered his mind that Karen could be serious about someone. Could have someone serious about her. Which was true stupidity on his part. She was a beautiful woman! What did he think? She existed in a vacuum?

Bette broke the silence. "Why don't the rest of us go up and take an early lunch? Lord knows if we'll have the opportunity to later. To hear Melanie tell it, the place is going to be overrun. And it could start at any time. You two come up when you're ready."

Diane and Manny agreed with the idea, but not without uneasy glances at Lee as they started for the stairway.

John made himself comfortable on a bar stool, a self-satisfied little smile tugging at his lips. "We did it," he said. "All we have to do now is sit back and let it happen."

"There's one thing," Lee said. "Something I need to talk to you about... Nate Barlow's headstone. Someone must have carried it off as a souvenir, because it's not there anymore. You don't want to make a fuss, though, do you? Not with the press coming so soon and all?"

John's smile disappeared as he absorbed what Lee said. He was startled, outraged, then alarmed, all within the space of a few seconds. "It's gone?"

"Uh-huh. And there's something else. Another headstone seems to be missing, too. For someone in the Harlon family. I thought it might be nice to have it replaced. What do you think?"

John stared at him. Now he knew for sure that Lee knew what he'd done. And that, so far, Lee seemed willing to look the other way. "Sure," he said slowly. "Sure, I do, too. I'll get on it first thing Monday."

"I'll even throw in a few bucks myself, to help out," Lee offered.

It was almost painful to watch John restrain himself from asking if Lee was the "someone" who'd carried off the headstone. He managed it, though, saying instead, "Right nice of you."

"Uh-huh."

A tight smile and a clap on the shoulder signaled to the older man that all was well. Then Lee said, "I'm going out for a drive. Tell Manny and Diane I won't be gone long."

Driving felt good to Lee. He hadn't been behind the wheel since the day they'd gotten here. It felt far more than two weeks ago. It felt a lifetime's journey, so much had happened. He remembered his thoughts going in, hoping to get Karen to listen to his apology, hoping to reclaim the Parker name. Now his goals had changed, shifted. He wanted Karen for himself. And now this interloper had shown up. To claim her?

He'd listened to instinct about the headstone, about keeping Twilight's secret. If he listened to his present instinct, the arriving press would have a lot more to report than a movie review. So what did he do? Wait and see? He wasn't very good at waiting.

KAREN DIDN'T THINK it fair to string Martin along, yet she didn't want to hurt him. "Would you like something to drink? Something cold, something hot? I can do either."

"I'd rather you answer my question."

She looked away and murmured, "That's the hardest thing of all."

Martin knelt at her side, taking her hand. He reached into his shirt pocket and brought out a ring case. "I've carried this with me, close to my heart. I'd like you to accept it, Karen." He opened it to reveal a diamond set with two dark blue sapphires on each side.

Karen looked from the ring to his face. He was such a nice man. "It's beautiful, but—"

"*I* come along with it," he stated starkly, and stood up, snapping the case shut before sliding it back in his pocket. He walked to the window overlooking the street.

Karen came up behind him and hesitantly rested her fingers on his arm. "It's not the way you make it sound."

"What is it, then?" He pivoted to face her.

"It's—"

"Rachel said something about an outlaw. An outlaw from your past. Was it one of those men in the saloon? The tall one with the dark hair and the pale eyes? He was certainly looking at you hard enough."

"I don't love you, Martin. Not enough. You deserve more...much more. Someone who'll love you the way you love her."

"But you love me some."

"I love you like a friend."

"Why didn't you tell me this before?"

"Because I didn't know it before. I didn't understand."

"And you do now."

"Now I—"

"It's him, isn't it? That man from your past. You've loved him all along. That's why you can't see beyond him to me."

"It's not as simple as that. Yes, it's him, but it's not him."

Martin seemed not to hear her last statement. "Nothing's ever simple when you don't want it to be. I love you, Karen. I'm willing to marry you with just the tiniest spark of hope."

She took his hand and pulled him back to the chairs. After they both sat down, she explained quietly, "I've wanted to love you. I've tried to love you. You're a very good man, Martin, besides being quite wonderfully nice looking. If it was only that... But I've learned something. The kind of love I'm talking about isn't a fix-it project you can do yourself. It either is, or it isn't. And it isn't for us."

"I'm willing to take that chance."

"I'm not. *I* deserve better, too, Martin. Not a better person than you, but the person I can love as much as I'm loved. Can't you see? I'm not trying to hurt you, even though I'm sure I'm doing it. I'm not the right person for you. And the sooner you accept that, the better off you'll be."

His words were tight. "I can't just turn off the way I feel about you."

She smiled slightly. "No. I understand."

"I'll have to live with it a little while."

She nodded.

"Rachel said this was going to happen," he murmured.

"Did she have another dream?"

"I'm not sure. She just said you were going to marry someone else."

That made Karen a little nervous. It was a few too many steps ahead.

She patted Martin's hand. "Would you like a tour of Twilight? It's particularly interesting with all the hustle and bustle going on. If you like, you can stay

the night. Either here or at the hotel. We have one
now. You can be my guest at the premiere.''

He was silent a long moment. "I might just do
that," he said quietly.

And Karen knew he was agreeing with the hope
that a new day might bring a new answer.

All she could do was give him a sad smile.

THE WHIR OF BLADES and the roar of an engine cut
through the afternoon quiet of the desert.

Everyone in town piled out to watch as a large
helicopter settled delicately to earth and perched, with
the blades still turning, while a group of well-dressed
men and women disembarked.

Melanie waited to greet them, dust and dirt and
loose bits of grass swirling around her. Once the people were at a safe distance, the helicopter lifted into
the air again, and Melanie took the group to one of
the newly arrived travel trailers on the outskirts of
town.

With the excitement over, the townspeople went
back to what they'd been doing and waited for more.

Then, shortly, more people started to arrive in air-
conditioned jitneys that were to ferry the media
around. Melanie had explained that most were flying
in, at studio expense, to a private landing strip, where
they would then be picked up and delivered to Twilight. From that point all their needs would be attended to by studio employees accustomed to putting
on these types of junkets.

Lee, Manny and Diane were kept busy recording
the arrivals and talking to the new visitors. Lee's
mind didn't want to focus. All he could think of was

Karen and that man. But professionalism won out and he did his job.

Late in the afternoon Lee, along with the invited media journalists, attended a meeting called by Melanie and her boss, Raymond Armstrong—Cryer Studio's top publicity specialist—in one of the large tents that had been set up by the studio for that purpose. They, along with the film stars' publicists, went over the ground rules for what could and couldn't be asked of the actors during their interviews the next day and what could and couldn't be expected from the studio and the townspeople. Handouts containing *Justice at Sundown* sheriff's badges were distributed, along with materials about the original movie and its doomed star Henry Ives and the "true" story about Nate Barlow, the child and the pursuing posse. Refreshments were served, then those who wanted to were taken in small groups to tour Twilight.

Everyone from town got into the act from that point, meeting and greeting the visitors and talking up Twilight's special qualities.

The visiting media ate it up. They loved the town, loved the townspeople, even loved the T-shirts and caps and pens and pencils—everything that John had ordered. Seeing this, Melanie bought large quantities as extra gifts for the participants. The media especially loved the Lady Slipper Saloon, the magnificent old-fashioned bar, the player piano, the quaint wall decorations…and Pete! With his scruffy desert-rat looks and loyal canine companion, he was a huge hit.

KAREN HAD PLANNED TO STAY inside as much as possible during this time, but with Martin here, and actually starting to enjoy himself, she couldn't spoil his day further. She'd seen Lee several times, but he'd always been working.

Now Manny wasn't the only professional cameraman in town. Almost everywhere she looked, someone was videotaping something. The well was popular, the hotel, the mercantile...anywhere on the main street. They seemed to love taking shots down the length of it. With no cars and some of the studio employees dressed in period costumes, it might have been the late 1800s again, and Nate Barlow just moments away from riding up.

As a surprise, an actor hired to help re-create the affair did ride up, go to the well, discover a "child," help him out, then have to face the arriving posse, who, after a little overacting, tied a noose around his neck and pretended to hang him at the tree.

The members of the local media, tipped off by John, turned out in force and intimated that the segments they shot were sure to make the national news.

John was over the moon, already making plans to order more souvenirs, to move forward the planned room expansion of the hotel, to quickly open the museum.

"I see what you mean when you say it's been crazy around here," Martin said when they at last went back to Karen's apartment to rest. "These people are determined to make this place into something. John's already made me promise to add some brochures about Twilight to the restaurant's tour display. Once he gets them printed, he's sending them on. The man's a dynamo."

Karen chuckled. "I've known him since I was six and that's never been my description of him. But I guess I have to change it now."

She collected fresh sheets and a blanket and glanced at her aunt's old room. "Are you sure you don't mind sleeping there? It's not like Aunt Augusta passed away in the apartment. She wasn't even in Twilight. But—"

"I'll be fine," Martin assured her. It turned out that the new rooms in the hotel had been so nicely done that Melanie had reserved all three for her boss and his higher-ups from the studio. There had been no vacancy. "I'm the unexpected visitor, remember?"

"Still…" Karen murmured.

"If you're offering me space in your bed, I won't turn you down," Martin said with a broken little laugh.

Karen smiled gently and shook her head. He was trying so hard to make the best of everything.

"I don't stand a chance, do I?" he asked quietly.

Again, Karen shook her head.

CHAPTER SIXTEEN

LEE SPENT A NIGHT fit for the damned. Never in his life had he thought himself the jealous type, and yet here he was, absolutely, totally and completely filled with green-eyed bile. He'd seen Karen and the boyfriend going upstairs to her apartment after being together throughout the day, enjoying all the events, and from that moment he'd been tortured by what might be happening.

Consequently, his disposition the next morning was that of a disgruntled grizzly. He snarled and snapped, and by the time he'd bitten Diane twice about something insignificant, he was told in no uncertain terms to stop it.

Good advice, when yesterday's madness only increased as the movie's stars, studio brass and numerous other invited celebrities began to arrive.

KAREN SLEPT MUCH LATER than she'd planned and was amazed she had, considering the uproar going on outside. She also was amazed that Martin had managed to sleep through it—her aunt's bedroom being so much closer to the street.

After peering into the shadowed room, though, she discovered why. Martin was gone. He'd made the bed, fluffed the pillows and left a note on top of one.

"Thanks for yesterday and all the days before. I hope your outlaw knows what a prize he's getting."

Karen closed her eyes. She would've liked to say goodbye. But maybe this was for the best. So he could make a clean cut of it. She held the note close to her breast and again thought what a nice man he was. A prize for some lucky woman. If she had a wish, it would be for him to find that woman.

She dropped down onto the couch and stared at the wall. What if she had another wish—one for herself? What would it be? She'd learned so much over the past two weeks. How easy it was to be mistaken, how silly it was to let that mistake rule your life, how running and hiding—in whatever form—from your true nature only set you on a course for mediocrity, how a passionate belief, even if it was only in a small town, could liberate you.

Someone tapped on the door. It was Bette.

"I just had to get away for a minute," Bette explained. "It's even crazier today than it was yesterday. I saw Johnny Mehan with his entourage…isn't that what they're called? The people who hang around a person and tell him he's wonderful? He is good-looking! But heavens, he can't make a move without three people showing him where to put his foot!"

She lifted Karen's chin to examine her face. "How are you today, honey? Holding up? I saw that boyfriend of yours leave early this morning. That's why I came over, really, to check on you."

Karen smiled. "I'm fine."

"He looks like the marryin' type. Is that what he wanted?"

Karen nodded.

"And what did you say? No, never mind, I'm not

really a relation of yours. I don't have any business poking my nose in.''

"You're as good as a relation. In my mind you are! You and John both.'' She paused. "I turned him down.''

A pleased smile flickered across Bette's lips at the elevation of status and at Karen's response to Martin. "I thought that, too. I just had to be sure. So why are you looking glum?''

"It's not easy to tell someone who loves you that you don't love them back.''

"I can imagine. John was my first and only love. He still is. It's the same for him, or so he says. And I think I believe him.''

"Do,'' Karen urged.

Bette reached for the doorknob. "I guess I better get back. John might be needing me.'' Still she paused. "You are coming to the premiere this afternoon, aren't you?''

Karen shrugged. "I'm not sure.''

"The music hall looks great. I took a peek. The new curtain's up, the chairs are arranged and they have this huge screen and speaker system set up by the pros. Too bad we won't be able to keep it.''

"I'll think about it,'' Karen promised, "but I'm not really very interested in the movie.''

"I know. Me, neither. But it should be fun.'' She paused again. "Something else... Did you know the 'Western Rambles' crew is leaving tomorrow? I didn't either, or if I did I'd forgotten. They have to get back to San Francisco so they can rush through editing all the tape and put their special together. Lee's promised to send us a copy as soon as it's finished.''

"Tomorrow?" Karen echoed hollowly.

"Sometime after lunch," Bette murmured. "Might want to keep your eye out to say goodbye."

Then she left.

Karen didn't move, struck still by what she'd learned.

"Tomorrow?" she repeated huskily. She hadn't expected it to be so soon! She hadn't thought... She needed more time!

More time to do what? a part of her whispered.

To apologize, to thank him, to tell him—what? *I'm sorry for thinking so badly of you, Lee. Thanks for what you did. Oh, and by the way, I love you.*

She remembered the wish she'd left dangling earlier. She hadn't known what to ask for then. Now she did, and closing her eyes, she wished for more time with Lee.

AS FAR AS LEE COULD SEE they'd covered every base. They'd talked with the stars of the movie, talked with the director, with the producer, with the set and costume designers, with Raymond Armstrong. Everything was in the can. Manny was going to record some of the critics' comments afterward, but that was it as far as coverage of the event would go on "Western Rambles."

As he sat in the music hall along with everyone else, waiting for the vaunted movie to begin, Lee grew antsy. Maybe it was having had only one hour's sleep last night. Maybe it was not having seen Karen all day, or the boyfriend.

What were they doing?

A frigging stupid question.

The music hall held an amazing mix of people—

from the wholly natural Pete to the glittery and glossy Andrea Wright, who was draping herself across Johnny Mehan in a way that at one time might have gotten them arrested for public indecency.

The movie's newly minted theme song started to swell. The lights went down. The chatter lessened.

And Lee couldn't take it anymore. He had to leave. Right then. That second.

He stepped past Manny's and Diane's chairs, pausing to murmur, "Tell me how it is," to address their puzzlement, and, "I'm going to pass for now," so they wouldn't continue to be concerned for him. They knew he was tired and had been existing on frayed nerves for most of the day.

They also knew what he'd done with the headstone. He'd told them earlier in private. They'd backed his decision one hundred percent, which should have done something to cheer him—but hadn't.

He ambled over to the well, the dry heat quickly taking the chill from the music hall's artificially cooled air, and breathed the sweetness of a West Texas afternoon. He was going to miss it when they left tomorrow. He was going to miss the town and its people. But most of all—

His gaze was drawn to the apartment above the antique shop. A jolt went through him when he saw Karen at the window, holding the curtain aside. She'd been watching him.

For a second he couldn't move. Neither did she.

Where was the boyfriend? he wondered sullenly.

Then she was motioning to him, as if she wanted him to come closer.

It was everything Lee could do not to turn around, to check if she was signaling to someone else.

But it was to him, he was assured when she motioned again.

In order not to make a complete fool of himself, he continued to amble, this time across the street. There were only a few people about in town, mostly technicians, whose business wasn't in the music hall viewing the film. The rest of the activity was taking place in the studio's temporary village, where preparations for the after-the-show festivities were under way.

He stopped a little out from the sidewalk to look up at her. With her fall of curly hair and beautiful features, she almost took his breath away.

"Could I see you for a minute, Lee?" she called down.

"Won't the boyfriend object?" he asked evenly.

She frowned, seemingly confused, and he mentally kicked himself for having blundered. *A beautiful woman, one you happen to be in love with, asks to see you...and what do you do? Throw up a roadblock.*

"Around back?" he asked, hoping to make amends.

"Yes...please," she said, then withdrew.

Lee no longer ambled. He hurried down the street and along an alley to the rear of the buildings, then trotted across the empty backyards. She wasn't waiting with the door open, so he bounded up the stairs and knocked. As he waited for her answer, he reclaimed the protective mantle of nonchalance.

KAREN DREW A DEEP BREATH and opened the door. "You didn't like the movie?" she asked, for something to say.

"It hadn't started when I left."

He looked so handsome standing there. Long and lithe, and coolly magnetic. She wordlessly invited him inside.

He came in and looked around, as if he expected to see something different. As if she might have changed everything around.

"Where's he at?" Lee asked at last, his gaze coming back to her.

"Martin?" she asked.

"Hmm."

"He went home. Back to Kerrville."

His features were like granite. "You going to meet him there soon?"

"I might, but—but not—" She took another breath and braced for what she'd brought him here to tell him. "Lee, I know what you did. Pete told me. He saw what happened. I—"

"What do you mean, *but not...?*"

"I want to thank you, Lee. What you did was wonderful. It—"

He stepped closer. "Are you going to meet him or aren't you?" he demanded.

"No!" she cried, and tried to turn away, but he caught hold of her. Why did nothing ever turn out the way she planned? She'd been going to thank him, tell him how much she appreciated what he'd done, tell him how much it would mean to the people of the town if only they knew.... Then she planned to tell him how she felt, if she could garner the nerve. But everything had become all confused. He seemed determined to take one course, while she took another. Obsessing about Martin—

Her protesting movements stopped. Obsessing

about Martin! She looked up at him. In his face she read determination, anger, a haggard sadness and a confused kind of jealousy. Her heart gave a funny little jump.

"No," she said again, only this time softer, more controlled. "I might meet him, but only as a friend."

"How close a friend? He stayed here last night, didn't he?"

"He didn't have anyplace to go. Melanie had booked the hotel."

"When did he leave?"

"This morning. Early. He left me a note."

Something shifted in Lee's demeanor. As if it were slowly becoming clear to him that the situation wasn't as he'd thought.

"Do you love him?" he demanded.

She issued a challenge of her own. "Why should that matter to you?"

Lee's eyes devoured her—her face, her body. He pulled her close. "It *matters* because I think I've been in love with you since I first saw you standing next to my brother and he introduced you as his fiancée. Since I had to come back inside that church two days later and deliver the news that he'd run away. You looked— I could barely handle the way you looked then. You were so vulnerable, so defenseless. I took you outside as quickly as I could, tried to comfort you, but it didn't do any good. You blamed me. So did your parents. They dragged you away as if *I'd* been the one to hurt you."

"That was you?" She relived the memory of being whisked out of church and held with her face pressed into a solid chest. She remembered how reassuring the embrace had felt in a world that had suddenly gone very wrong. "I didn't blame you," she said. "I was grateful."

"You didn't know it was me."

"I—I wasn't thinking. I was just...reacting. I barely knew what was happening. The embarrassment. Feeling stunned that Alex would—"

He placed a finger over her lips. "He's my brother, but he's done enough to come between us."

"Lee, I love you! I didn't want to, but— Like I told Martin, love isn't something you can make happen or keep from happening. It just is. I don't know why I love you, but I do! And I don't want you to go away without—"

He groaned and kissed her. As if it couldn't be held off any longer. As if the continuation of life itself hinged on the two of them finally coming together.

A wild kind of happiness sang through Karen's veins. She had to have him, just as he had to have her. Only there was more to it this time. The demand of spirit as well as body. The blending of two souls. She kissed him back as hungrily as he did her, and she soon led him to her bedroom, where all the unicorns frolicked.

Their disrobing was both short and sweet, a time of discovery, yet also of driving need. Karen marveled at how beautiful his body was.

But she wasn't allowed to marvel for long. His hands brought her to even greater heights, his kisses raining over her. Finally, when she didn't think she could stand it any longer, she reached the fullest satisfaction, and her fingers curled into his back, holding him, helping him. Wanting to bring him with her to the same wondrous bliss.

Slowly, panting—perspiration dampening their

bodies—they came down from the pinnacle to rest side by side in her narrow bed.

She'd never seen such an expression in his eyes before. Such satisfaction, such glowing happiness. She stroked his cheek, let her fingers play in his damp dark hair, smoothing it over his ear.

She loved his ear, she loved his hair, she loved his cheek, his eyes…his everything. She smoothed the muscles of his upper arm, ran her hand along his chest.

"Well—" he chuckled softly "—I'd say that was worth waiting for seven years."

Her dimples deepened and he kissed them both.

"I'd say so, too," she agreed just as warmly, just as softly.

His fingers threaded through her curls, trailed down her jawline to the pulsing hollow at the base of her throat, then on to the curves of her breasts. There, they trembled lightly.

"When did you know?" she asked.

His pale eyes, rimmed with dark lashes, met hers. "Not until I came here. I couldn't get you out of my mind, but I didn't know why."

"I blamed you most of all."

"Because I bothered you? Like a pesky fly?" he teased.

"Not exactly like a fly," she said, grinning.

"Zzz!" He moved a finger in a jerky zigzag simulation of flight that ended on the tip of her nose, which he then promptly kissed.

Karen said, "I'm realizing now that I must have fallen in love with you a long time ago, too, and didn't know it. I couldn't make you disappear like I wanted. And believe me, I tried. I was so angry and I buried it to survive.''

''You probably put my face on a wanted poster and shot the hell out of it every time you had the chance.''

''Public enemy number one!''

''I knew you were here when we agreed to cover the goings-on in Twilight. If I hadn't seen your name we might never have committed. We don't usually go to shoots on such short notice. And Manny and Diane were on vacation in Hawaii.''

''Where did you see my name?'' she asked, curious.

''John's letter. He wrote about your aunt Augusta, then said that she'd died. Did I ever tell you I was sorry about that? He said you'd be arriving soon. He wrote about other people, too, but I couldn't get past you.''

His hand dropped to massage her hip, but she caught it. ''I'd really like to know why you moved the headstone.''

''It was the only visible evidence that could give away the story.''

''Why?'' she persisted. ''I was thrilled when I heard about it. That's why I was in the saloon yesterday morning, looking for you. I wanted to tell you.''

He smiled slightly. She could sense him withdrawing emotionally.

She placed a hand on his cheek. ''What is it? What's happened?''

He still seemed hesitant, then he admitted, ''I didn't do it for you. I couldn't, not and live with myself. That was the hardest part. It would have been so easy to just coast along, let things go on as they were, make you happy. Make Diane happy. But I had to do what I thought was right. In the end I listened to my gut feeling. To instinct.''

''Do you believe now that what you did was right?'' she asked. Her respect for this man's honesty and integrity was growing with every word he uttered.

''Yes. Byron's the only person who might care, and I doubt he'd be too upset.''

She sat up suddenly, drawing his look of concern.

''What is it?'' he asked.

''I've just thought of the other Parkers! What would they make of this if they knew?'' She indicated the two of them together, in bed.

''Not a thing, I'd say.''

''What about your mother? What about *my* mother? Oh my heavens!''

He grinned. ''Maybe we shouldn't tell them…at least, not until after the first grandchild.''

''Grandchild!'' Karen exclaimed.

''Why not? If I'd married you in place of Alex, we could already have had five or six kids!''

''I wanted to slap you when you said that! I knew why you were doing it, but still—''

''I wanted to kiss you.''

Which he promptly did, because this time there was nothing to stop him, not even Karen, who fell against him in total complicity.

AN HOUR LATER, with the street still relatively quiet because the movie had yet to end, Karen and Lee sat down for a dinner of scrambled eggs and toast—in honor of the morning when she'd come to Bette's and they'd shared a first meal. Lee cooked the eggs again and she made the coffee and buttered the toasted bread. He was in the dark dress slacks he'd worn to the premiere and she was in her robe. Both were ravenous as well as completely happy.

They ate quietly for a few minutes before Lee said, "The Cruzes and I are leaving tomorrow. We still have to take a few shots of 'afters' here, then we go to San Francisco to put it all together. It'll be tough finishing in time, but to take advantage of all the publicity around the main premiere, we have to. I can't put it off."

"I know."

He reached across to take her hand. "If I had a choice, I wouldn't leave. You know that. But a few people have pulled some big strings to be sure the special airs close to the movie's general release date." He frowned. "After all this, I sure hope the damned thing's good!"

She laughed. "How can you say that when you walked out on it?"

He smiled crookedly. "I never gave it a chance. The music started and that was that. I wanted to see you. But I thought the boyfriend—"

"Martin is a very nice person. You'd like him."

"I didn't like him yesterday," he growled. "Or today."

"I'm going to miss you."

"You'll be so busy finishing up with your aunt's things you won't even know I'm gone."

"Yes, I will," she said huskily.

From that point the meal was ignored, as was the commotion that occurred sometime later when the movie let out. From the celebratory sounds that did manage to filter through, *Justice at Sundown* had been

very well received. But Lee and Karen no longer
cared.

THEY MADE NO SECRET of their togetherness the next
day. When it was time for Lee to join the Cruzes at
the saloon, Karen accompanied him.

"Is this what I think it is?" Diane asked, grinning
as she threw a meaningful glance at Manny.

"It" was hard to mistake. Lee had his arm around
Karen's waist, her body was tucked close to his.

"Another one bites the dust," Manny said softly.

"Manny!" Diane scolded.

"Well?" Manny said, defending himself. "It's a
married man's hobby to watch his buddies fall, one
by one."

"You're embarrassing Karen!" Diane maintained.

But Karen was smiling so broadly there was no
question of embarrassment. As was Lee. They
couldn't seem to stop.

"How was the movie?" Lee asked.

"Not as good as yours was," Manny teased.

"Seriously," Lee said.

"The critics liked it," Diane said. "They all gave
off-the-cuff glowing reviews. Even the few who paid
their own way liked it."

"It'll be a big hit," Manny forecast. "Stay at the
top of the list for weeks and weeks."

They were in the empty saloon, which had a
slightly fuzzy morning-after ambience. Used beer
mugs had been left here and there, bits and pieces of
paper littered the floor. Drink coasters had somehow
managed to collect in a corner.

"The townspeople came here after the show, while
the movie types had their good time under the tents,"

Diane explained. "We came here. We like being with the locals better. Then some of the others showed up, too."

The door to the upstairs apartment opened and Bette came out slowly. She saw the group downstairs watching her and said, "I think I survived. I'm not sure yet, but in a few minutes I might be. Lordy, I've never been so whacked in my entire life!"

She negotiated the stairs, then fell into a chair. "Looks like a bomb went off in here," she said, glancing around. Her gaze fell on Karen and Lee, taking in their closeness. "About time," she said with a pleased little smile, before her eyelids fell shut involuntarily.

A moment passed as everyone watched her.

"Is she asleep?" Karen asked quietly.

"I think so," Diane said.

Lee glanced at his crew. "Maybe we better get going, take those last shots. Give me ten minutes to change."

He was still wearing his dress clothes. They were a little rumpled, but he looked extremely handsome in them.

"Lee…you know? Maybe not," Diane said, arching a considering brow. "Why not wear what you're wearing? Morning after and all. I think it would work. What do you think, Karen?"

Karen thought he looked fabulous in any form. But she considered him—a night's growth of beard, his thick hair mussed but appealing. "Like you are," she agreed, nodding.

He shrugged and ran his fingers through his hair again, managing to muss it even more. Then he kissed Karen. "You want to come along?" he asked huskily.

She never wanted to be separated from him again! Yet she knew she would be. This would be a good test. Also, glancing at Bette, she knew where she was needed.

"Let me get Bette settled first," she said, "then I'll be there."

He made no protest. A friend took care of a friend.

And for the first time in a little more than fifteen hours, they parted.

KAREN DREADED THE PASSAGE of time. With every check of her watch the hands seemed to have leaped forward. After getting Bette safely back upstairs for a little more rest, she'd tracked down the "Western Rambles" crew and watched as they'd taken various shots, with Lee narrating most of them. He was an excellent off-the-cuff speaker, his words creating a colorful picture. He talked about the preview, about the way the sleepy little western town would never again be quite the same. He even talked about the Nate Barlow legend as he stood at the side of the well. And he used just that term: legend. Quietly, calmly, not making a big deal of the phrasing. Allowing the viewer, as well as himself, a little space.

Then the moment Karen dreaded most arrived. The Range Rover was packed, goodbyes had been said all around. The town's entire population turned out to see them off.

She and Lee had managed a half hour of privacy earlier, their lovemaking fevered, urgent. Joy had blended with heartache, yet there was the promise of more joy to come.

In the street, before other eyes, Lee held her tightly.

"I'll be back in two weeks," he said. "Don't you go anywhere. Understand?"

"Two weeks," she whispered, trying to smile.

"I'll call as often as I can," he said. Then he kissed her.

"I'll be here," she promised tightly. Tears collected on her lashes but didn't fall onto her cheeks.

As his arm dropped away, Bette came to stand next to her, offering moral support.

Then he was gone, the Range Rover's tires kicking up a plume of dust as it drove down the road.

Karen felt as if a part of her were being torn away. She stood for a long time alone—the others having wandered off. She could still feel his arms around her, feel his touch, feel his strength.

Finally she, too, walked away, returning to the antique shop, where she sat down and cried.

THE HOLLYWOOD PEOPLE TOOK leave of Twilight as suddenly as they'd arrived. By late Monday afternoon almost all trace of the little village on the outskirts of town had disappeared. The trucks that had become almost a fixture of daily life in Twilight started their engines and pulled away. All the media people had gone, all the celebrities, the two studio moguls. Many had disappeared after the premiere party.

It was as if a whirlwind had swept through the area, leaving most things untouched, yet what had been changed was changed forever.

The townspeople seemed deflated. "All partied out," was a term tossed around a lot. The entire weekend might have been a dream.

John, as usual, stepped in to be the driving force. He rubbed his hands together and said, "Okay, who's with me? We have to get those signs up. Otherwise people are gonna zoom right by the exit on the interstate! Come on...let's get movin'. We have a job to do here!''

And, once again, the people responded. They jumped right back into high gear, all wearing their hopes on their sleeves.

A WEEK WENT BY. Karen talked with Lee a number of times. The editing process was going well, he said. He and the Cruzes were putting in long hours, both by day and into the night. Then at the beginning of the second week their conversations grew less frequent. They were getting down to the crunch, Lee said, with very little time left. Karen tried to adjust. Then the second week drew to a close, and she heard nothing. All she got was his answering machine or the office voice mail.

"He's busy. You know that," Bette said, trying to offer comfort.

"I do," Karen agreed. She trusted Lee. She truly did. He said he'd be back at the end of two weeks, and she *believed* him. Even if it was past that time. She'd doubted him once before and wouldn't doubt him again.

She tramped down the seed of uncertainty. But like most seeds, harsh treatment didn't kill it. The thought arose time and again—combining with memories of the aborted wedding. Of Alex letting her walk all the way to the altar, to stand in front of family and friends, alone.... But she hadn't been alone. Lee had been with her. To help her, to protect her. Lee, who now swore that he loved her.

She believed him! She believed *in* him! And that made all the difference.

She would not listen to the nagging voice.

VISITORS HAD STARTED to show up in Twilight, tourists drawn by the publicity. *Justice at Sundown* had had its Hollywood premiere the night before, kicking off its national opening. Having collected great reviews, it was expected to draw huge audience numbers. As a result, word of mouth about Twilight was spreading, too. The town's dream was beginning to come true.

Bette came running over to the antique shop the next morning, waving a small package. "Look! It's from Lee! Sent by special messenger! It's got to be the tape of the show. Let me get everyone together. They'll all want to see it, too!" And she'd hurried away, leaving the package with Karen.

Karen stared at it. She'd never seen Lee's writing. It was strong, vital, confident and clear. There was no mistaking the formation of the letters. Just as there was no mistaking the man. She ran her fingers over the written indentations, hoping to feel a connection. The package had been mailed the day before, according to the shipping label. She hugged it to her breast.

A crowd of townspeople and a few visiting tourists followed on Bette's heels, and everyone piled into the saloon to watch the television and VCR John had brought down from upstairs. The set was turned on, the cassette inserted, and while the "Western Rambles" theme played, the screen showed one of Manny's sweeping views down Twilight's main street. The shot lovingly showcased the weathered wood buildings, the covered sidewalk, the hotel, the antique shop, the mercantile, the Lady Slipper. Then there was a long shot of the well and the music hall and the houses, both wooden and mobile. The effort was greeted with a loud cheer, then an even louder one when Lee appeared on-screen with a quick teaser about Twilight and the legend of Nate Barlow. Next, Bette's bedroom photograph of the old town was superimposed over a still of the present-day image, displaying how amazingly alike they were. Oohs and aahs continued to be drawn from the group as the tape rolled on.

Karen could barely stand it. She wanted the real Lee. His image flickering on the small screen only made her longing worse. Yet she couldn't tear her eyes away.

Someone sat down next to her at the bar. She edged closer to the set, trying to concentrate on what the recorded Lee was saying. But the person next to her started to murmur something. When the murmuring didn't stop, she frowned and cautioned, ''Sh!''

It did little good. As soon as Lee came on-screen again, the person murmured along with him, as if mimicking his words.

Karen gave a more impatient, *''Sh!''*

When it happened again, her temper flared. She didn't care if it was a tourist or not, they were going to stop! Her head whipped around, ready to take the person on, when she saw that her tormentor was Lee himself! Sitting there and smiling broadly at his little joke.

Karen squeaked so loudly that it drew the attention of everyone in the room. By the time the people farthest away had gotten the word about what was happening, she was in Lee's arms and kissing him soundly.

A loud whoop went up amid cries of happiness, and the tape was ignored until someone switched it off. It could be played again later.

"Did you think I was never coming back?" Lee demanded, reluctantly dragging his lips away. Everyone but the tourists, who were looking slightly puzzled, had crowded around them. Those closest were pounding Lee on the back.

"No, I *knew* you'd come!" Karen laughed even as she cried.

"Where's Manny and Diane?" John demanded, rushing over to greet Lee like a long-lost friend.

"In Hawaii by now, back on Maui. After these last few days we decided we all needed another break. We had some problems, but we fixed 'em. The special's airing tomorrow night."

"Tomorrow night!"

"And you came here to watch it with us?" John asked.

Lee's arm tightened around Karen. "I thought I would."

"Well, good! We'll have a party. We'll—"

"Down, boy," Bette teased, tugging on her husband's arm. "Give the young people a little time to themselves. Lee didn't come here to see what he's been neck-deep in for two weeks. He came to be with Karen."

John looked from Lee to Karen and actually blushed. Then, grinning, he made up for his blunder by bringing everyone's attention back to the tape. "Put it back on again," he yelled. "It hasn't gotten to the best part yet—me!'' Many hoots of derision followed.

When a jocular argument started as to who had given the best interview, Lee and Karen stole outside.

"I didn't know it was you!'' Karen said as they crossed the yard to her aunt's apartment.

"I wanted to surprise you.''

"Oh, you did that, all right!''

Lee couldn't wait. As they got to the stairs, he stopped her and kissed her again with all the love he'd been holding. Then he pulled back.

"Karen,'' he said as he took something from his pocket. "I know it takes all kind of gall to ask this so soon. But it's already been seven years, and I don't want to waste another second.'' He opened his hand and she saw a ring. A diamond solitaire—simple, yet beautifully cut to show off every facet. "Karen...will you marry me?''

Her wondrous gaze moved from the ring to his eyes. Those pale blue eyes that set him apart.

Who would have thought? she mused briefly. Certainly not her mother, whom she'd talked to earlier in the week but had not breathed a word to about Lee. Certainly not herself, not when she remembered how hostile she'd been to him initially.

She started to smile, and with all the exuberant joy of having him with her again, she answered with a resounding "Yes!'' And in case there might be any doubt, she kept repeating her acceptance. "Yes, yes, yes, yes, yes—''

Just as exuberantly, Lee stopped the flowing repetition with a sealing kiss.

EPILOGUE

TWILIGHT HAD NEVER GOTTEN around to building a church. The music hall had always done double duty when a traveling minister could be persuaded to stay around long enough to hold services.

It was pressed into double duty now for Karen's and Lee's wedding. Because it was the holiday season, bushels of holly cuttings had been rounded up by some of their friends and used by the florist as decoration, along with the more traditional wedding flowers.

A tiny sprig had been added to Lee's boutonniere. He glanced at it as he waited off to one side in the front of the hall. He knew Karen's bouquet would also have some matching sprigs. Then he looked out at all the people seated in the chairs the film studio had decided to leave behind.

His parents were there, as were Karen's... positioned about as far away from each other as the building would allow. Neither of their mothers had taken well to the idea of their marriage, but Karen had informed hers and he had informed his that the ceremony would take place whether or not they attended. It was to be their decision. Much protest had resulted, but in the end, when both women saw that their wishes were being ignored, they'd come around. At least enough to sit in the same room.

Numerous other Parkers were also attending. Those from the ranch and some from scattered areas across the state. Mae headed the delegation. There were also friends of Karen's. One, a pretty young woman named Rachel Anderson—Karen's maid of honor—was sitting temporarily with "the boyfriend," Martin Frederick, and a man Lee had been introduced to as Mr. Griffin, Karen's ex-boss. Lee had met them all on a quick trip to Kerrville when Karen had gathered the remainder of her things and moved them to Twilight. Lee still had reservations about Martin, but he'd liked Rachel immediately, even when she'd winked broadly at Karen and murmured something about him certainly having the look of an outlaw. Karen had refused to interpret.

Last but not least were the people of Twilight. Karen had made sure to deliver their invitations personally. Considering the way they'd been snubbed previously, she'd wanted this wedding to be done right. Everyone was dressed in their best, even Pete, who'd purchased a new shirt in town when he'd finally consented to see a doctor about his feet. He hadn't let Lee pay, though, but instead had used some of his share of the new tourist dollars.

Lee shifted uncomfortably. It was juvenile to be nervous, but he was. He glanced at Manny, his best man, who at his own wedding had been a basket case prior to the ceremony. Now he was cool and calm and gave him an easy thumbs-up sign. An old pro at this marriage game.

Lee adjusted his bow tie and waited for Karen. Where was she? It was already after four. She was late. His palms broke out in a sudden cold sweat. She wouldn't *not* show up, would she? To get back at him? This whole thing hadn't been some kind of elaborate scheme of revenge, had it? Panic delivered a sucker punch to his midsection, and his head jerked around again to Manny. Manny, sensing his alarm, stiffened and was about to say something, when the recorded music started to play.

His gaze flew to the rear of the building, where he saw Karen, much as he remembered her from all those years before—in another white gown that had a hard time competing with her beauty. He couldn't take his eyes off her and Manny had to tap him to remind him to walk forward.

The groom was in place this time as the bride neared the minister. It would take an army to drag him away! Especially when, her eyes dewy with love, Karen looked at him after parting from her father. And smiled. It superseded forever the terrible memory he'd held in his heart of her in pain.

He took her hand, made all the appropriate replies, gave her his ring while pledging his fidelity, listened as she slid a ring on his finger and pledged hers. Then, a much-too-short kiss later, it was done. The music swelled, voices rose. There was even clapping as their relatives and friends demonstrated their approval and enjoyment.

Since the same area was going to be used for the reception, everyone pulled their chairs aside. Then the tables holding the wedding cake and refreshments were brought forward.

Lee and Karen stood close, as if each other's touch were a lifeline. They laughed and talked, hugged and were hugged back repeatedly. Good wishes flowed all around.

Then it came time for Karen to toss her bouquet.

Amid squeals of anticipation, Rachel caught it, which tradition said would make her the next bride. Also following tradition, Lee flipped Karen's garter to a waiting group of bachelors. To Lee's surprise and consternation, Martin caught it. But Karen seemed so pleased that his irritation quickly vanished.

Still the newlyweds didn't leave. Lee's patience was stretching to the breaking point. He was accustomed to dealing with people, accustomed to how much they liked to talk, and normally he enjoyed it. But he wanted to be with Karen now. Just the two of them. Alone.

What seemed eons later, the moment finally arrived, and amid showers of confetti, they ran out to Lee's waiting car.

WHEN KAREN SHOOK HER HEAD confetti flew from her curls, causing her to laugh, which made Lee laugh, too.

She waved to the crowd until she couldn't see them anymore, then she leaned against Lee's shoulder, enjoying the short kiss he gave the top of her head.

"That was wonderful!" she said. "So much fun! It certainly makes a difference to have the right bridegroom!" She tilted her head to look at him. "Do you know who I heard say that? Mae!"

"Alex was smart to lie low. She's still gunning for him."

Karen sighed. "Actually, one day I hope he does find the right person. Right now I want everyone to be as happy as we are. Do you think he'll ever settle down?"

"He called me last night. Wished us luck. Made excuses for not coming. That surprised me."

"Maybe he's finally growing up."

"First he has to develop a conscience."

Karen hugged Lee's arm—her husband's arm. "If he'd had a conscience back then, things might have turned out very different. I'm glad it happened the way it did." She paused. "Did you see Rachel and Martin? I'm hoping something will start there soon. They've always fought like cats and dogs, but I've begun to wonder if that isn't a cover. Like with us. Sometimes the stronger the antagonism, the deeper the feeling."

"That's why you were happy when Martin caught the garter."

"I made sure Rachel caught the bouquet! I thought you knew."

"Nope, pure chance."

"Did you see Diego? You can't tell which are his real teeth and which are the replacements. They look wonderful. He's so handsome. He always has been, but—"

"Hank showed me his truck. First thing I had to see when I got into town this time."

"Pepper has her new living room set, too."

"Did Mary show you her savings book?"

"No! Did she show you?"

"Oh, yes."

"They look on you as a friend, Lee. Someone who helped make their dreams come true. Aren't you glad you got rid of the headstone?"

"I was glad right away."

"You realize they're making you an honorary citizen of Twilight?"

"Well, I seem to be with you more than I'm in San Francisco, when the crew's not on the road."

"They hope to convince us to stay."

"Do you want to?"

"I want to be with you, wherever that is. I used to think living in Twilight made the difference in me. Gave me the freedom to be myself. But it was in me all along. All I had to do was listen. I can take that with me anywhere."

He squeezed her hand. "I'm listening to something right now."

"What?" she asked, even though she had a good idea of the answer.

"I want to get you inside that fancy hotel room we have reserved, pick you up, carry you into the bedroom, rip all your clothes off and have my wicked way with you."

She giggled. "It's going to take a while to get there."

"Not if we follow Mae's plan."

"Oh, dear."

"Her neighbor has his own plane and he's willing to fly us directly to Cozumel."

"She's already asked him?"

"That's Mae."

"Mae's really very sweet, isn't she?"

He laughed. "Don't ever let her hear you say that!"

"She reminds me a lot of Aunt Augusta in the way she watches out for the people she cares for."

"I'm going to have to take your word for that." He laughed lightly. Then he gave her an estimating look. "What do you think your aunt would make of us right now?"

"I think she'd be very happy."

"Karen Parker." Lee tried out the legal blending of his last name to hers.

"Karen and Lee Parker," she murmured back.

Lee couldn't wait any longer. He pulled the car to the side of the road, took her in his arms and didn't notice that the sky was once again resplendent with color as the sun sank slowly beyond the mountains in the west.

HARLEQUIN SUPERROMANCE®

He's the guy every woman dreams of.
A hero in every sense of the word—strong, brave,
kind and of course, drop-dead gorgeous.
You'll never forget the men you meet—or the
women they love—in Harlequin Superromance®'s
newest series, **LOVE THAT MAN!**

BECAUSE IT'S CHRISTMAS
by Kathryn Shay, December 1998

LOVE, LIES & ALIBIS
by Linda Markowiak, January 1999

Be sure to look for upcoming **LOVE THAT MAN!** titles
wherever Harlequin Superromance® books are sold.

HARLEQUIN®
Makes any time special ™

HARLEQUIN SUPERROMANCE®

COMING NEXT MONTH